THE MANY WALKS OF LIFE

RANDY BLALOCK

To Marlene
Randy Blalock

ISBN: 1511468742
ISBN 13: 9781511468749

*Dedicated to everyone who has played a role in my life
but especially to my loving wife, Cindy and my fellow Murphy War
Eagle classmates*

INTRODUCTION

This is a work of fiction. Yet, at the same time much of the story and vignettes found here are semi-autobiographical in nature. Some happened- some didn't. No, my ego has not gotten so large that I think the world deserves to hear about my life. It is just that many of the things that have happened to me during my life have probably happened, in some common form, to many of you who will read this and those episodes will make you think about good times, good friends, and good memories.

First of all, to the best of my knowledge and God's grace, I do not have a terminal disease but that was my starting point to set up the plot for the rest of the story. However, many of the streets mentioned actually do exist in and around the East Atlanta area where I grew up and most of the people mentioned are real people; people very near and dear to me. While the people and places won't mean much to those who didn't grow up there, I am sure you can recall similarities from your youth. These classmates and friends that are mentioned have played significant roles in the makeup of my life and, for that, I thank them. For the sake of their privacy, I have only used first names but they will know who they are. If any are offended by their inclusion, I apologize.

I actually did take the walk that is detailed to commemorate the 150th anniversary of the Battle of Atlanta that took place on July 22, 1864. Growing up only a few hundred yards from where the battle's first shots were fired, that part of our nation's history has always intrigued me. As a young boy, I would often find artifacts like Minie' balls, belt buckles, and other parts of Union and Confederate uniforms. Some of the events that are described during that section of the story are purely fictional, however. Again, I'll let you decide, dear reader, which is which.

It is estimated that the average person walks approximately 7,500 steps a day. That means that if they took their first steps at age 1 and lived to the age of 80, they have walked 216,262,500 steps in their lives or over 108,000 miles. All of a sudden, I just became very tired. Some of those steps are routine and mundane but some, in the total fabric and scope of our lives, have great significance. This is the story of one man's steps taken in his MANY WALKS OF LIFE.

CHAPTER 1

MY WALK TO THE DOCTOR'S OFFICE

The walk I took that day from the doctor's office to the garage where my car was parked was one of the longest I had ever taken. The total distance was not that great. The burden I carried making it, however, weighed me down. Each step felt as if I was walking in quicksand. I felt like I was sinking into the ground below me. Let me tell you about the first phase of that walk- the walk to the doctor's office and what led up to it first.

The appointment today had been a follow up to my annual physical I had taken a few months prior. Nothing major seemed to be wrong with me at that time. Blood pressure a little high- could lose a few pounds but, other than that, I was feeling pretty good. I was going to be turning 67 in a few months so the things the doctor suggested I work on to correct were nothing a man of my age didn't normally experience.

I had been active all my life. I played sports as a kid and had continued that in adulthood with lots of tennis, softball, and running.

When my joints and back told me it was time to slow down that jarring activity, I had started a regimen of walking and weightlifting. All in all, for a guy my age, I was in pretty good shape.

I'm often told I don't look my age and I guess I have my parents to thank for that. My dad had lived to be just 15 days short of 100 years old and my mom is still up and at em' at 97. Pretty good genes, right? You'd think so but, unfortunately, I apparently got one bad one.

A few days after my initial physical, I had received a call from my doctor's office asking me to come in to have some additional tests run. "No cause for alarm." The nurse said. "We just want to check on a few things." Those "few things" had turned out to be a reason to go in three more times. Sure, I was worried, but the doc, using his best bedside manner, kept saying that there was nothing to be concerned about. He was wrong.

I had arrived for my appointment about ten minutes early but that was the story of my life. I was always early everywhere I went. You could say that I was punctual to a fault and you would be correct. I have wasted a lot of time in my life being early. Waiting at airport gates, waiting in business offices where I had meetings scheduled, and waiting in movie theaters thirty minutes before the previews were even supposed to start. My kids always chided me for getting to the theater so early when I took them to the movies when they were kids. "Dad," they said, "we're the only kids we know who watch the movie ushers clean up the candy wrappers and popcorn boxes from the previous show."

I pulled my car into the parking deck and found a space on the third level. I turned off the ignition and took a deep breath. I am a praying man so, I took a moment to raise a little prayer. When people, even faith-filled, prayerful people pray they don't always pray for the right things. Rabbi Harold Kushner in his wonderful book, _WHY BAD THINGS HAPPEN TO GOOD PEOPLE,_ said that we are usually too specific with our prayers. I knew that whatever was going on in my body was already there so it made no sense to pray that the doctor's findings were either positive or negative. The better prayer was for God to help me through whatever the news might be. If it was nothing serious, great. But if the news was not good, I prayed for Him to help me accept it and to be with me as I dealt with it.

I got out of the car and headed toward his office. As I said, I was early (surprise!) so I walked down the ramps to the ground floor instead of taking the elevator. As I was exiting the garage, I looked down and there on the ground was a shiny new penny. Find a penny, pick it up and all day long you'll have good luck. I hoped that was a good omen.

I entered the lobby of the large medical complex and pushed the button on the elevator for the 6th floor. The elevator began to rise and I whistled along to the music coming from the speakers. It was an instrumental version of *Stairway to Heaven*. How strange, I thought to myself. A song about a stairway in an elevator but then, I've always been told that I have a weird sense of humor. I could only hope that the irony of the heaven part didn't materialize.

I entered the waiting area, signed in at the window and joined the other half dozen people waiting their turn. And now, here I sat, alone with my thoughts, in a doctor's office waiting for my name to be called. After all these follow up visits, I couldn't help but be a little concerned. Truth be told, I was more than a little concerned. I was terrified. I had not told my wife about these follow ups because I didn't want her to get upset. Stupid, I know, but, hell, I'm a man and we are innately stupid when it comes to matters like these. And the female congregation said......AMEN!

When my name was finally called, Mary Ann, the doctor's assistant, smiled and even gave me a reassuring pat on the back as I walked through the door. She showed me to the room and told me the doctor would be in shortly. Yeah, right! There is never anything short about that wait, is there? In the meantime, all I could do was wait. Being a creature who knows his faults, I always came prepared for any down time I might have to endure. I opened my iPad and started playing Candy Crush. I've been stuck on Level 245 for quite some time now but that's still pretty good. Right?

Examination rooms are always so sterile and cold. There is very little on the walls except diplomas and posters detailing the inner organs and skeletal system of the human body. The furniture usually consists of two chairs- one for you and one for the doc, a counter where the jar of tongue depressors are kept and that torture rack with the scratchy piece of cloth you have to lie on. You have to have something to take your mind off those surroundings so, I attempted to do just that.

The Candy Crush level stumped me again and, for some reason, the human form diagrams caught my eye again. The human body is a miraculous, incredible, and wonderful thing. And to a young boy, the female form begins to be something that you appreciate in ways you never considered before. The young boy, just on the cusp of puberty, is drawn to it like a magnet. I know I was at that age. I remember when I took........

CHAPTER 2

MY WALK TO MANHOOD (PART 1)

I grew up in Atlanta, Georgia. Specifically, the southeast quadrant of the city that contained two vibrant communities- Kirkwood and East Atlanta. My house was equidistant from both so, as a young boy, I spent a good deal of time in each.

The church that my mom and I attended was Kirkwood Baptist where I was baptized at age 8, but when I went to the movies on Saturday afternoons, it was in East Atlanta at the old Madison Theater. I'll talk about one of those Saturdays a little later.

My house was on Memorial Drive, a major thoroughfare that went from Stone Mountain all the way to downtown Atlanta. I lived only about 10 miles from the heart of downtown Atlanta but when I was a child, it seemed a continent away. Hundreds of cars went by our house each day on their way to and from downtown. This was about a decade before the interstate systems were built in Atlanta.

I can even remember the old trolleys, or maybe some people know them as streetcars, that ran up and down Memorial before the diesel buses came along in the late 50's. The roads were grooved with the rails that the wheels fit into and up above, electric lines that gave the trolleys their power looked like massive spider webs against the sky. Occasionally, the trolley would jump out of the track and the passengers would unload to try and help get it back into the groove. And sometimes, the rod leading from the trolley itself that made contact with the power line would come disengaged and the conductor would take this long, insulated pole and push the rod back into place. When they connected, there would usually be a big spark that looked like fireworks on the 4th of July.

My dad used to love to sit in our front yard and, literally, watch the world go by represented by the cars. Sometimes, I would sit with him and we would play a game we called "Red car, blue car." As the cars whizzed by, Dad would count the blue cars and because red was my favorite color, I would count the red ones. The first one to a set number, usually 50, would win. For reasons I never understood then, Dad almost always won. I only found out later that most car manufacturers of that era made three times as many blue cars, because blue is a much more soothing color, than they did red. Dad was playing with a stacked deck but I was too naïve to know it.

My house was situated midway between Clifton and Wyman. Seven brick houses had been built in the late 40's, all with exactly the same floor plan, and ours was exactly in the middle- three on our left and three on our right. My playmates in those early years were nothing but girls and they outnumbered me so I never got to choose the games we played. But when it came to our make-believe games, being the only boy, I always got to be the dad or the male movie star so, that helped secure my masculine identity.

There was another girl in the neighborhood who became the first person in real life that I really looked up to. Sure, I had my sports heroes: Eddie Matthews and Ted Williams from baseball; Bill Russell from basketball; and Paul Hornung from football but she was my first that I could say hi to everyday. Her name was Sharon and she was six years older than me. Sharon was an excellent high school athlete and I really credit her with a lot of my future athletic abilities because she was the one who took time to work with me on basketball and baseball fundamentals.

When I got to be about 10 or so, Sharon started teaching me sports-related things that Dad never cared about doing with me. We would shoot hoops together in my back yard and we would play toss with a baseball or softball for hours. She'd hit grounders to me and we'd even toss and kick footballs back and forth in the Fall. Whatever the season, Sharon and I could usually be found playing some kind of sport together.

Of course, I would be very remiss if I didn't give additional credit to my early sports training to my cousin, Bobby. My dad was the third youngest of ten children, four girls and six boys. I can't imagine how my dads' parents came up with the names they gave their children. The girls were Nellie, Myrtie, Edna, and Lucille. The boys' names were even stranger: Ottis, Oather, Elmer, and Horace, my dad. I guess they ran out of off-beat names by the time the last two boys came along because they were named Lawrence and Dennis.

Most of my cousins were much older than me because I came late in my parents' marriage. They had been married for ten years before I was born. They married in 1937 and Dad didn't want a child until he was, in his mind, financially secure. In fact, I was never really sure that he wanted a child at all from the way he treated me but that's another story.

Just about the time my parents felt they could afford to have a little one around the house, WWII came along to derail their plans. Dad enlisted in the Marines and when the war ended, it was the same thing all over again- they had to wait to get their financial feet back under them. I was born on June 9, 1947 at Crawford Long Hospital in Atlanta.

Bobby was 20 years older and was married with two girls of his own but that never stopped him from including me when they would go to the old Ponce de Leon Park in Atlanta to watch the Atlanta Crackers play or to a dirt-track stock car racing venue called The Peach Bowl long before the college football game of the same name. Those races were always entertaining because there were as many wrecks on the track which led to subsequent fights in the pits among the drivers and their respective crews as there was racing action. Remind me to tell you a story later about one of the great fables involving the Crackers and one of their greatest players ever, Bob Montag.

We lived, at one time, within a half mile of Bobby and I would spend as much time at his house as I would my own. Bobby worked with me diligently helping me with my baseball skills and later, when I was playing high school baseball, he would come watch me play- the only one who ever did.

Bobby had a nickname for me that stuck until the day he died. He always told me that I was tough for my size and very competitive. He was right about that. I hate to lose at anything- anything. So, he called me "Rawhide". I loved that nickname. I signed the card accompanying the flowers I sent to his memorial simply "Rawhide." He knew who they were from. He was a great guy with a tremendous sense of humor and I miss him a lot since his girls, his wife, all his friends and I lost him to cancer a few years back.

Anyway, back to Sharon. There was no question that Sharon was a tomboy but there was also no mistaking that she was a girl as I found out most accidentally. In the 50's, there was a very lax and lenient attitude among neighbors. You didn't call them on the phone before you visited to make sure it was okay and, heaven forbid, there was no such thing as knocking on the door. You just walked in the house and yelled your arrival. It was a safer world it seems because we rarely ever even locked our door when we left the house.

I guess I was 10 or maybe 11, making Sharon around 17. I never thought of Sharon as a girl. I didn't think of her as a boy, either. She was just my friend- my buddy. It was a Saturday and I walked down to her house to see if she wanted to play some baseball. I walked in her house but for some reason I didn't announce myself this time. I walked back to where her bedroom was located and as I walked into the hall, she came out of her bathroom stark naked.

Now, other than getting my hands on some of my dad's old girlie magazines one time, this was the first naked woman I had ever seen. Certainly, the first one in the flesh. And even though it was a long time ago, I remember it being really good flesh. Heck, I didn't even realize Sharon had boobs before then.

I don't know who was more embarrassed. We both kind of froze in place for a few seconds before I was able to make my feet work again. I ran out of her house straight to mine where I sprinted to my room and locked myself in. I just knew the police were going to break down my door any minute and arrest me for being a pervert, even though I had no idea what that was.

It was obvious that I was acting funny because Mom asked me why I wasn't eating my dinner. "Do you have a fever?" she asked. Apparently, in the 50's, a fever was the first sign of (a) a broken arm (b) mental illness or (c) anything else that could be wrong with you. I assured her I was okay. I told her that I was just worried about a test I had Monday at school.

I spent the rest of that night and the next day moping around the back yard or by myself in my room, not knowing what to do. Then, a marvelous thing happened. Sharon spotted me sitting gloomily by myself in the backyard. She walked two houses down to our house and opened the gate. I was certain she was going to walk up to me, pull me up by the seat of my pants and proceed to beat the snot out of me. But she was smiling as she came up to me, fully clothed to my great relief. She sat down next to me and there was an awkward silence until she said tenderly, "Sweetie," she said, "it's all right. Nothing has changed between us. You're still my best pal." There was a prolonged pause as we both silently sat there until she said, "Can I ask you something?"

I nodded with my head hung down.

"Was I the first girl you've ever seen without clothes on?"

Again, I gave her nothing but a nod.

"Look at me." she said as she took my chin and lifted it so I had to look her in the eye. "When you get to school tomorrow, you can tell all your buddies that you've seen a girl naked. You'll be the envy of them all. You'll be king of the 5th grade. Now, you wanna play some catch?" I think it was the first time I was ever in love.

By the way, I never told a soul.

I have to tell one other quick story regarding Sharon that is probably the funniest thing my mother has ever said. After Sharon went off to college, I lost touch with her. I have no idea where she is today or even if she is still alive. She'd be in her 70's and the odds are pretty good that she's still with us but you never know. We heard later that she had moved in with another girl and that her lifestyle had changed fairly dramatically for the mid-60's. Couples weren't as open with their sexuality as they are now. I guess it was never meant to be between us because, if the stories were true, her romantic preferences didn't include penises.

Mom and Dad were visiting with us one Sunday afternoon and the subject of the old neighborhood came up. We were playing the "Wonder What Happened to So and So" game and Sharon's name came up. I said a very sexist thing and hinted that she was probably living with a woman and was a Phys Ed teacher at a private women's school somewhere. Without a beat, Mom said, "You know, I always wondered if she was Lebanese." It was all Cindy and I could do to keep from breaking into hysterics so we wouldn't embarrass her.

Sorry, I have had to take a quick break from writing because even today, every time I think of that it breaks me up.

Seeing a woman naked for the first time was, while a nerve-wracking event at the time, a wonderful memory. Some years later, I would take an even better walk. That would be ……….

CHAPTER 3

MY WALK TO MANHOOD (PART 2)

T he great Southern columnist, Lewis Grizzard, once defined the difference of being *naked* versus being *nekkid* this way. Naked means you don't have any clothes on. Nekkid means you don't have any clothes on and you're foolin' around. I have always loved getting nekkid. I saw Sharon naked but I certainly didn't have any fantasies of getting nekkid with her. Those thoughts would have to wait a few years.

Before I get into the story of this particular walk, I have to relate to you a couple of my favorite Lewis Grizzard antidotes. Grizzard, was a marvelous storyteller as well as being a talented writer. You can get a semblance of his sense of humor and wit just from the titles of his books. Some of his best are: _If Love Were Oil, I'd Be About a Quart Low, Daddy Was a Pistol and I'm a Son of a Gun,_ and the ab-solute best _Don't Bend Over in the Garden, Granny – Don't You Know Them Taters Got Eyes._

Being a University of Georgia football fan, my favorite Grizzardism relates to our beautiful, well, he's beautiful to us, English Bulldog mascot that we lovingly and adoringly refer to as Uga (pronounced UGH-A). The Seiler family out of Savannah have been supplying the school with these mascots since 1956 and they are named sequentially so, we are up to Uga IX. Uga IX's eight predecessors are all buried at Sanford Stadium. During the game, Uga enjoys his air-conditioned dog house that is located on the sidelines right in front of the cheerleaders and the student section. Before a game, the most popular locale for fans is underneath the bridge where Uga can be found posing for pictures or just having his ears rubbed by adoring fans.

Lewis and a buddy were attending a game on a glorious autumn afternoon in Athens, Georgia waiting for the start of the game. The seats were filled with fans dressed in red and black waiting for the Dawgs to be led onto the field by Uga.

Finally, the moment arrives and Uga runs, or maybe a better way to phrase that is waddles, to midfield, led by his handler, ahead of the team. As Grizzard tells it: "Upon arriving at midfield, Uga sits back on his haunches and proceeds to lick himself where only a dog can lick themself." Grizzard nudges his buddy and says with a sly grin, "Damn! I wish I could do that." Whereupon, his buddy looks at him strangely and says, "THAT DOG WOULD BITE YOU!" _

The second story relates a situation that Gen. William Tecumseh Sherman found himself in after his Union army had taken Atlanta during what we true Southerners refer to as the War of Northern Aggression. Sherman and his army of 150,000 were leaving Atlanta and were on their way to Savannah when they went by Stone Mountain. For those of you who have visited our wonderful state and seen the largest solid, exposed piece of granite in the world with its carving on the side of three Southern heroes: Robert E. Lee, Jefferson Davis, and Stonewall Jackson, you will understand its magnificence. To Sherman, it was just a big rock and, of course, it didn't have the carving then.

As they passed by, they heard the taunting cries of a lone Rebel soldier at the top of the mountain hurling down curses and threats to the Yanks. Gen. Sherman ordered the toughest man in the army to go up the mountain and get rid of that Johnny Reb.

Only a few minutes passed before that Yanks' body came flying off the mountain landing at Sherman's feet. "Send up ten men!" Sherman shouted, but no sooner had these ten men gone up than their bodies, too, came flying off.

Totally exasperated, Sherman sent 150 men to get rid of this Rebel. About fifteen minutes passed before one solitary Union soldier staggered back down the mountain. He was bruised, cut, and bleeding from every portal of his body. Sherman asked him, "What in the world is going on up there?" The soldier replied, "It's a trick, General. There's two of em!" This would be where Dixie starts playing softly in the background.

For young men, that first walk to manhood takes many forms and happens in a multitude of ways. It might be in the back seat of a car, the luxury of a bed found in a seedy motel room, or some might not get to take the walk until their wedding night, which, as I recall, is actually the mandated way. For me, it was a sandy beach in Panama City, Florida.

I was never one of those little boys who hated girls. I never thought of them as having cooties or being yucky like some do. Maybe it was because I grew up in a neighborhood full of girls and I had to get along with them just to survive. But I took it beyond tolerating them so I would have someone to play with after school- I really liked girls.

From my earliest years, I always remember having girlfriends. There was Pam P. in the first grade. She was the first girl I kissed. I did it on a dare from my cousin, Terrie, one of Bobby's girls who I spoke about earlier. Pam was a very pretty little blonde and the three of us were out riding bikes one day. We stopped to rest awhile and Terrie, a straight-forward girl then and no different now, proceeded to throw out the dare. Pam didn't seem to object so, I leaned over and gave her a quick kiss square on the mouth. It may have lasted all of 1.2 seconds but it was wonderful. I don't remember anything about the rest of that day.

I went through some lean years between 2nd and 4th grades, I guess, because I don't remember any steady girlfriend. Then, there was Marsha H., a blonde, in the 5th grade; Alaine C., a blonde, in the 7th; and Glenda P., a blonde, in the 9th. Detecting a theme here?

But sandwiched in the middle of those sweet girls was my 6th grade love, Devon S. While she is a blonde now, back then she was, and these are her words, a mousey brunette. Devon was actually a year younger than I. We were in a combined 5th and 6th grade accelerated class. Miss Mitchell was our teacher and probably my favorite grade school teacher. All of us in her class loved her because on Fridays, if we had behaved during the week, she let us clear our desks from the middle of the room and she allowed us to have a dance party.

We were able to bring our own 45's from home and she would act as deejay and spin the discs. Elvis, Frankie Avalon, and Connie Francis filled the air. And on occasion, she would even play a slow dance. If someone passed by our room and looked inside they would have seen a strange sight. Tall and leggy Devon, wearing my stylish black leather jacket, towering over short, tiny me. Cute as hell, for sure, but still, quite the sight. I get to see Devon occasionally at high school reunion gatherings and she is just as pretty now as she was then. But at least I am taller than her now.

I didn't have my major growth spurt until I was in high school so, I probably was no more than 4 ½ feet tall in the 6th grade. I always hated those class pictures that were taken every year because

I was always on the front row, sitting cross-legged with the other short boys while the girls in the class were behind me followed by the taller guys on the top row. Oh, how I wanted to be on that top row.

I call my Sophomore and Junior high school years my "big brother" years. They're called that because I was more like a big brother to the girls than someone they would consider going out with. I'd be standing in the hall between classes and I would see a young lady who I was attracted to walk up to me. My heart would pound in my chest in anticipation only to have it shattered when they would ask, "Do you think Kenny likes me?" or "Why won't Kenny ask me out for a date?" or "Would you tell Kenny I think he is cute?"

It was always Kenny M. Kenny was tall with wavy, blonde hair, very smart, and a great athlete. He reminded you of those surfer- dude types that we saw in the Frankie and Annette Beach Blanket movies. The girls were crazy for him and many of them thought, I guess, that I ran interference for him. They knew he was my best friend so, they figured they could go through me. And like the little obedient dog and to win their favor in case they were ever willing to "settle", I'd trot off and deliver their message to him. If I had charged a delivery fee, I could have paid for my college education.

Now, it wasn't that I was an ugly kid- I was just sort of, well, geeky. Even though I played on the varsity basketball and baseball teams, I was known more around school for my trumpet virtuosity so, as my wife is prone to do when she looks at my annual and sees my picture, she says I was a Band Geek and popular girls don't want to date a Band Geek. I prefer to think of myself as a Jeek rather than a Geek. That's a combination of a Jock and a Geek. Nevertheless, and for what ever reason, I couldn't even scrape a date for my Junior-Senior Prom. They were probably all waiting to hear from Kenny.

But then came my Senior year and that meant Cathy H. Cathy, a Junior cheerleader, and I started dating early that school year and it's kind of ironic how it came about. She used a neighbor of hers who played in the band with me to deliver a message that she was interested. I took one look and fell head over heels. She was a statuesque blonde (go figure) and she was gorgeous. OK, I've got to be honest with you at the risk of totally embarrassing Cathy. Cathy had matured quite dramatically for a 16 year-old so to say that she was bountifully blessed in the chestal area would be a fair assessment. I got the nerve to call her up one night and I asked her to go to that week's football game with me and she immediately agreed. I was in heaven the rest of the year.

Rare were the times when we were not together at school unless we were in class. Since I lived across the street from the school, I always got there first and waited for her to walk in the door. We ate lunch together, we talked in the halls between classes, and at night we would talk on the phone for hours.

We went to the football games together and I spent more time watching her cheer than I did watching the game. But she told me she was always listening for me to play "Charge" and during halftime she didn't take her break with the other cheerleaders- she stayed in the stands to watch me march and play my solos with the band.

Some of my proudest moments during basketball season that year were hearing her call out my name during the "He's our man" cheer. You old farts like me know how it goes- "Blalock, Blalock he's our man. If he can't do it nobody can." And after those games was the best part. East Lake Park. Submarine races. Making out. Sorry, Karen and Michael (her two children) but mom did have a life before she met your dad.

I am not sure that Cathy's dad ever trusted me or even liked me after an incident early on in our dating life. We had been on a date and had gone to my favorite location for some good old-fashioned lip-locking. The "road" where most of this activity took place for us was an unpaved pathway with nothing but sharp rocks as its base. When it was time for me to take her home we discovered, much to our dismay, that I had a flat tire caused, I'm sure, by the conditions of the road.

Now, to say that I am mechanically inept, even at this stage of my life, would be a correct assessment of my skills. At 17, all I knew about a car was where to put the gas if I had to pump it myself so, putting the spare tire on a car was well above my pay grade. Somehow, I did manage to figure out the jack and how to use the lug wrench to get the tire off and replace it with the spare but it was a very time-consuming task. I delivered Cath to her door well after curfew and we were met at the door by her scowling father. Even showing him the flat in the trunk didn't seem to appease him all that much. Thankfully, he was gracious and forgiving enough to allow her to see me again.

Because of Cathy, my Senior year was very special. We shared a wonderful night together at Prom. Our Prom was held at the Georgian Terrace Hotel in downtown Atlanta and she was beautiful in her pale blue gown. I didn't look too bad either in my tux, I might say. After a night of dancing, we went to Renee's house where her parents had prepared a great steak dinner for us. Along with Cathy and me there was Lloyd H. and Renee G., Kenny and Peggy H., and Floyd H. and his date.

My graduation night was very bittersweet. I was happy to be moving on from high school but, at the same time, sad to be leaving Cath while I was away at college. I think that was the real reason she broke my heart later that summer. She didn't mean to hurt me and I believe she was hurting just as badly as I was, but I think the reason she broke up with me was that she was just scared to be alone. She told me years later that she just couldn't face not seeing me when she walked in the school each morning. We've stayed in touch over the years and even though I wouldn't change a thing regarding the way my life worked out, it is impossible not to wonder what might have been. But Cath, if you read this, you were my first <u>real</u> love.

It was that same summer when, at least for one night, I was able to forget my heartache. That was when I took my first steps on my walk to manhood.

Unlike many of our classmates who took off immediately after graduation night to either Daytona or Panama City to celebrate their big achievement; Kenny, Floyd, Lloyd, and myself waited until later in the summer for our adventure. As is the case with most of my memories of my high school years, those three names are always fairly prominent.

Kenny had been my best friend since grade school and I probably spent as much time over at his house as I did my own. Floyd and Lloyd, yes they are identical twins, came to Murphy from Tennessee during our 9th grade year and the four of us became inseparable. All three were excellent baseball and basketball players but the twins had special baseball talents. Floyd played shortstop and Lloyd was our first baseman. In fact, they were both so good that they later played college baseball for Georgia Tech, a fact for which I have never totally forgiven them, being a University of Georgia fan.

The girls in the school could absolutely not tell them apart which led to several interesting double dates during those years. I would go to their house thinking I was picking up Lloyd before we went to get our respective dates and out would come Floyd, or vice versa. One would decide at the last minute that they didn't want to go and the other would take his place. And the girls they were dating would never suspect a thing- or, at least, they never let on that they knew the other twin was their date for the night.

The girls never seemed to figure out that even though they were identical in facial features, Floyd was right handed and Lloyd was left handed. If the switch was on, I would always remind the substitute to sit on the girls' proper side. That is, left side if it was Lloyd so he could put his right arm around the girl and the opposite for Floyd. Sit on the girls' right side.

The twins' proper names were James Floyd and William Lloyd and we would often tease them and ask why their parents didn't call them Jim and Bill. Floyd related the story to me many years later.

The twins had four older brothers and their parents were desperately trying for a girl. When they were born, it was a double surprise. You have to remember that back in 1947, the year all of us were born, parents didn't find out the sex of the baby nor did they often know when the births were multiple so you can imagine their surprise when not only wasn't it a girl, but the reality was that it was two more boys.

Their dad was a preacher and the boys were born early one Sunday morning so after checking on them, their dad did what he always did on Sunday. He went to church and preached. The congregation asked if he had any news and from the pulpit he told them that he had some good news and some bad news. The bad news was that they didn't have a girl. The good news was, with a broad grin on his face, that it was TWO boys. A deacon approached their dad after the service and told him, "Preacher, I'll give you $20 if you'll name them boys Floyd and Lloyd." The $20 bill went in his pocket and they've been Floyd and Lloyd ever since.

I had lied to my mom and dad about the trip because I knew if I told my dad where I was going and the real reason for the trip, he would never allow it. We were only going to be gone for a long weekend so I told them I was going to the mountains with Kenny's family. We worked our trip to coincide with a weekend when Kenny's family was actually going to be gone. I felt relatively safe that they wouldn't check up on me.

We headed out early one Thursday morning in Kenny's hot 57 Chevy, expecting to return that following Sunday. Floyd and Lloyd, who would drink an occasional beer, had gotten one of their older brothers to get us a supply. Somewhere around Dothan, Alabama I had my first taste. Unlike my beautiful wife who loves her beer, I have never had much of a taste for it and that first swig may be the reason. It was lukewarm, at best, and just didn't appeal to me at all. But if Cindy is asked what her favorite beer is, her reply is one word- cold.

One of the other little nicknames Cindy has for me along with Band Geek is Goody Two-Shoes. She is 12 years younger than me and things were a little looser and more experimental when she was a teenager compared to my era. So even though I was a child of the 60's when drugs were just beginning to take hold of my generation, I NEVER partook of any substances. No, not even one marijuana cigarette and certainly no mind-altering drug has ever entered my system.

We got to PC and checked in- all of us in one room to save money. We got in our trunks and immediately went on the prowl. PC has always had a reputation as being a party town but, again, things were considerably tamer then than they are now. There were no wet t-shirt contests or Wild Girls of PC videos but there was plenty of drinking and lots of female skin which made four horny guys from Atlanta very happy.

At some point that first night Kenny and I lost the twins. To this day we don't know where they went or what they did and neither do they. They showed up around noon the next day ready to start our girl search all over.

That night, we went to one of the local bars which we knew, by reputation, was a great place to pick up girls and they were lax about asking for ID. Again, the twins, after an hour or so, were nowhere to be seen and Kenny had latched on to a girl from South Carolina.

I was standing near the bar by myself when she walked up. She was, and this will surprise you greatly based on my prior history, a very pretty redhead, wearing black shorts and a red bikini top, a great combination for a guy who was entering the University of Georgia in just a few months. She seemed to have everything in the right places and maybe she could have been called just a few pounds overweight but when your hormones are raging like mine were, you tend to overlook some things.

"What're you doing standing here all by yourself?" she asked.

I've never been known for my glib tongue when it comes to pick up lines but I have to admit that when I said, "Right now, I'm just enjoying the scenery." was one of my best.

We started talking and it was evident that even though I didn't really look the part, she mistook me for a college guy. Since I would be real soon I didn't contradict her thinking. I discovered that she would soon be entering her second year at Millsaps, a small college located in Jackson, Mississippi. Holy jackpot, Batman! An older woman.

The rest of the night was spent talking and dancing a little. I drank Cokes while she did a pretty good job of trying to deplete their stock of beer. Around 11: 30 we decided to go get some fresh air on the beach. She was in dire need of it and I just wanted to get her alone.

We held hands as we walked on the beautiful white sand of PC. We got to a quiet, secluded area that had some beach lounges left out from that day. She had taken the role of aggressor from the beginning of our conversation but she really took charge at this point. She led me to the lounge and pushed me down. She climbed on top of me and we began some very active kissing and fondling. I removed her bikini top and well, I won't go into the details but, as I'm sure you can guess, we did the deed. Que the fireworks, explosions and rockets blasting off.

For the life of me, I cannot remember that girl's name and I am sure she doesn't remember the name of that young boy from Atlanta but I will never forget the night. We promised each other, after I had walked her back to her room, that we would stay in touch. I knew, deep inside, as I walked back to my room, that that would never happen. She had a life to live and so did I. That life did not include each other. It was just the story of a young woman cutting loose and getting rid of some inhibitions and a young boy who was ready to receive whatever she was prepared to share that night. I hope she has had a good life with lots of blessings.

The tapping on the door brought me out of my daydream and back to reality. "It's Dr. South." the voice said. I replied, "Come on in. I'm decent."

My heart started racing as I prepared myself for……..

CHAPTER 4

MY WALK TO DISCOVERY (PART 1)

The doctor entered the exam room and gave me a big hand-shake and started with the usual pleasantries of asking about my family. It's a little ironic that now that I live in a small town northeast of Atlanta that my doctor would be from the same area of Atlanta where I grew up. He had gone to our rival high school and I never knew him then but, what are the odds that two guys from the same part of town would wind up in the same little town.

While I was listening to him ask me about my family, my inner voice kept saying, "C'mon, get on with it. I'm dying here." Bad choice of words I told my inner voice.

His face then got stern as he gave me some background as to why he had run so many follow up tests. I won't go into the details of what he then told me. Most of it was medical mumbo jumbo that I didn't understand then and don't really understand any better now after all the research I've done on the disease. The one thing I did understand, however, was his diagnosis was serious and he still didn't have all the answers as to why the illness had attacked my system what with my family history of no known cases of cancer. The bottom line was I had contracted Acute Lymphoblastic Leukemia, or ALL, which is, basically, too many lymphocytes in your blood. Mine had apparently progressed at an alarming rate and, eventually, I wouldn't be able to fight off its effects on my body.

He knew of nothing that had been proven to be effective in battling the disease after it had gone this far and that it would eventually allow any little virus or infection I might pick up to take over my body. I asked him to give me a time frame and I am sure my face got white as a sheet when he told me, "Unless you decide to live in a sterile bubble world, no more than a year because it is impossible for our bodies to avoid coming into contact with something that someone with your disease can't handle."

We discussed what could be done in the meantime and he gave me some prescriptions for medication that could delay but not prevent the inevitable. He expressed his heartfelt regret to have to give me this news and we shook hands once again and said goodbye.

The world around me collapsed. The implosion going on inside me was not being felt by the outside world, however. On my walk back to the parking lot, a little boy smiled and said hi; nurses gathered in the coffee shop in the lobby of the building; and the parking lot attendant was just as surly as ever as I paid my fee and watched the gate rise allowing me access to that world. A world where, except for a select few, no one gave a damn about the news I had just received because they had problems of their own.

The drive home was, luckily, uneventful as my mind was certainly not on my driving. It was as if the car was on autopilot because I don't remember making the turns necessary to get me to my destination. And the big proof showing that my mind was absorbed with the news I just heard was the fact that I had turned off my satellite radio.

Music is always with me. It is my biggest pleasure in life. And the beauty about my radio system was that no matter what type of music I was in the mood for, it was there at my fingertips waiting for me to hit the button. If I felt like a little Perry Como or Nat King Cole, bam! hit the 50's channel; Beach Boys, Temptations, or Beatles, boom! punch the 60's; and if I wanted Chicago, Journey, or Rod Stewart, zap! the 70's were right there. Country, show tunes, jazz, and blues were always available, depending on my mood. My mood today was silence.

Yes, music has always been a huge part of my life. It is one of the few influences my dad had on me. The radio or our hi-fi system was always on when I was young. I grew up listening to the orchestras of Hugo Winterhalter or Paul Whiteman, the big band sounds of Glenn Miller, and on Saturday nights it was a-one and a-two Lawrence Welk with his Champagne Music Makers.

I started playing the trumpet when I was 7 years old and once I started down that musical pathway, I didn't want to stop. Being able to play a musical instrument allowed me the opportunity for.........

CHAPTER 5

MY WALKS ON STAGE

Through music, I was able to meet the man who, as I look back on my life, probably had the greatest influence on me. Certainly, there are many men and women who affect and shape the person you become, but none had the profound influence that Charles I. Bradley had on me.

I have no recollection about my decision to begin taking music lessons and why I chose the trumpet. As I said, music was always playing in our house and I guess that had some bearing on it but why the trumpet out of all the other instruments, I just don't remember. Unless it was because one of dad's favorite recording artists was Harry James, the great trumpeter, and, subconsciously, the beautiful sounds he made with his horn influenced me more than I thought at the time.

I'll give dad credit for one thing- when I told him I wanted to learn to play an instrument, he never hesitated in his willingness to make sure I had the best instrument money could buy.

Mr. Bradley was the director of an organization called the East Atlanta Elementary Band. It was comprised of students from several grade schools in that section of the city. He would come to each school one day a week and meet, individually, with the students who were members and then the entire band would practice after school one or two nights, depending on whether we had a big concert coming up or not.

When I decided to join, I met with him one day when he came to Burgess, the elementary school I attended. He, very sternly, told me what I would have to do to play in the band. He laid out a time-consuming practice schedule for me- a schedule that would considerably cut into my play time after school, but I wasn't deterred. I had made up my mind to master that trumpet. I do remember that he told me that I had made a good choice for my instrument since I appeared to have excellent lip structure. He added, with a little twinkle in his eye, that trumpet players made the best kissers in the world due to the muscle they developed on their upper lip from their playing. That information had little affect on me at that young age but I secured that fact in the back of my brain for future use.

I practiced hard each day and was so proud when, after just a few weeks of practicing, I could play "Twinkle, Twinkle Little Star." I remember like it was yesterday playing the song for Mom and Dad that night when they got home from work. When I finished playing for them, Dad told me to pick up my trumpet and music. He marched me next door and told me to play the song again in front of my first audience. I think their dog howled the entire time.

The music bug had bitten me hard and I kept at it until I had improved enough to join the "B" band. This was a group made up of beginners who weren't ready to join the "A" band quite yet. We still needed a good bit of development in learning how to play as a unit instead of by yourself as you practiced at home. I had now advanced to the point where I could play the old hymn "Abide With Me", "Happy Birthday", and a few other simple melodies. I was so excited the day I would go to that first practice. Upon arriving at the practice location, that excitement turned into pure terror, however.

The "A" Band was finishing up their practice as I entered the auditorium and took a seat in the back. Mr. Bradley was at the podium with his baton waving back and forth as the band played "Washington Post March" by John Philip Sousa. All of a sudden, he rapped the baton on his music stand and started yelling at the clarinet section that had entered two bars early. "Count your measures! Count your measures!" he screamed.

Wait a minute, I thought to myself. This is the not the same nice man who greeted me warmly that day at school when I told him I wanted to be in his band. This is not the gentle person who told me I would be a great kisser one day. This is a mean man who yells at kids. I started tearing up and wanted to run from that auditorium as fast as I could. The only thing keeping me from doing so was the thought that I would hear even worse yelling from my Dad if I had made that decision.

So, I mustered up the courage to take my seat when it was our turn to practice and I never once regretted that decision. Just a few months later, way ahead of the normal schedule, I was chosen to join the "A" Band where I had some of the best moments of my life as well as some of my best memories.

When I shared the news with Dad that I had made the big time, he smiled and said go get in the car. I thought, "Oh, boy! He's gonna take me to Miss Georgia Ice Cream Shop in East Atlanta, to reward me for making the "A" Band. Instead, we drove down Memorial Drive to the Cecil White Piano Company. Mr. White sold, not only pianos as the name indicated, but all types of musical instruments, including trumpets.

Dad told him he wanted a top of the line trumpet and Mr. White said he had the very thing. It seemed that a member of the Atlanta Symphony had ordered a French hand-made Besson trumpet from him but had backed out and it had just come in the day before. He showed it to Dad and even to my untrained eye, it was a thing of beauty. The brass gleamed brightly, the valves worked like pistons, and, after playing a few notes, I knew I could make beautiful music with this instrument. Dad opened his wallet and paid him the $300 retail price, a small fortune in those days, on the spot. I still have that trumpet today almost 60 years later and it still has a beautiful tone when I play the correct notes.

The next few years were spent learning at the feet of a master conductor. Remember, we were just a bunch of fifth, sixth, and seventh graders yet, we were playing stirring marches, wonderful symphonies, and marvelous overtures from the world of musical theater and we were playing them better than most high school bands around. We won awards and superior ratings at every festival we entered. We traveled to Hattiesburg, Mississippi, making a fun stop in New Orleans afterwards, to play at a conference for band directors from all over the country and we were fantastic. The reason- Charles I. Bradley.

Looking back on those years I often define him to others as a taskmaster. He was quite strict, allowing absolutely no horseplay or talking during practice. He frequently said that to be a good musician, you had to have discipline and we believed him because even at that young age, we wanted to be the best. And we were.

Competition was keen between the members of each individual section. It was an honor to play in the first section and an even greater honor to be first chair. That meant you were the best of the best. Mr. Bradley had a points system that went a long way in determining where you sat within your own section. He would award points for excellent play or for practicing even more than you were supposed to. But he would also take away points if you cut up during band practice and he would do this in front of the rest of the band which was always humiliating.

By the time I entered fifth grade, I was already in first section battling against two older boys and my arch rival, Johnny W., who was in the same grade as I but who went to another grammar school. Then came sixth grade and I was promoted to second chair behind Alan P. who was a year older. The three of us, I believe, gave Mr. Bradley great comfort in having a quality trumpet section because all three of us were advanced musicians for our age.

Mr. Bradley suggested early on that I take private lessons to enhance my skills. He gave me the name of a man who gave lessons out of a downtown music store called Ritter Music Company. The store was located on Auburn Avenue, which meant that each Saturday I had to ride the bus, by myself, all the way downtown to take these lessons. Now, before you label my parents as careless by sending their 8 year old son on a bus ride like this each week, you need to remember that it was a different era.

My tutor was a man named Carl Stewart and in a strange twist of coincidence, he was the same Atlanta Symphony trumpeter who intended to buy the trumpet that I now owned. He certainly helped hone my skills and made me an even better trumpeter than I could have ever been on my own.

One Saturday lesson proved to be quite embarrassing for me. I went through my regular Saturday morning routine- bathed, dressed, got my trumpet case, and went to the corner bus stop to wait for #10 to come along. I thought the case felt lighter than usual as I departed the bus and made my way to the store but didn't give it much more thought than that. Mr. Stewart called me in to the small studio where we had our lesson each week. I laid the case down and opened it and realized why it felt so light. No trumpet.

"Very difficult to have a lesson without your instrument." Mr. Stewart said trying hard to hold back his laughter. Then I remembered. I had been cleaning it the night before, oiling the valves making sure they worked efficiently, and I had simply forgot to put the instrument back into its case. Maybe that was the lesson I was supposed to master that day- always put your trumpet in its case.

I took great pride in wearing the green and white uniform of EAEB even though it did look rather tacky being topped off with a beret-like hat that never seemed to sit correctly on my head. We wore green pants with a green vest atop a white shirt. On one side of the vest was a white, embroidered shamrock while the other side was adorned with the medals we had won, both individually and collectively. Those medals are still with me in a box and I want them to be with me when I'm cremated because they still are some of my most prized possessions.

One medal stands out from all the rest, however, and was the basis for my first walk to a stage. At the end of your seventh grade year, Mr. Bradley would award some special medals to his most-prized students. There were some lesser awards; perfect attendance, most points, etc. but the most coveted awards were the ones he awarded to the best brass, woodwind, and percussionist player in the band.

I wanted that medal badly but knew that there was stiff competition. We had two great trombonists, Gary W. and Tim A.; an excellent French horn player, Howard M.; and Tom H. was a talented baritone player. And then there was my good pal, Johnny W. While I sat first chair most of the year, the truth was that we were really 1a and 1b when it came to ability. Nevertheless, I was extremely nervous when it came time for the awards to be meted out.

The night was doubly meaningful because it was one of the rare occasions when my Dad came to a concert. As I've indicated, Dad always supported my musical interests, he just wouldn't get out and go to the concerts. Said he didn't like crowds. So, for most concerts, Mom and I would catch a ride with Gloria W., a cute trumpeter that I secretly had a crush on, and her family. But on this night they were both there.

We finished our concert to a rousing standing ovation. Mr. Bradley took his bows and then asked for quiet. The Best Brass Player Award, or Brass Achievement Medal as he called it, was the last to be announced and I fidgeted the entire time. But then came time for our award. I can still remember his words to this day.

"I have had many fine musicians pass through this band over the years," he said, "and some of the finest are playing for you tonight for the last time. I feel a twinge of heartache in losing many of these students because this has been the best group I've ever had." Every head of every member of that band went higher and every chest puffed out more with the pride we felt in hearing those words.

"But in my 15 years of being associated with this organization, I don't think I've ever had a student work as hard and perform as well as this one. It is with great pleasure that I award the Brass Achievement Medal to........." C'mon, Mr. Bradley, you're killing me here. "Randy Blalock."

My heart leapt. I stood and before I could take a step, Johnny did something that I'm not sure I would have been big enough to do if our roles had been reversed. He grabbed me and gave me a huge bear hug- an act not really in the character of a seventh grader. I looked around me and there was nothing but a sea of smiles from my fellow band mates. I was a "cute kid with a great personality" as the yearbooks always said, but I think most of the members of the band were truly glad that I had won. A lot of neat, wonderful things have happened to me in my life, but I have never felt as accepted as I did in that moment.

I looked out to the audience and saw my Mom crying. I looked at Dad and he was smiling broader than I'd ever seen him smile, before or ever again. As I approached Mr. Bradley, always a man of extreme poise and correctness, I knew I was supposed to have a semblance of decorum but my body would not allow me to be reserved. I started running to him and jumped in his bewildered and unexpecting arms. I know I embarrassed him but there was no other act or demonstration that would have properly shown my admiration and, yes, my love of him. At that moment, all the yelling, all the hours of practice, all the effort was worth it.

As I look back on that walk I took with him, the thing that separates him from other teachers was his passion for the subject. Music was his life and he wanted to pass it on to others.

In the 70's there was a show on every weeknight evening that did features of people and places around Atlanta produced by WAGA-TV. I wrote them and suggested that they do a feature on him and they agreed with my suggestion and even asked me to be interviewed on air. I jumped at the chance to share my feelings for him to the world.

During that show, Mr. Bradley summed up his own personal philosophy regarding his love for teaching music so well. He said, "Children are like flowers. The more you feed them with the wonderful things in life, the more they grow. Music makes them grow into beautiful gardens."

When Mr. Bradley died, I was asked to be one of his pall bearers. The walk I took that day from the hearse to the grave site was one of the most difficult I've ever been asked to make. Saying goodbye to your mentor is never an easy thing.

August 18, 1965. That was the date of my second walk to a stage and it also is one of the most significant in the history of the great city of Atlanta.

It was a Wednesday and muggy. The temperatures were in the low 90's by mid-afternoon but the city was ablaze with the anticipation of who was arriving later that afternoon and who would be performing at Atlanta-Fulton County Stadium that night. And the excitement for five guys from the southeast part of that city was even greater because we were going to have a small part in that historic night. We were going to be one of the opening acts, and the only band strictly from Atlanta, to open for the Beatles during their concert here in Atlanta.

Our group, The Noblemen, had won a Battle of the Bands contest sponsored by the local AM radio station, WQXI, back in the Spring and the prize for doing so would be to play at this concert. Yes, long before satellite radio systems, cassette players in your cars, 8-tracks, and FM stations, there were AM stations.

The journey to get to this point had started a few years earlier in Jimmy R's garage. Kenny had started messing with a guitar when he turned 14 and he had a pretty good voice. Like he needed anything else to win the hearts of the girls, now he was going to be a rock n roll star. I couldn't let him outdo me so I started messing with an old bass guitar that one of my neighbors owned. We self-taught ourselves how to play and decided our Junior year in high school that we were good enough to start a band.

We teemed up with two other classmates and started messing around with some of the songs of that time in the garage of one of the guys so that the noise I'm sure we were making didn't disturb too many people. The names of the four guys were: Jimmy, Ernie G., Randy, and Kenny so one day when we were trying to come up with a name, Jimmy, the funny man of the group, took the first letter of each of our names and said loudly, "That's it! We'll be The Four Jerks!" It stuck and that was the start.

We played at the baseball field that summer and at classmates pool parties. When school started, we played a few concerts but we just weren't clicking. That was when Kenny and I were approached by a guy that had graduated high school two years earlier. Freddy had a bit of a reputation as a bad boy but we knew he could play and sing after hearing him at different talent shows.

So, the Four Jerks split. Jimmy and Ernie formed a group called The Misfits and they became the hit of the school. Kenny and I joined Freddy W. and two guys he knew from where he was working and we became The Noblemen. Freddy was the lead singer, a darn good lead guitarist, and self-appointed manager and before we knew it, we were playing all over town.

Freddy had gotten connected with a couple of the deejays at the radio station and they booked us for a lot of events that the station sponsored. This gave us exposure all around the town and we quickly developed a following. We'd see the same group of girls at FunTown, Misty Waters, and other local teenage gathering places that the station had us playing. And because of our name, the station even had us outfitted in British period clothes, much like Jerry Seinfeld's puffy shirt he later made famous.

Let me tell you a little more about Misty Waters because it was quite an interesting place. MW was located on Candler Road and was a gathering place during the summer for teenagers of several schools in the area, including Murphy. Its main attraction was the man-made lake with an actual beach area where you could actually lay out a beach towel and soak up the sun. Of course, the guys spent all of their time patrolling the beach looking at the girls or swimming out to the 15 ft. tower where they could show off by jumping off into the icy-cold, spring-fed water. If you weren't into the beach scene, there was also a traditional pool.

At the top of the hill at the rear of the property was a building that served dual purposes. During the week it was a skating rink but on the weekends it was converted into a teenage club. Local groups would play and several of them, at least the headliner of the group, went on to future stardom. Mac Davis and his band, the Zots, along with Tommy Roe and Joe South all got their starts there. Most of the time MW was a pretty calm venue but when fights broke out they were legendary.

If you're not familiar with Mac Davis, maybe you remember one of his biggest hits, *It's Hard to be Humble:*

> *O Lord, it's hard to be humble*
> *When you're perfect in every way*
> *I can't wait to look in the mirror*
> *Cause I get better lookin' each day*

To know me is to love me
I must be as helluva man
O Lord, it's hard to be humble
But I'm doing the best that I can

We played there on many occasions by ourselves but we also played on the same bill as Sam the Sham and the Pharoahs of "Wooly Bully" fame as well as a young Ronnie Milsap before he skyrocketed to country stardom. Between school and then basketball practice and games for Kenny and I who were still in school, we didn't have much time to practice and it was evident this was getting on Freddy's nerves because he really wanted to do something with his talent and for Kenny and I, it was just something fun to do.

We entered the contest I mentioned feeling that we had a good chance since we were already doing a lot of Beatles cover songs. There were five bands that made it to the finals and we were to perform second by luck of the draw. We were to do three songs before a live audience and the winner would be decided based on audience reaction and the votes of three judges. We were doing Atlanta Idol before there was an American Idol, I guess.

We thought long and hard over which three songs to perform but, as always, Freddy's decision won out. We opened with "For Your Love", a song that had been recorded by The Yardbirds earlier that year. Then, we knew we had to do a Beatles song that featured Freddy's voice so, "All My Loving" was chosen. To finish our set we broke away from the British sound and paid tribute to Roy Orbison by doing "Pretty Woman" but we put a twist on it that involved the audience. Before we played, each of us went out to the crowd and picked a girl to come on stage and stand beside us as we played the song. That did it! We won in a landslide even though we probably weren't the technically tightest band of the contestants.

The summer was spent practicing in every spare minute we could find. We knew this would be the largest gathering we had ever played in front of but we were also realistic. We knew that the crowd that would be there was not going to really care a gnat's behind what we did or how we sounded. Those screaming girls were there for the Beatles and rightfully so.

The day arrived and Kenny and I decided we needed to get out of our respective houses before the big night. He picked me up and we drove by the stadium. We were amazed to see hundreds of people already lining up outside even though it would be several hours before the gates opened up. Never have figured out why so many people were there so early since it was reserved seating and they already had assigned seats but then my wife doesn't understand why I have to be in my seat for a University of Georgia football game an hour before kickoff either.

We had met with the concert promoters and the two deejays, Tony Taylor and Paul Drew who would act as emcees for the show, the previous week to get the guidelines and all the Do's and Don'ts of what was expected of us. It was at that meeting that we were told we would actually be introduced to the Fab Four and we would be allowed to spend a few minutes with them but in no way were we to harass or bother them.

The five of us, in two separate cars with one pulling a trailer filled with our clothes and equipment, arrived at the stadium at 4:00. The concert was scheduled to start at around 8 PM and we would go on at 8:10 after a brief fashion show put on by one of the local department stores.

We got dressed in a little cubby hole they called our dressing room and walked around the underbelly of the stadium. We could hear the crowd coming in above us and, for the first time, I got nervous. Freddy wanted to do a quick tune up and run-through but we had to play with no amps, making it very difficult to get a good read on how well we were blending. The radio station wanted us to do the same exact set we had done at the contest and they had already checked with the Beatles' people making sure they were not doing "All My Loving."

We ate a quick bite and about 6 PM, Paul Drew came and got us and escorted us in to meet the Beatles. We entered a smoke-filled room and it was evident at first sniff that they weren't smoking Winstons. George and Ringo were over in a corner sharing a joint giving us a mere head nod to acknowledge our existence. Paul was at a piano, ignoring us completely, playing the melody line that we would recognize later when it was recorded as "Paperback Writer". But John was another story.

He jumped up from his chair, held out his hands, and said in an awful imitation of a Southern accent, "Hi! How ya'll lads doin'?" We laughed at his attempt and each of us shook hands with him. He congratulated us on winning the contest and said he was sorry he wouldn't be able to hear our set but wished us good luck. Knowing that Freddy was our leader, he whispered something in his ear and, to this day, Freddy has never told us what he said.

Now, there was nothing to do but wait. We did just that as we waited outside one of the dugouts while the roadies for one of the other opening acts that was on the tour with the Beatles, Cannibal and the Headhunters, took our instruments and did a sound check on the stage.

The crowd was buzzing and every time there was even the slightest movement from the third base dugout, the screaming would start. The minutes crept by until it was our turn to go on. Freddy gave us his usual pep talk when he looked at us and said, "Don't fuck this up!"

Tony Taylor took the mic on stage and welcomed the fans giving them a few kind words of instruction. One of the points he made was to give explicit details as to where the medical stations were. I think I've read that over 100 girls were treated that night for various reasons. I'm sure many more were treated by their personal doctors for sore throats in the weeks following.

Tony then told the crowd, "And now to start us off tonight, please welcome the band that won Quixie in Dixie's (the nickname for the radio station) Battle of the Band Contest, Atlanta's own—The Noblemen!"

We stepped out of the dugout to polite screams and cheers and walked in a brisk manner, as we had been told to do, to the stage. I remember nothing after that. We made it through the set and we did great. No foul-ups; no broken guitar strings as Paul would later experience; no missed notes that we could tell. The sound system, for an open stadium facility, was pretty good because one thing a band needs is to be able to hear everyone else.

We finished the last notes of "Pretty Woman", took our bows, which were orchestrated to be low, sweeping bows from the waist, very regal-like, and walked back to the dugout where the next group was waiting to go on. Again, the crowd was polite and I even heard one girl sitting near the dugout call out, "Freddy, you're cute."

We were allowed to stay in the dugout to watch the rest of the show but like the others gathered there that night, we cared only about the Beatles. Paul Drew took the stage at approximately 9: 30 and after a few more thanks and words of instruction brought them on with two simple words, the only two words necessary- The Beatles!

Their entire show only lasted about 40 minutes but it was packed with eleven songs. I wrote down the list of songs they did that night on a piece of paper I found in the dugout. That smudged piece of paper is the only thing I have left from that evening other than my wonderful memories. The songs, in order, were:

Twist and Shout
She's a Woman
I Feel Fine
Dizzy Miss Lizzy
Ticket to Ride
Everybody's Trying to Be My Baby (Ringo's solo)

Can't Buy Me Love
Baby's in Black
I Wanna Be Your Man
Help!
I'm Down

There is no way to truly describe the feelings each of us felt that night. When you rank the Top 10 important days in your life, one like this has to be ranked in that list. Some years later, the magnitude of that day became even more important.

Like many other people, I was watching Monday Night Football on the evening of December 8, 1980. It was a little after 11 PM and John Smith, the placekicker for the New England Patriots, was lining up to attempt a game winning field goal against the Miami Dolphins. Howard Cosell interrupted Frank Gifford's commentary with the news that John Lennon had been shot twice in the back outside his New York City residence. He had been rushed to the hospital but had been pronounced DOA.

My jaw dropped and after a few moments, when the words sank in, I cried. I didn't always agree with his political, moral, or religious views but I admired him as a musician. He was, without question, the most influential musician, along with his writing partner, Paul McCartney, of my era. I looked down at my right hand, the hand that had shaken his, and realized that I had met and touched greatness. Then when George died, a part of my youth also died. There will never be another group like the Beatles.

The Noblemen broke up about a year and a half later because we lost our leader. The radio station continued to use us for many of their shows and one of them turned out to be the big break Freddy was looking for.

In the autumn of 1966 the station sponsored an event called The Atlanta Teenage Exhibition at a downtown building referred to as the Merchandise Mart. It was a weeklong affair but on the final two nights the station brought in Paul Revere and the Raiders to do concerts both nights. We were to be their opening act.

The nights went so well that a few months later, when one of the Raiders was drafted into the military, Freddy got a call from Paul Revere[1] himself asking him to join them and become their new Raider. Obviously, he jumped at the chance and went on to perform with them for the next few years. I admit that there was a twinge of envy as I would watch Freddy perform with the group on the TV show, "Where the Action Is" or on Ed Sullivan but I knew that's what Freddy wanted more than anything. After leaving the Raiders, Freddy went on to make a good living in the country music industry releasing several albums along the way. I haven't seen him in many years but I hear he lives in Nashville and is still writing and producing for other singers. Thanks Freddy for pushing us.

I pulled into our carport and opened the door to the home I had shared with my wife for the past 26 years. The sound of my wife's voice brought me back to the now where I continued ....

---

1 Paul Revere Dick died on October 4, 2014

MY WALK TO DISCOVERY (PART 2)

"Honey! Is that you?" her voice from upstairs called. Somehow, I had made it home without difficulty despite the fact that I remember nothing about the drive back home from the doctor's office.

I answered, "Yeah, sweetie. It's me."

One of the prevailing thoughts that I recall discussing with myself on the drive home was how I was going to break this news to her. Of course, the other thing that keeps going through your mind is "why me?" I believe that my faith is pretty strong but you can't help but wonder why you've been dealt this bad hand when all you've tried to do all your life is be the best you could be. You don't smoke or drink to excess, you pay your taxes, you attend church and even teach a class, yet, this has happened to you. You just can't understand it and your initial reaction is to get angry with God for allowing this to happen.

It's only later, when you've had a chance to absorb the impact of the message that you realize that God didn't allow this to happen. Just because we have a strong faith, no matter what our religious beliefs may be, we are not immune to the evils of the world. In fact, some times we are given tests to see just how strong our faith is but I strongly believe that faith-filled people have an advantage over non-believers because we have God right there beside us, helping us face the challenge. This, for us, was going to be a challenge. But I was confident that with God's guidance, we could face it.

I knew that Cindy was a very strong woman. She was highly regarded at her company because of her strength in making very difficult Human Resource decisions. She had a great deal of responsibility in the bank she worked for and was respected and thought highly of by those that reported to her as well as those she reported to.

But she had inner resolve to handle personal things as well. When her father passed away two years ago, she assumed the mantle of responsibility and helped her mother get through the emotional and financial problems they faced. She did this not only because she was the oldest child, but because she knew it was what her dad would have wanted. She amazes me more and more every day that we are together.

When we met, Cindy and I both worked for the same bank in downtown Atlanta and both of us were going through our mutual separations and divorces from our first spouses. My breakup had hit me hard leaving two children behind and so, when asked by some fellow workers to go out to a local club one Friday night after work in Buckhead called *Studebaker's,* I thought that would be something I needed.

Studebaker's specialized in oldies, which at that time meant music of the 50's and 60's. Since this was the music from my youth, I loved the place the minute I walked in.

Cindy and I knew each other in passing at the bank but this was the first time I had seen her outside of working hours. I had always thought she was gorgeous but, that night, she looked especially good.

I've always enjoyed dancing so I made the rounds with several of the ladies who said their husbands never danced with them and even had a few fast dances with Cindy. Boy, did she look good on the dance floor!

The club's deejay would have a routine of playing several upbeat songs and then slow down things a bit by playing three slow songs in a row. When one of these sets started, I got up my nerve and asked Cindy if she wanted to dance. She agreed and I held her in my arms for the first time.

I have no recollection of what the first two songs were but I will never forget the third because it changed my life. During the first two songs we chatted while dancing but then *"Chances Are"* by the great Johnny Mathis started playing. I found myself pulling her closer to me and we swayed to that beautiful melody without saying a word. Then, as the song was reaching its last few bars I did something that has made all the difference.

I don't know what made me do it but we looked at each other and I gave her a soft, little kiss. No great passion exhibited with it but at the same time I meant it to be more than just a friendly "thanks for the dance" kiss. Wow! What a little kiss can do. After that, I was absolutely smitten and she has since told me that she felt something special as well.

It is sometimes the smallest things, things we felt were insignificant at the time, that can wind up having the biggest impact in our lives. What might have happened if John Wilkes Booth had been detained by anyone in Ford's Theater that fateful night? How would history have been changed if Alexander Fleming had given up and penicillin not been discovered? And while it does not rank up there with other far more important acts in the history of the world, what would have happened if I had not kissed Cindy that night? Would we have wound up together anyway or would she be spending her life with someone else meaning that my life would be totally different from how it has been these last twenty-seven years? But I did kiss her and that little act has made all the difference.

We started seeing each other regularly after that. She is a very fun-loving person and never meets a stranger (she got that from her dad who would talk to the wall if he thought he had a chance of the wall talking back) and we had so many wonderful moments together. I knew she cared for me so, I decided I would try this marriage thing again. When I decided to ask her to marry me, I knew there was only one way to propose to her.

I had bought her ring and asked her to go to the place where it had all started one Friday night after work. We went to *Studebaker's,* of course, and while she went to the bathroom, I went up to the deejay's booth and told him what I had in mind. He thought the idea was great and added, "Keep her back to me while you're dancing so she won't see what I'm doing." Everything was in motion.

Shortly after her return the deejay started one of his slow sets and we went out to the dance floor. Again, I have no idea what the first two songs were but I knew what the third was going to be.

As the first notes of *"Chances Are"* began, the deejay began motioning with his arms for the other couples to move back off the dance floor. Now, with no one else around us, I got down on my knee, pulled the ring out of my pocket, and popped the question. She gave me that big smile of hers, the one that lights up an entire room. She nodded. We kissed. The crowd cheered and applauded. And I became the luckiest man in the world.

We married on May 28, 1988 in a private ceremony performed by Rev. Chalmes Holmes, the pastor of First Baptist Church of Winder at the time. Only the immediate family attended. Being the consummate romantic I wanted to do something special for her- something that would make this an especially memorable day for the both of us. So, during the ceremony, I recited a poem I had written to her for the occasion. Here it is:

I wake each day into a world
With many wondrous sights
The beauty of the rising sun
The sparkle of star light
I know that God's been good to me
As I have oft' confessed
For all the things He's given me
I surely am quite blessed

He's given me my health, my job
Two parents that I love
And then He gave a boy and girl
Two gifts from up above
And when I thought there'd be no more
That He could possibly do
He sent another gift to me
Then God gave me you

I have never regretted for one minute that decision and here we are, twenty-six years later. Do we have squabbles and disagreements? Certainly! We both are rather strong-willed and I can be quite opinionated and controlling from time to time which does not go over very well with her, but I love her with all my heart and even though I am the more romantic of the two and more inclined to show it, I know she loves me. This news would tear her up inside.

She came down the stairs and gave me a hug and a kiss. It was unusual for her to be home on a workday but we were getting ready to go on vacation the next week and she was home getting a head start on her packing.

My girl is stylish, to say the very least. At the very most, she is a shopaholic. Don't get me wrong, I am always so proud to be seen with her because she always looks great but it takes her a long time to select her wardrobe for a trip because she has so much to choose from. We have a running joke that I know both the UPS and Fed Ex delivery men on a first name basis because they make a stop at our house most every day. If it's not a Talbot's delivery, then it is definitely something from QVC. My other clothes joke on her is that when I go shopping for her, I walk into a store and ask for the gaudy section. The more sequins, sparkles, and glitter the better.

She has got to select just the right outfits for us to go to dinner in each night but the really tough job comes in the selection of which shoes to take to match the outfits. Then, her jewelry must match that. And, of course, she has to try on each outfit to make sure it looks just right. It easily takes her a full day to pack for a five-day trip. When we went to France last year for two weeks to celebrate our 25th wedding anniversary, I didn't see her for a full week.

"Are you packed?" she asked. "We leave on Sunday, you know."

"Yeah, babe. Remember, you picked everything out for me a few days ago. All I have to do is put them in my hang up bag."

Of course, for me it was an easy task. Two or three swim trunks; a pair of dress shoes and a pair of Crocks for the pool; three pairs of shorts; a few polo shirts; some dress shirts for dinners; two pair of slacks; underwear and I'm good to go. From the looks of her clothes that were laid out in the floor, we would need a U-Haul-It just to get to the airport.

Then came the moment I dreaded. "How'd things go at Dr. South's? Why'd you have to go take all those extra tests?" she asked.

I looked into those beautiful brown eyes and I just couldn't do it. Here she was, so excited about going down to Mexico and laying out in the sun for a few days with good friends. I just couldn't take that away from her by giving her the news.

Nothing was going to happen over the next few days so I just said, "Oh, he just wanted to monitor my white blood cell count that had gotten a little high to make sure I wasn't becoming anemic." Not a total lie I justified to myself. He was monitoring those things. I just conveniently chose to leave out the seriousness of the matter.

I wasn't sure if she sensed then that there was more to it than that but she let it drop and went back upstairs to finish her project. I felt guilty about not being honest with her but this was a trip when even she had been counting down the days until our departure. This was a chance to reconnect with two couples that lived hundreds of miles away from us in Indianapolis, Indiana who had become four of our closest friends in the world. And the way we met brought back memories of............

MY WALK TO FRIENDSHIP (PART 1)

This was going to be our third visit to a location outside of Cancun that had become one of our favorite places in the world. It was an all-adult, all-inclusive location with an incredible pool and a swim-up bar where the drinks, make mine a Miami Vice and Cindy will have a beer, flowed freely. To use the word opulent in describing the resort is an understatement.

We were originally introduced to it back in 2010 by Cindy's sister and husband who went there just about every year. They always raved about it but I had always pooh-poohed the idea of going there since the beach and I are not on the best of speaking terms. I'm not a big water person and I've had some history with skin cancer which hinders my sun intake. Besides, there is nothing more boring to me than baking in the hot sun with sand in your butt crack. But for Cindy, knowing how much she loves the ocean, I had decided to make the most of it and give it a try. If nothing else, I thought, the food and drink could entertain me. After that first experience, I'm not sure why I ever considered going back in 2012. But because of what happened to us during that visit, we were now returning in 2014.

On the day we arrived at the resort, my brother and sister in-laws were on their last day of their annual trip there. We partied in the pool all afternoon and somehow found our way to the restaurant that night. To be cool, I had worn a pair of loafers with no socks. That was the beginning of my downfall.

After dinner we decided to walk to the shopping area that was located in the complex- a walk of about a mile from the resort. While the girls looked in every store, Cindy's sister has the same shopping addiction that Cindy has, the guys followed close behind. When they had made several purchases, we walked back to the resort. Remember- no socks.

Before I go further I need to tell you that after years of pounding on pavement while jogging, considerable time spent running up and down basketball and tennis courts, and shagging flies in the outfield my feet had lost the viability of the nerve endings. In layman's terms, I had no feeling in the soles of my feet so, I did not realize the damage that had been done that night from all the walking.

Both of us had imbibed that night so upon arriving back at our room, we crashed. I am an early riser so I didn't want to disturb my Sleeping Beauty by making coffee so I left the room in search of same and to explore this beautiful resort. I didn't bother putting on my shoes.

I located a pot of coffee, poured me a cup, and headed back to the room. Getting nearer to the room, I noticed what appeared to be small droplets on the pavement. Looked like a trail of blood. Loving a good mystery, I followed the trail just like Sherlock Holmes or Hercule Poirot would. Strange, I thought. They look like they were going in the direction of our building.

Sure enough, the trail continued through the open-air lobby of our building and down the hall toward our room. I was further amazed when they stopped at our door. I used the key, opened the door, and there in the foyer of our room they appeared again. The bathroom was covered in these droplets which I now recognized definitely as blood. I pulled the lid down on the toilet, sat down, and lifted my foot so that I could see the bottom of it. Lifting my left foot I discovered a blister the size of a half-dollar, bleeding like the proverbial stuck pig.

Being the helpless man that most of us are, I screamed for Cindy. Drowsily she came into the bathroom, took one look at my foot, and screamed, "What have you done? Did you step on some glass?"

Meekly I mumbled, "No, I think it is a blister I must have gotten last night."

I could have guessed her next words. "I told you to wear socks, didn't I?"

We bandaged it up, declined any medical assistance from the hotel, and spent the next few days monitoring it for infection. It seemed to be doing okay until the day before we were due to leave when I developed a fever and saw that the foot was swelling with little red veins climbing up my leg.

As we packed to go to the airport the next day, I could barely get my left shoe on. It was an agonizing flight back home but finally we made it.

The next morning was Sunday and I was due to teach my class until Cindy saw that my leg was now purple. She looked at me and said, "You're not going anywhere but the hospital."

Knowing that she never left the house unless she was fully made up, I thought I'd be a smart-ass. I told her that if she could get ready in five minutes, then we'd go. She called my bluff and off to the emergency room we went.

Long story short, I spent the next four days in the hospital full of IV tubes trying to stop the infection. This was my second trip to a hospital and it was just as unpleasant as the first that I'll tell you about later. The doctor said that what I had contracted was cellulitis along with a flesh-eating virus that had gotten in my system through the blister. He also said that if I had not come to the hospital when I had, the infection could have gone to my heart and killed me. Needless to say, Cindy has never let me forget this and I have never, uncool or not, worn shoes without socks again.

So, in spite of this experience, we went back in 2012. That's when we met Jeff L. and his wife, Dawn, and Mark and Cathi S.

Cindy and I had a fairly regular routine while at the resort. We'd wake in time to see the sunrise which is always breath-taking, go workout in the gym to get rid of the calories we would be replacing during the day, go get breakfast at the buffet, and go to the pool. All of this took place before 9 am.

One day, we had staked out or lounges near two ladies who were already sipping their first drinks of the day. I noticed two guys at the bar, who I presumed were their husbands since no one else was at the pool yet, and asked Cindy if she wanted anything. I was ready for my first Miami Vice. For those of you who may not know what that is, it is a combination pina colada and strawberry daiquiri.

I walked through the warm water over to the bar and did something that I rarely do but by doing so this time it has developed into this incredible friendship. I struck up a conversation with them.

I admit that I am not the world's most outgoing individual. I am rather private so it is rare when I initiate a conversation with a stranger. Cindy is the exact opposite of that and there is no question that she got this trait from her father. Her dad was one of the most personable people you'd ever want to meet. He would talk to anyone, anytime, anywhere. I gave the family eulogy when he passed away shortly after we had returned from this trip and one of the things that I lovingly said was that after fifteen minutes in heaven, he knew everybody's name, where they were from, and who their momma was.

On those rare occasions when I have struck up a conversation with someone, Cindy has always been quick to respond, "My, aren't you the little Ambrose (her dad's name)?"

The three of us sat at the bar and started talking about various subjects but when three guys get together, the conversation usually turns to sports. We talked about our sports' bucket list; those events we want to experience before we're called to the great arena in the sky. I mentioned that I had just gotten to scratch one off my list the past April by going to my first ever Masters Golf Tournament. Sorry, but that's a good story as well.

I used to write a weekly sports column for one of our local newspapers. The column was called *IN MY OPINION* and it was exactly that. It provided me with an outlet to vent some of my frustrations with what is going on in the world of sports today, both collegiately and professionally. One week, however, I wrote about my bucket list and said that the Masters was definitely included.

The next week at church, Dr. Ron Saunders, the retired Superintendent of our county school system, walked up to me and said, "I really enjoyed your column this week." After thanking him he continued, "So, you've really never gone to the Masters?"

"No, Ron. In spite of living just a few hundred miles from Augusta all my life, I've never had the opportunity."

Those of you who follow sports and particularly the world of golf know that the waiting list to get season tickets is significant. There have been major court battles and families have been torn apart in this state over who gets the tickets when the owner dies. Masters tickets are treasures so his next words were totally shocking.

"Well, you're going this year."

"What do you mean?" I stammered.

"I've been lucky enough to have tickets for over 20 years and I always try to find someone who has never been and let them go to the first round played on Thursday so that they can experience the beauty of the course." he told me.

I was dumbfounded. I was awestruck. I was speechless. Finally, I got out, "Are you serious? That is just so generous."

He assured me he was serious and he told me he would give me the details as the date got closer. For some reason, Cindy did not go to church that day and I couldn't wait to get home to tell her this exciting news. But in my head, I was going to take my son with me. He is much more of an avid golfer than I am and I knew he would enjoy it greatly.

I ran in to the house, called for her, and told her what had happened. "I can't wait to call Brian and tell him." I said, apparently stupidly.

"Like hell you're taking Brian! I'm going with you." That, as they say, was that and we had a great day. Unfortunately, we had had an early blooming period that year in Georgia so the lovely dogwoods, azaleas, and other flowers were not in their full beauty but we still had a marvelous experience. An added bonus was that we got to see Tiger Woods up close and, also, that was the year Bubba Watson, a University of Georgia alum, won his first green jacket making it even more special.

Knowing that both of them lived in the Indianapolis area I added that, even though I am not a big racing fan, I've always wanted to go to an Indy 500 race. Jeff looked at me and said, "I can make that happen." He stated that he worked for a company that got tickets so if I was serious all I had to do was let him know next year and he'd get me some tickets.

Then it was their turn. Both of the guys had attended the University of Indiana which has had some great basketball teams in the past, especially when the legendary Bob Knight was their coach, but their football teams have been less than stellar.

Almost in unison they said, "We've watched Big 10 football all our lives but we think seeing an SEC game in person would be an awesome experience." Being a season ticket holder for over 40 years I knew they were right so I said, "I can make that happen." I explained that I had 4 tickets and would love to have them (the guys) come down for a game later that year.

By that time we had made it back across the pool to where the wives were and introductions were made with them. It was just amazing how all six of us hit it off from the start. Actually, they had already befriended another couple from Colorado, Ron O. and Tracy, so the eight of us, under the heavy influence of the never-ending libations, started cutting up and got to know each other better.

This was actually the Indiana groups last day so after a few hours in the pool together they had to sadly make their way back to their rooms to pack up for their flight back home. We exchanged emails and telephone numbers but I think secretly none of us thought we'd ever hear from the others again. You all know how those things go. You have good intentions but you never carry through because the trials and tribulations of everyday life get in the way.

Unless your name is Jeff and you make the effort. The following week our phone rang and it was Jeff from Indiana. We chatted for a while and he said his main point in calling was to tell us how much they had enjoyed meeting Cindy and I and that he was dead serious in us coming up to see the race some time. I followed that by telling him I was serious about all four of them coming down to see the Bulldogs play that Fall.

From the time we met in the pool to this long distance conversation, something between the two of us clicked. To this day I'm not sure why he chose to befriend a guy some twenty years older than he but I'm glad he did. We call each other brothers and it is a rare week that goes by that we don't talk at least once on the phone.

Mark and Cathi were not able to come down for the game but through our continued phone conversations, Jeff and Dawn made plans to come down for the Georgia-Tennessee game that year. I wanted Jeff to get the taste of a real rivalry game and, boy, did I pick a good one for he and Dawn to see.

During that summer we continued making plans for their trip and at the same time that Jeff and I were becoming good friends, Cindy and Dawn were also developing a close bond. That leads to a great story that we now often laugh about regarding our friendship.

Originally, when both couples thought they were travelling down, I had made hotel reservations for them in a local establishment. But when Mark and Cathi had to back out I told Jeff that it was ridiculous for them to stay in a hotel several miles from our house, they could just stay with us for the weekend.

When I told Cindy about the invitation I had made that night when she got home from work, she looked at me and said, "Are you nuts? We've known these people for a few hours in a pool in Cancun and you're inviting them to stay in our house. They could be serial killers for all we know." I know what you ladies are thinking. Typical man.

The weekend arrived and we picked them up at the airport. We're driving through Atlanta, showing them the sights of this great city, and I hear Dawn giggling in the back seat when I told them what Cindy had said about my invitation. Through the laughs she admitted, "When I told my sister what we were doing and where we were going, she asked me if I was crazy. They could be axe murderers for all you know."

Neither one of us turned out to be serial killers or axe murderers although Jeff did get a little worried when he arrived at our house and saw the woods that make up our back yard. He told me straight off that he was not going to take a chance and walk back there with me.

We were lucky in picking an exciting SEC game for them to see. The Tennessee Vols were coming to town and I knew this would be a great rivalry game for them to witness. Boy, did we get our money's worth. Georgia won a close one by holding them off on the last series. I was having a nervous breakdown and Jeff was hoping the game would go into overtime. The added bonus was that they got to have their pre-game tail-gating meal from the Varsity, makers of the best chili dogs in the universe.

Since then, Jeff and Dawn have visited again for Christmas in 2013 and the two guys came down for the Georgia-LSU game that same year. We also surprised Dawn for her 40th birthday by joining the gang at the sister resort in Jamaica of where we stay in Cancun in 2013. And this year, a few weeks after we return from Mexico, Jeff will make good on his end and we'll travel to Indianapolis so Cindy and I can experience our first Indy 500 race.

Friendships are a precious and wonderful gift we're given and they should never be taken lightly. Each one is unique in how it starts and where it leads. Yet, sometimes we let the tiniest, most insignificant thing ruin them. Let me pontificate for just a moment. If you find yourself at odds with someone you once held dear, whether family member or a friend, go find them and work things out. It's the hardest thing you might ever do but to renew a friendship is also the most rewarding thing you'll ever do.

I am a great believer in fate and it was definitely a work of fate that made me talk to two guys from Indy that day. There is no doubt in my mind that destiny meant for the six of us to know each other. I cherish the friendship of both couples and look forward to building one with another couple that will join us this year for our holiday. Two neighbors of Jeff and Dawn's, Jim and Jennifer, will be there with us to share in the fun. I refuse to let my news get in the way of that.

Remembering that friendship made me recall another strange situation that resulted in four guys from different parts of the South bonding together in friendship. Ironically, that, too, began around a swimming pool. It was in Dallas, Texas that I took.........

CHAPTER 8

MY WALK TO FRIENDSHIP (PART 2)

F or most of my working career I was a banker. I joined a bank after graduating from college and I stayed in the industry until 2001 when I had had enough of the changes in the wonderful world of banking, primarily regulatory, that were taking place. It quit being fun to go into work each day and when that happens, it's time to move on to something else.

I got my license and tried real estate for awhile but I didn't enjoy that. It was then that I realized what my problem was. I had reached the stage in my life when I didn't want to work for anybody else. I didn't want to answer to anybody else. I wanted to call my own shots and be my own boss so I started a company and did recruiting work. I became what they call in the vernacular, a headhunter, specializing in what I knew best and where I had the most contacts- banking.

The job had a great many perks. My commute was great- twelve steps down to the office I had built in my basement to accommodate my needs instead of battling daily traffic jams. Maybe I need to add that I didn't build the office, I had it built by a contractor who knew what they were doing. Heck! I can't even hammer a nail in straight. I've never been a handy man of any type. I'm not a yard man and I know nothing about the inner workings of a car. My Dad, who was a pretty good tinkerer around the house, always got mad at me when I told him I was having work done at the house.

"Why don't you learn how to do those things yourself?" he would ask.

"Dad, that's why I went to college to learn how to write a check and pay someone else to do it." I didn't mean that to be snide or condescending, I just have no interest at all in those "manly' endeavors.

The other advantage to working from my own home was that I only had to deal with one other employee the entire day. She was the perfect employee because she never asked for a raise, never called in sick, and didn't share her problems with you. The only thing she required was for her ears or her belly to be rubbed occasionally, taken outside from time to time so she could do her business, and be given a treat. My schnauzer, Lucy (more on her later), was the best company a man could ask for.

Being a recruiter was great until the economy, especially in my part of the country, took a big hit with real estate. Banks that had been vibrant a few years before were now having serious troubles because of real estate loans they had made that had gone bad. And when losses occur, banks don't hire. Since my focus was on small to medium sized banks, my placements began dwindling rapidly.

I tried to fully retire but Cindy was having none of that. "I'm not leaving you everyday in bed while I go to work. You go find something to do!"

About that time, the Financial Secretary position became available at my church and I submitted my resume. It was a part-time position that would allow me a good bit of flexibility to do some of the things in life I wanted to do so, when I got the job it satisfied my darling wife and it allowed me to give something back to the Lord who had always been so good to me.

But I do have some very fond memories that took place during my days in banking. Some of the best involve my association with an organization called the American Institute of Banking, or AIB. I began climbing the ranks of the Atlanta chapter in the mid to late 70's and eventually became President of the Atlanta chapter. This position allowed me to go to the annual regional and national conventions and it was at one of those that the Four R's came together.

The first of the R's that I met was Rick from the Fort Lauderdale, Florida area. We became friends at a convention in New Orleans in 1980 shortly after the eruption of Mount St. Helens had made all the headlines. We stayed in touch after the convention and were excited when we would have the chance to reconnect the following year at the convention in Dallas.

One afternoon during the convention there were no activities planned so a group of twenty or so including June S., Paul, the two Susans, Karen G., and Owen decided to just relax by the pool and have a few beers. Also included in the group were two guys from Alabama; Roger, from Montgomery and Russell G., from a small town near Huntsville.

At some point during the afternoon, the subjects of birthdays came up and since mine was coming up in just a few days, I said, "mine's June 9th."

"You're kidding me." Rick said. "Mine is June 11th."

Roger said, "Mine is June 13th."

To which Russell replied, "Mine is June 16th."

Now I ask you, what are the odds that four guys from different parts of the South gathered at a banking convention in Dallas, Texas would have birthdays within a week of each other? Mind you, we didn't share the same birth years, but that was immaterial at that point. Someone in the group then brought to our attention that the dates fell in order according to our names as well and said "You guys are the Four R's." That sealed it. We were ready to become blood brothers at that point.

Then, to make it even cornier, we gave each other code names. I became R1, Rick became R2, Roger was R3, and Russell, was, naturally, R4. And that was how we were known from then on.

We continued seeing each other at conventions for several years after that but we talked on the phone all the time and even visited each other when we were travelling in one of the other guy's area. There are a lot of stories, some I can tell and some I can't, involving us. One that I can involves a trip to Nashville.

By this time, our "fame" had grown within the organization so when we arrived in Nashville, one of the ladies who had known us and had been a part of that original group at the pool in Dallas, had t-shirts made for us. On the front they said "Four R's" and the back had our code names listed to identify us individually.

All four of us were taking a walk on the streets of downtown Nashville wearing our shirts when we were spotted by some girls who looked to be college age. Probably Vandy girls. They ran up to us and, seeing our matching shirts, asked us if we were a country singing group. Roger thought quickly and told them that we were the backup band for the Oak Ridge Boys. They squealed with joy and asked us for autographs. We obliged and the girls ran off thinking they had just scored a big coup in the world of autographs. I wonder if they ever found out that the names they got that day were just from four crazy guys instead of being from would-be celebrities. Great times with those guys but, again, that's what friendship is all about.

Over the years we've shared in some joys and some sorrows. Rick got married to Maureen and now has three children, the youngest going off to college next year. Gosh, that makes me feel old. Roger left banking and became a forest ranger and, unfortunately,

I have lost touch with him. And Russell, stayed in banking, went through a divorce but remarried a great lady named Pat.

We had to say goodbye to R4 a couple of years ago. He passed away and when Pat called me to tell me the news, I felt as if I had lost a brother. Truth is, I had. I knew exactly what he'd want me to do. When I hung up the phone I went to my liquor cabinet and poured myself a Wild Turkey on the rocks- his drink of choice. It burned all the way down but it helped ease the pain.

Saying goodbye to a loved one or a friend is never easy. A few weeks after Cindy and I returned from our trip to Mexico, I had to take one of those walks again. I was faced with ………..

CHAPTER 9

MY WALK WITH GRIEF

When we returned home from our Mexico trip, we had a very nice surprise waiting for us. That Spring had been spent in the planning, the designing, and the hiring of the contractor we planned to use to do a big project at our home. Cindy wanted to tear down the existing deck we had on the back of our house for the last twenty years and build a new two-tiered masterpiece.

The construction had begun in March, about the time I had gone to the doctor for my check-up. In fact, the crew showed up on the Thursday when March Madness started. It is easy for me to remember the date because nothing in the world of sports gets me as pumped, well, maybe Georgia football, as the NCAA Basketball Tournament. I love it! I work my schedule around those games for that three week period.

But the last phase was the complete remodeling and re-landscaping of our backyard. This was to be completed while we were in Mexico. The job was being done by the owner of the lawn maintenance company we had used for the last few years. His name was Cody B. Cody and his crew did a wonderful job and along with the new deck, we now had a backyard to be proud of and, needless to say, we were.

But Cody was more than just the guy who mowed and edged our lawn and planted flowers for us from time to time. He and his wife, Amie, and in spite of the major age difference between us, had become very close friends to Cindy and I. They had just had a beautiful baby girl the past December named Ayla and they were beginning their life together.

Cody and I, especially, had become extremely close. Don't ask me what he saw in this old guy but he genuinely seemed to like me. And I certainly thought the world of him. We both shared an intense love for North Carolina Tar Heel basketball and we were even planning a trip for next season to go see them play in Chapel Hill. Being a young (only 29) businessman, he would often ask my advice on business matters and he loved to talk sports with me; usually, over Dairy Queen Blizzards.

Actually, Cody loved to push my buttons about sports and he was an expert at it. Cody knew that I am an opinionated person, especially when it comes to sports and modern day athletes, and he had a knack for getting me on one of my soapboxes. Knowing that I am not a fan of Lebron James, an example might go something like this:

Cody: "Man, didn't Lebron have a great game last night?"

Me: "Don't tell me you actually watched that overrated, self-promoting jerk play."

Cody: "Yeah, you should have seen the dunk he made."

Me: "I hope the Heat (the team he played for before he left them to go back to Cleveland) lose every game they play because of how he manipulated putting that team together."

Cody: "Well, they beat the Celtics by 20 last night."

Me: "Damn!" (sputter, sputter, mumble, mumble)

But the real value in Cody was his heart and his smile. I can never remember a time when he wasn't smiling. His smile was one of those that could light up a room and his heart was full of goodness and love. You always felt better when you were around him.

It was also a treat to attend a wedding that Cody was invited to because sometime during the night, he would do his famous Tonto Dance. If you want to see him in action, just go to YouTube and enter "Cody's Tonto dance" and you'll see what I mean. He loved people and he loved life.

No sooner had Cindy and I returned from Mexico than it was time to pack again to go to Indy for the big race. What an experience! As I said earlier, I've never been a big racing fan so I had no idea just how exciting it could be.

Jeff's company was located close to the Speedway so we had a parking space waiting for us and he knew the back roads that kept us out of the horrendous pre-race and post-race traffic. We breezed to the track. Jeff, Dawn, Mark, and Cathi were our hosts.

Jeff gave us a tour showing us the garage area and the plaza. I had my picture made kissing the bricks that represent the start-finish line and then we made our way to our seats for the pre-race festivities.

Indy is all about tradition. Since I am too, I ate this up. Florence Henderson, Mrs. Brady to you Brady Bunch fans, sang a stirring rendition of *America.* Then, former winners of the race paraded around the track accepting the cheers and applause of the crowd. But the real treat was next.

Jim Nabors of *Gomer Pyle* fame has sung *Back Home Again in Indiana* for over twenty straight years but due to health issues this was going to be the last time he could make the trip to Indy from his home in Hawaii. You can't imagine how beautiful the sound of nearly 250,000 people singing along with him was. I looked around me and grown men had tears in their eyes. I did too. But that sound was nothing compared to what I would hear next.

When the immortal words, "Gentlemen. Start your engines." is uttered- that's when the real excitement begins. Those engines rev up and the ground shakes. You think the sound is enough to tear down the grandstands but, luckily, they stand firm and the drivers slowly pull out and begin their practice laps.

And just when you think the sound couldn't be any more deafening, the starter waves the green flag, the cars accelerate, and thirty-three bullets come barreling down the straight-of-way going 200+ miles per hour. I've never experienced anything so thrilling in my life. I will never forget Jeff and the gang for making this dream come true. It was not likely that I would cross off all the events from my Bucket List, but at least I could say I had attended an Indy 500.

The next day was Memorial Day and the eight of us who went to Mexico had a tremendous holiday feast. I only thought of my news one time during that great weekend and that was when Jeff asked me if I liked the race enough to come back the following year. I grinned bravely and told him that I couldn't wait knowing I probably wouldn't be able to follow through with my words.

We flew back on Tuesday and Cindy and I were back at work the next day. That Wednesday evening, however, we met and had a 26th wedding anniversary celebration dinner at one of our favorite restaurants- Bonefish. We had our usual appetizer of Bang Bang Shrimp accompanied by a couple of their wonderful specialty martinis. The dinner was delicious, as usual.

On Tuesday of the following week, I called Cody to tell him to come by and pick up his check for the landscaping work he had done. Yes, I could have easily put the check in the mail but having him come over to pick it up was just an excuse for me to have a chance to sit and talk with him. I'm glad I did.

He came over late that afternoon and we sat on our new deck and chatted about the usual things. My birthday was coming up on Monday of the following week and the four of us were going out to dinner that weekend to celebrate. Cody had never been to one of the better restaurants in Athens, The Last Resort, and I told him about their menu to whet his appetite. Cody is a basic meat and potatoes kind of guy, as I am, but I assured him he would love it. When it was time for him to leave we gave each other man hugs and said to each other that we'll see you on Sunday.

On Wednesday, June 4th, 2014, my phone rang about 5: 00 pm. It was my mother-in-law.

Knowing that Cindy and I were both very close to Cody and Amie she said, "Have you heard the horrible news?" Before I could respond she said, "Cody was killed in an automobile accident this afternoon."

I have no recollection of what I said next or if I said anything. I was in complete and total shock. Finally, I managed, "Are you sure? Where did you hear about it?"

She told me that one of her best friends had called her and that it was definite because she had heard it from her granddaughter who did the books for the company Cody owned.

I told her I had to go. When I hung up, I fell to my knees and began sobbing. I was that way for at least ten minutes. I gathered myself and called Cindy's cell phone. That's our mutual sign that the call is important; otherwise, I call her office phone and leave a message.

All I could say was, "Get home! Right now! Cody's been killed in an accident!"

The next few days are a blur to us but I cannot begin to imagine what they were for the young woman who had just lost her husband. She showed amazing strength during the visitation and the funeral service- strength that had to have come from the faith that she and Cody shared. I'm sure that she collapsed later but for those few days, she was a rock.

It is a wonderful testimony to Cody to have as many people come out to honor his life as there was. The church was completely packed. But why not? He was a beacon in this sometimes world of darkness.

Cody had a remarkable maturity for being still relatively young. He had shared with me on several occasions his philosophy of life that he called 'Where Will Diamonds Be?' What this meant to him was that you can never be sure who will be diamonds among the people you meet in your life. We should never judge by first impressions. Some people, like a diamond, have to be formed just right and then they have to be polished so that the luster they have inside them can come out in its truest form. And just like a diamond is formed under pressure, sometimes the best qualities of an individual don't come out until they are tried and tested by life's pressures. He may have been the wisest man I've ever met and I am so blessed to have been one of his friends. I wear a Carolina blue bracelet everyday that has the initials "WWDB" (Where Will Diamonds Be) as a reminder of his very positive take on life.

WWDB also stood for World Wide Dream Builders, an organization that Cody and Amie believed in and promoted. Their mission statement says: "Believing that my life and business should be built upon a foundation of integrity, character, and standards of excellence." Sometimes a unique individual intersects your walk of life and influences you to take steps in directions you hadn't considered before. Such an individual was this young man.

When things like this happen, our natural question is "Why?" Why Cody? He was a wonderful young man who had just started his walk with beautiful Amie. They had just shared in the joy of the birth of their daughter- a daughter who would never have the opportunity to know her father. And there is no doubt in my mind that he would have been a remarkable father. We can ask ourselves "why?" all day but we're never going to get all those answers this side of heaven.

I will admit that I got mad at God for a few days afterward, but you know what? It's okay to get mad at God. He can take it. The secret is not to let the anger simmer and allow it to separate you from God. God never leaves our side. It is us that move away from him so, even though we might not get all the answers we want, reconnect and give him your sorrow. Remember, he watched his own son die on a cross. He's used to sorrow.

I, like all of you, have been touched by sorrow many times in my life. I guess losing Papa Blalock when I was about 8 or 9 was the first. Then I lost my beloved Nanny, mother's mother, in 1962. Nanny lived with us for awhile and I was her baby. As I said earlier, I was a late baby for my parents and because of that I was the last grandchild of hers. There had been three girls born earlier but they were all adults now so Nanny doted on me as much as she could.

Her special treat for me was her wonderful lemon meringue pie. My mother-in-law makes a great one for me today but, Beverly, I hope you understand it when I say there is nothing like Nanny's.

My dad's mom died when I was about 19 but living so far away from her, I didn't see her all that much so I was never really close to her. Along the way I've lost some high school classmates, some aunts and uncles but within the last few years I've said goodbye to three very close cousins.

I told you about Bobby, the person responsible for my love of sports, earlier. But I had two others, a cousin and her husband, who were like my second parents to me.

At one point in my life we lived next door to Carmen and Jug. Yes, you read it right- I said Jug. His real name was James but he had gotten the nickname Jug during his military service and that was what everyone now called him. Carmen was the daughter of one of my dad's sisters and she loved me like I was her own. She and Jug took me everywhere.

Jug always loved telling the story on me about the time they took me to the Atlanta Zoo when I was four. We went into the elephant house and the ventilation system was not as good as

The Many Walks of Life

it is today. The odor must have been pretty bad because Jug said I yelled at the top of my lungs, "Jug! Somebody's pooted in here!"

Jug and I would often have lunch together after Carmen died and I think often about those conversations we had. He always sympathized with me and could never understand why Dad had treated me the way he had. I would never let him pay for lunch. It was the only way I knew to pay him back for something he did for me when I was a kid in high school.

I wanted desperately to go to a basketball camp that was being held the summer of 1964 at Wofford College in Spartanburg, South Carolina. Three other guys from Murphy were going and I wanted to improve my skills as well. The camp was being run by Press Maravich, the father of the great "Pistol" Pete Maravich and Dean Smith, the legendary coach of the North Carolina Tar Heels. My admiration of Coach Smith started here and he is the reason I became an ardent UNC basketball fan for the rest of my life.

The cost of the camp was $200 but Dad had emphatically refused to pay for me to attend. Jug gave me the money and that caused a rift between he and Dad that lasted many years. I always loved Jug for telling me later that he would rather have me as a friend than my dad anyway.

My most endearing recollection of Carmen was the day she taught me how to ride a bike. I had received a new bike for Christmas and had ridden it with the training wheels on but now came the time for me to learn without them.

Dad took me out to the street and went through some minimal instructions. He then lifted me on to the seat, held me until I got my balance, then gave me a push and expected me to be able to do the rest. I went about 10 feet before I came crashing to the ground. Again and again I tried but I just couldn't get the hang of it. With each successive crash, his anger grew which meant he

76

would yell more which made me begin crying, both from fear and from the pain of crashing on the road.

Finally, dad had had enough. He yelled at me that if I didn't ride the bike he was going to take me inside and whip me. I didn't. He did.

I have always thought that my dad had an undiagnosed chemical imbalance of some sort that would send him into the rages he would have when his anger got the best of him. Carmen told me later after I had become an adult that she had witnessed the entire episode and heard my cries from her house as the belt lashed against my skin. She told me she had wanted to come over to our house and beat my dad senseless for doing that to me but people, even caring, loving people didn't interfere with others in the discipline of their children in those days.

Carmen didn't work so I was always dropped off at her house in the mornings and she would take me to school. The day after the incident, however, she called in to the school telling them I was sick. She swore me to secrecy and I stayed home with her. She took me out for a special lunch and when we got home she said, "Let's go learn how to ride that bike."

It's amazing what a little patience and a lot of love can do. After a couple of failed attempts, the switch clicked and all of a sudden, I was gliding down the street- a little wobbly, but upright.

I must admit that I was more than a little jealous when Carmen had two beautiful girls, Karen and Pam, of her own. Jug and I continued to see each other regularly for lunch after her death and when I lost him from my life earlier this year, a huge part of my childhood went with him. It's a great blessing to have people like these in your life walk and I'm so thankful for the steps I got to take with them.

But, perhaps, the biggest personal loss I've dealt with is the loss of Cindy's dad. We live in a small town and the night of his visitation service, the entire town showed up to pay their respects for this beloved man. I have yet to hear one person ever say they didn't love Ambrose. In fact, the City of Winder lowered all the flags to half mast to pay homage to this man. How many men get to have that as a legacy?

Brose never met a stranger; at least they weren't strangers for long. He, very simply, was the finest man I've ever met in my life. The hardest job I have in my marriage is trying to live up to the example he set. He spoiled his girls rotten. I try my best but I will never be able to fill his shoes in Cindy's mind.

But as we walk through life there are others that can touch us and leave us with sadness that is sometimes as difficult to bear as the loss of a loved one. They're called pets. These creatures come into our lives and become like family. That was definitely the case with our beautiful miniature schnauzer, Lucy.

I never had a dog growing up. A few parakeets, some goldfish, and one Easter mom got me a little dyed chick. It lasted maybe a week. I was determined that my children would enjoy this part of their childhood. In fact, our first dog was purchased before Brian was born so that it would be house-trained by the time of his arrival.

We searched the want ads and did some research on dogs that were good with children and decided on a miniature dachshund. We picked him up from the breeders and immediately named him Dooley after the legendary Georgia football coach, Vince Dooley.

By now Jessica had come along and after Dooley passed away, we got Doc. Jessica named him as I recall, using the logic, "He's Doc the Dachshund."

So, after Cindy and I had been married a few years and had settled into our home, we decided to get a dog. Truth is, I decided and Cindy went along with the idea because she loved me and she knew I really wanted it. She insisted on three things: (1) it must be a female (2) it must be a breed that did not shed and (3) I was responsible for house-training it. I agreed to all three conditions.

I did research on different breeds but the real swing factor was that I worked with a man who had schnauzers and he raved about them. Again, we searched the ads for breeders in our area and saw one that was in Athens. We called and set up a time to go see the new litter. It was love at first sight.

As most schnauzers, who will eventually have salt and pepper coats, Lucy was coal black as a puppy. We had an advantage in being able to see both the mama and the papa and to get an idea if they were high-strung or not. Both seemed to have the demeanor we wanted in a dog so, we made arrangements to pick her up after she had been weaned and had her initial shots, etc.

I will never forget the night we went to pick her up. The cold-hearted woman who wanted no part of a dog couldn't keep her hands off her on the drive back home. Cindy nuzzled her and loved on her all the way home. We sat on our front stoop and just glowed as we watched our new addition waddle around her new front yard.

Some of you who are dog lovers will not like this next part. During our research, we had made the decision to crate her at night rather than letting her sleep in a basket somewhere in the house. I will never regret doing this in spite of what some of you may feel is cruel and inhumane. I'm sure Lucy whimpered for a few nights but it hastens allowing the dog to get used to her surroundings. It is also the best way to house-train them since they will not soil their immediate surroundings. In any event, Lucy adjusted rapidly.

By the time she was a year old, we set up a bed downstairs but Lucy was having none of that. We'd hear her little paws scampering up the stairs after the lights had been turned out and before you knew it, Miss Hard Heart was reaching down and picking her up to put her in bed with us. I never said a word.

I know I am offending cat lovers, but there is nothing like a dog. Have you ever seen a YouTube video of a cat welcoming its master back home after they have been away for a lengthy period? No! But dial up one of those videos and see the pure joy displayed by a dog on seeing its owner.

We held on to Lucy much longer than we should have. It was our own selfishness that kept us from making that very tough decision. She had started ebbing away from us several months prior but we just couldn't stand the thought of saying goodbye to this very significant part of our lives.

I used to write a weekly sports column for one of our local newspapers in Winder. The day we finally had the courage to put her out of her misery, I wrote this column. Even though it had nothing to do with sports, my editor kindly published it. I think it sums up our loss, our walk with grief in ways that you who have said goodbye to a pet will understand.

Tribute to Lucy

My wife and I said goodbye this morning to a dear, dear friend and companion. Lucy, our 16 year-old schnauzer, our only child, quietly went to sleep. Now, she can run and play again like she did when she was a puppy. She can chase tennis balls, dance for her treats, and speak to her hearts content. But for the two she left behind, our days will be a little less joyful; a little less blessed; and a lot less loved because if Lucy gave us anything, she gave us love.

I never had pets as a young boy growing up. It was only when my two children got old enough to talk about having a dog that I even considered having a dog around the house. They wanted a dachshund so we searched the papers and found a breeder that lived close by to us and went to see the new puppies. Both Brian and Jessica immediately fell in love with one right off the bat and so we brought Doc ("after all, he is a doc-sund" my daughter said and so the name stuck) home.

Cindy and I had been married about five years. We had recently moved to Winder and, for some reason, I started hinting about getting a dog. Cindy was dead set against it. We both worked a good distance from Winder at the time and I think she was reluctant to having a dog wander around the house all day. She gave in, however, and so I started doing research on dog breeds.

I came across some articles on schnauzers and I also worked with a guy who had two schnauzers of his own and he absolutely raved about them. I knew that I wanted a small, lap dog and Cindy wanted a female- those were the basic requirements. We found a breeder in Athens and her female had just had a litter so we went to go see them. Lucy's mother's name was Jasmine and the sire lived next door. The scoundrel had already abandoned them. Lucy had a brother that we called cocked head because he had been born with a muscle deficiency that didn't allow him to hold his head up straight so he wobbled around as he tried to get to us. That's why Lucy made it to us first and at one glance it was all over for the both of us. The hard-hearted woman who wanted no part of a pet, melted like ice cubes in a glass of tea on a hot summer day.

As we have reminisced this morning through both tears and laughter, we recalled the first night we brought the little fluff ball home. Her little legs could barely hold her up as she waddled around the yard getting used to her surroundings. We crated her for the first year of her life at night and during the day while we were at work and for any of you who might be considering a new puppy, I still say that this is the best training method there is. She was never a chewer and she was trained in just a few months. I know that there are many who feel that this is cruel, but we never experienced any negatives from this training method at all.

I taught Lucy a few tricks. She could speak on command, sit, shake hands, roll over, and dance for her treats. But my favorite trick of hers was when I would say, "Lucy, would you rather be a dead dog or a Yellow Jacket." She would immediately roll over on to her back with her legs straight up in the air. A "Good girl!" would spring her back to life where a treat was always awaiting her.

I am sure that Dr. Richard Duffey and his staff at Winder Animal Hospital would say that we doted on Lucy and, you know what? They would be absolutely right! But I must take a moment and thank them for their tender care of our special girl over the years. And don't worry ladies. I'll still bring you my special fudge every Christmas.

Lucy was not a barker but, boy, was she a snorer. She would sleep with us at night and if you women think your husbands are bad, you've never heard Lucy. She had a variety of different snores but each of them were done at decibel levels that would rival a stock car. It is going to be very hard tonight not hearing those snores. Please tell me that this hurt will go away some day.

Pets can play a very significant role in the lives of our families. Lucy was our baby and I've often said she was the best of my three children because she never talked back and she never once asked for money. All she wanted from us was two good meals a day, a little belly or ear scratchin and a lap to take a nap in. In return, she gave us unconditional love. Lucy was not a dog who licked, but she could look at you with those big, black eyes and you could see the love she had for us.

I will miss my little girl so much that it is difficult for me to type these words right now because they are filled with tears. Call me a big baby all you want! Cindy and I loved that dog and our hearts ache with her loss. One of the last things I told her was to wait on me in heaven. Till I get there, have fun. Chase balls, run, jump and take your naps but I expect you to be waiting on me so we can play together. I love you and I will never forget the happiness you brought to Cindy and me.

Lady Lucy Waverly
July 13, 1993- June 8, 2009

After Cody's death, the rest of the month was a blur. We celebrated my birthday a few days after the actual date because neither of us wanted to go to dinner that weekend. Before we knew it, the Fourth of July came around and we spent it with our good Winder friends, Don and Melissa.

I always enjoy watching the 4th of July specials with their great music and the incredible fireworks displays. Every time I hear

Stars and Stripes it takes me back to my band days when we played it both in my elementary band as well as my high school band. I am proud to be an American and I have never felt that patriotic pride more than when Cindy and I had a chanced to visit the American Cemetery at Normandy.

For our 25th anniversary, we had taken a river cruise beginning in Paris that travelled up the Seine. To see the Eiffel Tower, the Louvre that houses the Mona Lisa, Winged Victory, and Venus di Milo, Napolean's Tomb, the Arc de Triomphe and all the other magnificent sites of this city was just the tip of the iceberg. As we sailed past beautiful countrysides, stopping in quaint French towns along the way, Cindy and I were enthralled by the sights.

But the highlight of the cruise was our visit to Normandy and Omaha Beach. The cemetery, with its 9,000 crosses commemorating the sacrifice made by these young men and women, was inspiring enough but the gesture made by our tour guide was even more moving. She gathered us at the front entrance courtyard and asked us to turn and face the American flag and sing the National Anthem. Forty voices cracked with emotion as we sang this nation's anthem. Never have I felt more proud of my heritage than at that moment.

She then gave each of us a rose. Cindy and I decided to find two Georgia boys who had given their all and lay the rose at their grave site. One interesting fact about the cemetery that I did not know before; the men and women resting here are buried in American, not French, soil. The dirt used to build this immaculately-groomed cemetery was shipped over from America. Rest easy, my fellow Americans.

Melissa and Cindy have been friends since high school and M, as I call her, is one of The Shopping Queens. Seven ladies, including Cindy and Melissa, go on shopping trips together each year. When I say shopping trip, I don't mean a quick trip to the mall; these are three and four day excursions. While they do a good bit of actual shopping, I've always felt that the real purpose was eating, gossiping, and complaining about their husbands- not necessarily in that order.

While the girls were busy in the kitchen preparing our dinner, Don and I sat on the new deck discussing varied topics. Don is a history buff like me so a lot of our discussion centered around a little hike I was planning to take in a few weeks to commemorate the 15oth anniversary of the Battle of Atlanta. This was going to be ....

CHAPTER 10

MY WALK THROUGH HISTORY (PART 1)

Early on the morning of Friday, July 22, 1864, Confederate forces under the command of Lt. General John B. Hood marched in southeast Atlanta attempting to surprise Union troops headed by William T. Sherman in an effort to regain important rail and supply lines that had been taken near what is now Decatur, Georgia. Thus, when the first actual shots were fired, commemorated by a historical marker on Memorial Drive and Clay Street, the Battle of Atlanta had officially begun.

This battle took place in the middle of what is now referred to as The Atlanta Campaign, following random skirmishes in the area as well as the Battle of Peachtree Creek, and was significant in many ways. By cutting off the Confederate supply lines, Sherman essentially secured victory for the North. As he continued on his famous March to the Sea, Sherman sealed off much of the South's ability to obtain much-needed supplies destroying what little morale and hope the Confederate soldiers may have had. This victory was also responsible in propelling Lincoln to a second-term Presedential win.

The Union, however, did suffer some significant losses themselves. Included in the deaths of approximately 3,700 soldiers was the loss of Major General James B. McPherson, Sherman's second in command and the second highest ranking Union officer killed in the entire conflict, during the afternoon of the 22nd. His death could have possibly been prevented were it not for the stubbornness of Sherman, his commanding officer.

Sherman believed that the Confederate troops had been defeated and that they were evacuating their positions. McPherson from his high-ground observation point on Bald Hill, strongly disagreed. During their arguments Confederate troops had enough time to gather themselves. When McPherson rode back out to scout the area he was ambushed by Confederate sharpshooters and as he attempted to retreat for cover, he was shot and killed.

Clinging to survival, the city held on and did not actually fall until September, 1864 after a six-week siege by the Union forces. Sherman showed his anger with the veracity of the city and its people by torching the city as was vividly depicted in the classic film *Gone With the Wind.*

Much of the fighting took place in the immediate area of southeast Atlanta where I grew up. As a young boy, I would often discover artifacts from that time. I dug up lots of Minie' balls, belt buckles, and once even found a Union soldiers cap that was authenticated by Civil War experts as original. I later donated these findings to the Atlanta Cyclorama, a Civil War museum located in Grant Park, also the site of much of the fighting.

Allow me to play Chamber of Commerce representative for a bit. If you ever visit Atlanta, the Cyclorama is a must-see. In the very near future the diorama is being moved from its present location to the Atlanta History Center in Buckhead.

I loved going to see this wonder as a boy. It was amazing to me to see this combination sculpture/painting. The painting is 42' high and if unrolled would stretch out 358', more than the length of a football field. There are many stories-within-the-story in the painting. There is McPherson sitting on his horse overlooking the battle; the Confederate soldier giving water to his Union brother who has been wounded; the eagle soaring over the battle in the sky; and, if you look closely, you can see Clark Gable.

The story goes that after the premiere of GWTW, the cast was taken the next day to view the painting. Gable is claimed to have said that the only way the painting could be any more magnificent was if he were in it. The statement prompted management to add his features to one of the mannequins in the diorama. To get the last laugh, however, his features were added to those of a dying soldier.

But the real feature I always loved was being able to pick out the area in the painting that depicted the very ground where I lived. I guess this explains why I have always been a Civil War buff but it is the same feeling I get whenever I have stood on historical ground. I am spellbound standing in Dealey Plaza. I was awe-struck walking through Westminster Abbey. And standing in the amphitheater in Ephesus where Saint Paul preached brought me to tears.

July 22, 2014 would mark the 150th anniversary of the Battle of Atlanta and I had decided to do a walk through the primary battle sites that day as my way of paying tribute to those, from both sides, who fought so bravely that day. Even though I was in pretty good shape for my age because of the exercise regimen I was already doing, this hike promised to be lengthy and strenuous so I thought it would be a good idea to check with my doctor before I undertook this rigorous trek.

I got him on the phone, explained what I wanted to do, and he asked me to come in and do a quick blood test to see if the count had gotten better or worse. After I had the blood drawn he came in and said it would be better if I didn't take this exertion on since it might hasten my body's inability to fight off anything that might happen. But after explaining that there was a secondary reason of just wanting to see the old stomping grounds again, he knew he was not going to be able to talk me out of it. Reluctantly, he said I could go ahead with my plans.

I had mapped out my route in my head and I knew it was going to be a long hike so I packed a few power bars and a couple of bottles of water and I headed out from Winder about 8 that morning. I make this same drive several times a year when I venture to East Atlanta and visit with old high school friends. We meet on a quarterly basis thanks to the hard work of Harriett C. who sends out all the information and makes the arrangements with the restaurant where we meet. Generally, about 20-30 of us show up but you can always count on Jerry and Judy B.; Harriett's brother, Tom C.; the Blissett sisters, Jackie and Linda; Linda W. and Sue H.

My plans were to start my walk at the corner of Glenwood Avenue and Wilkinson Drive near where I-20 crosses under Glenwood. This is also the site of Walker Monument, the location most often associated with the first casualty of the battle.

General William H. T. Walker was born in Georgia near Augusta and had served with distinction in the Mexican-American War. When Georgia seceded and joined the war, Walker surrendered his rank and joined the Confederate cause. Walker was scouting the area the morning of the 22nd when he was shot from his horse by a lone Union sniper who had gotten separated from his unit. Walker's division was taken over after his death by Brig. General Hugh Mercer who led his troops on a march to the site where the actual first shots of the battle occurred- the route I was going to match that morning.

I parked my car at a convenience store on the corner and began walking. There are homes on the right side of Wilkinson but the left is now comprised of an open grassy area where the original DeKalb Memorial Little League baseball diamonds were situated. A little further down the road finds a playground and picnic area where the locals can spend some quality leisure time.

About 200 yards further down Wilkinson is the entrance to the second phase of DeKalb Memorial and the location where I spent many, many hours as a young boy and later, as a teenager, play-ing baseball and swimming in the community pool situated there. The only thing that remains from where once stood two baseball fields, a concession stand, and the pool is grass and woods. It was amazing to see a stand of pine trees in the spot where the pool once was. At some point in the past the building housing the changing areas for the pool had been demolished and my guess is that the pool itself had been filled in with dirt. Whether the trees rising above where I used to get up enough courage to jump, not dive, off the high board were planted or had grown naturally, I can't say. But no semblance of the pool can be seen today.

And then I turned to my right and looked sadly at what once was the big field. This is where you played after you turned 13; behind it was where the Little League field was located. Gone are the outfield signs that carried the sponsorships of local merchants like Archie's Sporting Goods, Miss Georgia Dairy, Trust Company Bank, Colonial Store, and Merita Bread Company. Gone are the terribly uncomfortable wooden bleachers where spectators watched the action. And gone was the concession stand where most of the activity took place.

The little kids were always hanging around purchasing that hard as rock baseball card bubble gum and those luke-warm hot dogs that spun on the rotisserie heated only by a 30-watt light bulb. And any time a foul ball carried over the back stop screen there was a wild scramble for the ball because the reward for retrieving it and bringing it back to the concession stand so it could be used again, was a free Coca-Cola.

But the reason the older boys hung around the concession stand when they weren't playing was the teenage girls that could always be found there. Oh, do I have some great memories of those very short shorts that were the style in the early 60's, displaying those tanned legs. Sweet, Jesus the female form is marvelous and for a young boy with raging hormones there was no better place to be than the ball park during summer.

I say with some amount of bias that this organization was the premier youth baseball association in the entire city and it had this reputation because of the tireless work done by the parents and officers of it. The playing field was always immaculate; the dugouts were as good as most high schools; and even the parking lots were swept and kept free of litter.

Dad, of course, refused to help in any way. He would get calls from time to time by some of the dads of my friends asking if he could help but he would tell them in no uncertain terms that he had no intention of being a part of their little "men's club" as he called it. In fact, he didn't want me playing there because he thought it was a waste of my time since I was never going to be a major league player. Mom wound up paying my registration fee to play.

But for me, it was an honor to play there and some of my fondest memories center around that park. That's why the day I was able to contribute in a big way to the success of the organization has always meant so much to me. It was the day I took........

CHAPTER 11

MY WALK TO GLORY

B aseball has always been an important part of my life. So important, that I set a goal a few years back of trying to see a game in every Major League stadium. I may not be able to reach that goal now but I came pretty close seeing all but four stadiums. It's been difficult to keep up with them as fast as they build new ones to replace stadiums that are not that old. They're doing that here in Atlanta. Turner Field was opened for baseball play in 1997 to replace Atlanta-Fulton County Stadium and now, just 17 short years later, a new stadium is being built in Cobb County.

While many view the game as slow and boring, I contend that you can't have a full appreciation for the game and its subtle intricacies unless you have played it. There is so much that is going on between pitches that is critical to the outcome of the game that would make the game far more interesting to the casual observer if they realized what was happening. However, there are many things that are going on in the game today that I don't like but most of those distractions deal with players and the way they treat this sacred game rather than the game itself.

I know that many may classify me as a fuddy-duddy when it comes to some of these matters that upset me but that is just the way I feel. My wife gets so tired of my rants regarding the way that current players wear their uniforms, but it just drives me crazy. The baggy pants with the cuffs hanging over their shoes and the way their straight-billed caps fall over their ears and are cocked to the side are ridiculous. To me, they are disrespecting the uniform and the organization they represent.

The major complaint I have, however, is the meism that has invaded not just baseball, but all sports. I heard the great Cincinnati Reds Hall of Fame catcher, Johnny Bench, once say, "It appears to me that some of the guys playing the game today care more about the name on the back of the uniform than the name on the front." How true that is!

I can guarantee you that if a player had ever dared to stand at home plate and watch the ball go over the fence for a home run before he started his trot when Don Drysdale, Bob Gibson, or Nolan Ryan was pitching, the next time they came to the plate they better be wary because it would be very likely that they'd get the ball thrown at their head. There's just no place for showboating in baseball or any other sport.

There was an incident last year in pro football that shows this meism attitude to perfection. A defensive lineman sacked the quarterback and got up and started celebrating his play. He jumped in the air, landed wrong, and tore his knee up and was lost for the rest of the season. The problem was that he celebrated one lousy sack when his team was losing by 28 points. I doubt that this "look at me" mentality will end but it is ruining sports at all levels.

I went to a youth basketball game recently and saw a nine year-old boy fist pump and beat his chest after scoring a basket. Where did he get this idea? From watching pro athletes do the same thing. C'mon guys! You need to be better role models. As Coach Mark Richt of the Georgia Bulldogs football team says to his players after they score a touchdown, "Don't celebrate! Act like you've been there before."

Atlanta has a long, rich history as a baseball town. I can remember my cousin, Bobby taking me to games when I was very young. At that time, long before the Braves came to town, Atlanta fielded a minor league team called the Crackers. For most of my youth, the Crackers were a AA team in the Southern Association. The Southern Association was comprised of eight teams: the Nashville Vols, Memphis Chicks, Chattanooga Lookouts, Mobile Bears, Birmingham Barons, Little Rock Travelers, and New Orleans Pelicans as well as the Crackers.

The Crackers played their home games at Ponce de Leon Park near downtown Atlanta across from the old Sears building. The park had many notable characteristics. There was a big 40 foot scoreboard in left field and a magnolia tree that stood on a little incline in dead away center field beyond the center field fence. But the most prominent feature was the three-tiered right field wall that had its own set of ground rules.

It was possible for a ball hit to right field to land on one of the ledges that separated the three tiers. If the ball landed and stuck on the first tier, it was a ground rule double. If it landed on the second tier, it was a triple. Of course, if the ball went over the top tier it was a home run. Running across at that point was a railroad track used by the now defunct Southern Railway System and often during the game, a train would come roaring through. This railroad track is the source for one of the best legends the game of baseball has ever had.

The game of baseball is known for its legends. Perhaps, the most famous is whether Babe Ruth actually called his home run shot in the 1932 World Series, the Series pitting his mighty Yankees against the Chicago Cubs, by pointing to centerfield or was he simply pointing at the pitcher. Did brash Dizzy Dean exude confidence in his pitching skills so much that he told the batters what he was going to throw?

But one of the best legends in baseball centers around the longest home run ever hit. Most baseball historians acknowledge that one hit by the great Mickey Mantle at Griffith Stadium, home to the old Washington Senators, travelled 565 feet. But I say, as do those who witnessed it that night, that the longest was hit by an Atlanta Cracker player by the name of Bob Montag.

Montag never had a Major League at bat spending his entire career in the minors, mainly with the Crackers. While a powerful hitter, Montag was a defensive handicap in right field and he possessed a weak throwing arm. He would have made a perfect designated hitter, but, unfortunately for him, his era was long before that was instituted. On that night in 1954, however, he made history.

During an at bat in the fourth inning against the, ironically as you will see, Nashville Vols, Montag hit a towering drive over the right field fence. The timing of the blast was such that the baseball flew in the open door of a box car of the train that was passing at just that moment. The train did not stop until it got to its destination in, you guessed it, Nashville, Tennessee. So, the argument could be made that it travelled some 240 miles from its Atlanta origin to its Nashville destination.

The Crackers were also special to me because that is where I started following the player who would eventually become by baseball idol, Eddie Matthews. Matthews began his career with the Crackers who were then an affiliate of the parent Milwaukee Braves, the team where he would have most of his success. It was there that he would team with the true home run champion of all time, Henry Aaron, to set the mark for most home runs by teammates in major League history.

And, yes, even though there are thousands who say they were there the evening of April 8, 1974, the night Hammerin' Hank broke Babe Ruth's career home run mark, I witnessed the historic home run in person. And I have the Super 8 movie that I took that night to prove it.

My first father-in-law worked for the City of Atlanta Water Department and he would often get tickets to various sporting events. We had seats about 20 rows up, just to the first base side of home plate. When Aaron came up to the plate, I would start the camera just as Al Downing, the Dodgers pitcher that night, went into his windup. His first at bat, Aaron walked on four straight pitches to a rousing chorus of boos from the crowd. The second time up with a man on first base, Aaron hit the second pitch over the left field wall and as Milo Hamilton, the Braves announcer said, "There's a new home run champion of all time and its Henry Aaron."

No matter what the current record books might show, I will always recognize Aaron as the true champion. His name and his home runs are not blemished in any way with steroids or other chemical enhancements like Barry Bonds and the others. He achieved his records honestly. With what he went through, he remains one of the classiest people to ever play the game.

So, playing baseball as a young boy came as natural as breathing in and out. Being an only child and the only boy in my immediate neighborhood, I would spend hours throwing tennis balls or rubber balls against the front porch steps. I can't tell you how many screens were knocked loose by errant throws that had to be replaced on the front door. Because of all that practice I became a pretty good fielder.

I only played one year of Little League ball at Dekalb Memorial because, for some reason, they changed the boundaries and our house was outside the area even though we lived less than a mile from the park. But for the year of 1962, they widened their area and I was then eligible to play. By that time I was old enough to play in the league for 13-15 year olds called Babe Ruth League. It was during this time when I really got to know Floyd and Lloyd.

The twins had moved to Atlanta and entered Murphy that previous September at the start of our 9th grade year. They were placed in the same home room as I and we became friends. After playing intramural (home room against home room) sports that year, I knew that they were terrific athletes. When tryouts were announced for the summer Babe Ruth League, the boys were part of another twins' trick that was a classic.

Everyone, whether you played in the league the previous year or not, had to go through tryouts. This would be where the coaches for each of the teams would put you through some basic skill sets; batting, fielding, and throwing to see the level of your ability. Then, after the tryouts, the coaches would bid on the players to make up their respective teams.

One of the coaches in the summer league was also a coach at the high school and he had seen the boys play during these intramural games so he knew how good they were. Since one of the guys was right-handed and batted right (Floyd) and the other (Lloyd) was left-handed and batted left, he convinced them to tryout pretending to be the other so they wouldn't tip their hand as to how good they were for the other coaches. Floyd would throw and bat left and Lloyd right. This way, he could bid very low on them and get two excellent players without spending too many points on them. There may be no crying in baseball but there was certainly conniving.

His ruse worked to perfection because they were, as you might expect, just awful during tryouts. He got both players and with the help of a good-fielding second baseman- me- we won the pennant that year. When it was discovered what he had done, he was not allowed to coach there the following year.

After the season, an all-star team was named that would go on and play in various tournaments leading to what we hoped would get us to the Babe Ruth World Series that was going to be played in Farmington, New Mexico later that summer. All three of us, along with some other really good players, made the team.

The first step was winning the region tournament. We breezed through that defeating a team from North Atlanta led by a pitcher named Billy Payne. Payne would find some success later in life by being one of the organizers for the Atlanta Olympic Committee that successfully brought the Olympics to Atlanta in 1996. And then he topped that by being named Chairman of Augusta National, the home of the annual Masters Golf Tournament. You can see him every year awarding the winner the cherished green jacket. But on that day we bested them 4-1 and I went 2x3 and drove in a run with a double.

We then went to Columbus, Georgia to play in the State Tournament and won that. Next stop was Nashville for the Southeastern Region. The winner there would go to the World Series.

We left late one afternoon and stopped in Chattanooga to spend the night so we could visit Rock City. This was my second visit here but the first one had been when I was only 6 or 7 so I really didn't remember much about it other than the swinging bridge over one of the gorges. I was not looking forward to cross-ing that. I was sure that some of my teammates would try to make it swing as much as it could and the thought of that made me very nervous. I survived the walk across and we even went to Ruby Falls just down the road from Rock City.

I was sharing a room with David and Kenny when we got to Nashville and we got into a little trouble the second night we were there. Our room was located on the fourth floor overlooking one of the main downtown Nashville streets that had lots of pedestrian traffic. David got the idea to toss water balloons out in an attempt to hit the passers-by. Our aim, perhaps luckily, was not too good and we didn't hit anybody but we came close a few times. Close enough that one of them complained and she was even able to identify which room they came from. Coach came to the room but all the evidence was gone so he couldn't prove we had been the culprits and, of course, we denied it vehemently. We ran a few extra wind sprints the next day at practice anyway.

We were playing well and even though some of the games were very tight, we had managed to win them all. Here was our chance. We would play for the championship. Winner take all. Win and we'd go to the Series. Lose and we'd go home.

We were matched up against a team from Montgomery, Alabama. They had a very hard-throwing lefty who had dominated in the games he had pitched. Jimmy, our pitcher, was a crafty right hander with excellent control and a wicked curve ball.

The game went back and forth through the first six innings and we held a slim 3-2 lead. We only needed three outs since our games only went seven innings and we would be champs. But Montgomery rallied and scored on a sac fly to send it to the bottom of the seventh all square.

Chris led off with a sharp single up the middle. Our coach, playing good percentage baseball, called on Floyd to bunt him over, which he did to perfection. Runner on second, one out. Lloyd was next up and for a moment we thought it was over when he smashed a drive down the right field line. It hooked at the last minute, however, and curved foul. The pitcher was shook by the blast and proceeded to hit Lloyd in the leg with his next pitch. Runners on first and second.

Coach surprised us by, again, calling on the next batter to bunt. But Gary laid down such a good bunt that no one could field it and he made it safely to first. Bases loaded.

That brought up Jimmy, our pitcher, to the plate and I moved to the on-deck circle. I admit that I said a little prayer that Jimmy would come through so I wouldn't have to bat with the game on the line. This guy had my number. I couldn't touch him. I was 0x3 with a strikeout, a popup to short, and a weak grounder to second. "C'mon, Jimmy. C'mon." I whispered to myself. Jimmy wasn't listening. He popped up to the catcher on the first pitch. Now the bases were loaded but there were two outs.

"Now batting- #13, second baseman Randy Blalock." came the voice from the press box. My knees wouldn't work properly and I waddled, more than strode, to the plate. I heard the encouraging words of the guys in the dugout and the fans, mostly parents who had made the trip, in the stands. I went through my routine to compose myself. Bend down and pick up some dirt and put it on the bat. Tap my left foot with the bat. Tap my right foot with the bat. Slide my right had up the barrel of the bat and step into the batter's box.

The coach from the other team came out to the mound just to make sure that the infield knew exactly what to do. I hoped that he would take the guy out but no such luck. He took his place on the mound and looked in to get the sign from the catcher. I guessed that he would throw nothing but fastballs since I hadn't been able to catch up to one of them all day. I was right. The first bullet came out of his hand and I took it for ball one.

He surprised me with the second pitch by throwing a good curve that buckled my knees. I took it and the umpire called it a strike.

Then he followed that with a fastball on the outside corner of the plate. I swung as hard as I could, hoping I would get lucky and make contact. I didn't. Strike two.

His next pitch came deep inside- a purpose pitch trying to get me to back off the plate so he could paint the corner with his next one and I wouldn't be able to reach it. Count was now 2-2.

Now the battle really started. I fouled off four straight pitches, one of them a liner down the third base line that was nearly fair. It would have been a game winner but my swing was just a tad too early and it went foul.

I could tell he was beginning to get frustrated and I was gaining a little confidence. His next pitch was high making the count 3-2. If I could just force another ball, that would score the deciding run.

What followed next was called "the best battle between pitcher and hitter" that the sportswriter covering the tournament said he had ever seen in youth baseball. I fouled off pitch after pitch, one of them another close call, this time down the first base line. My coach told me later that I had stayed alive for thirteen pitches.

I was exhausted but I guessed my opponent was just as tired, maybe even more. I stepped out of the box, took a deep breath, and stepped back in. I was determined not to strike out even though no one would have criticized me for it if I did. He had given me his all and I had managed to fight it off. But the job wasn't done yet.

We glared at each other from 60 feet, 6 inches away. I saw on his face a little smile which almost said, "Well, you've been lucky so far but now you're gonna get the best I got." He toed the rubber and didn't even bother with a sign. Everyone in the place knew it was going to be the fastball.

He went into his windup and an absolute rocket came out of his hand but it didn't look like the others. Its trajectory was a little off and in the split second it took the message to go from my brain to my hands, it told me "Don't swing." The ball landed in the catcher's mitt and the world stopped until the umpire yelled out "Ball four! Take your base!"

I was stunned. For a second, I didn't know what to do. Finally, things kicked in and I trotted down to first base looking around the diamond to make sure that Gary went down to touch second, Lloyd to third, and that beautiful sight of Chris touching home with the winning run. When I stepped on first, my teammates came running out of the dugout almost knocking me down with their congratulatory pats on the back.

We celebrated for a few minutes and from the melee, I saw the Montgomery pitcher sitting on the pitcher's mound crying. He didn't deserve to do that so I slowly left my buddies and went over to him and put out my hand to help him up. He looked up at me and after a few seconds took my hand and boosted himself up. We never said a word to each other and he walked off to join his teammates in their dugout somberly watching us on the infield grass.

This was the closest experience I ever had to being a hero. I never threw a game-winning touchdown pass or hit the game-winning bucket and this certainly wasn't the way you dream about doing it when you're in your backyard. No, I hadn't smashed a home run or even gotten a lousy single. I had walked. But on this day, that was enough and I will never forget the feeling I had that day until the day I die. I imagine that one of the first things I will tell God when I get to heaven will be that I appreciate that gust of wind that pushed that ball outside.

We went to the Series and played respectably but came up short. It was a double elimination tournament and we went to the final game against a team from Tulsa, Oklahoma. Each of us had one loss so the winner would be Babe Ruth Champs. Tulsa had a pitcher who was ambidextrous. So as to not tire out, he would throw one inning right handed and the next left. We led 5-2 going to the bottom of the seventh and we were already hoisting the trophy. Unfortunately, Tulsa had other ideas helped by some sloppy play by us. They scored four runs and beat us.

As I sat in that dugout, sobbing with my head in my hands, I knew exactly how the Montgomery pitcher felt. We had accomplished so much but none of that seemed to matter on that long three-day bus ride back home. We were met by over two hundred people at DeKalb Memorial. All the other guys had their parents there, greeting them warmly and shuffling them into cars back to their homes. I looked around and there was no one there for me. No Mom. No Dad.

I picked up my duffle bag and started my lonely trudge home. On the walk home I imagined that Mom would have a special dinner waiting for me and that Dad would surprise me by loading us in the car and driving us to get an ice cream.

I walked in the house and mother greeted me with a big hug. Dad sat in his chair working a crossword puzzle. He didn't congratulate me, say "welcome home", or any other cordial greeting. He never said a word about the trip other than, "Heard you lost. Go pack your room. We're moving next Saturday."

CHAPTER 12

MY WALK THROUGH HISTORY (PART 2)

The moving van pulled into the driveway that Saturday morning and I thought it was the end of the world. I was caught totally off guard and unprepared for this life-altering change. Dad had never said one word about moving to me and Mom told me later that she had not been consulted either. When Dad decided to do something– that was the end of it.

I had been able to say goodbye to most of my closest friends but many of them only found out about my move when school got back in session a few weeks later.

The reason for the move was the influx of black families moving into our area. Dad was a closet bigot and he didn't want to live that close to anyone whose skin was darker than ours. He wanted to be the first in the neighborhood to move before, in his words, "the property value went down because of those people." Those people, indeed. One of those people had possibly saved his life when he was wounded in World War II but that, of course, was a different story.

We settled in to our newly-constructed home and I must admit that it was very nice with a big back yard and a spacious bedroom of my own. It was a tri-level and I was on the bottom level next to a huge family room containing a new pool table Dad had bought. I met a few kids I would be going to school with in the Fall and one was a big surprise. Johnny W., my main trumpet competition from elementary school band, lived in the area and he introduced me around.

"Family" life was drastically different in the new location from what it had been on Memorial. I put quotes around the word family because no one could have ever mistaken us for the Cleavers (Leave It To Beaver) or the Nelsons (Ozzie and Harriet). We were more like a tv family that would come later- the Bunkers. Dad was Archie, the bigot; Mom was Edith, the Dingbat; and I was the Meathead.

Suppertime was where the most drastic change had occurred. Mom still worked at the downtown Rich's so her commute on the bus was over 90 minutes, meaning that she didn't get home until after 7: 00 pm most nights and the lord and master of the manor couldn't wait that long to have his evening meal. She would prepare meals ahead of time and Dad, who had gotten home much earlier but couldn't dare be caught in the kitchen, would have me warm them up for the two of us. We rarely sat down at the table together which, at least, had been our habit on Memorial.

While Mom was an okay cook, I could never say that she was a great one. But, then, she didn't have much to work with since both Dad and I were very picky eaters. Her options on what to prepare for us were very limited so you could usually tell what day of the week it was from what was on the table.

Sunday- roast beef, meat loaf, or fried chicken

Monday- leftovers from Sunday

Tuesday- ham and eggs (I still love breakfast for dinner)

Wednesday- pork chops (my favorite day)

Thursday- country-fried steak and occasionally liver

Friday- she worked late so I would fix myself a tv dinner

Saturday- Dad would grill a steak or we would get fried fish from a drive-in called The Shrimp Boat

No matter what was being served, with the exception of Tuesdays, Dad had to have corn bread. He would have one portion with his meal but his dessert was to crumble up the corn bread in a glass of buttermilk (yuck!). And if the corn bread was not perfectly prepared, poor Mom would catch hell. On one such occasion, Dad was not pleased with it and he went into one of his rages. He swept the plates and dishes off the table into the floor and proceeded to break practically every glass in the house. You always sat on pins and needles until he took his first bite, never knowing what to expect from him. Always quick to voice his displeasure, I don't think I ever heard him compliment her one time.

I was going to attend Southwest DeKalb High School, a much larger school in total enrollment than Murphy. I quickly discovered as I stepped into those halls that September day in 1962, that the kids here were just as fun, just as cool, and just as friendly as those I had left making my transition a little easier.

There were two things about the school that I found quite enjoyable from the start. One was the band because of its director, a great guy named Moe Turrentine. Mr. T, as we called him long before there was a more famous Mr. T, was a trumpet player himself and he took special pride with his brass section. I liked him immediately and he seemed to take an instant liking to me as well. I quickly established myself as second chair behind a Senior and when the practices started for football season marching band, I knew playing in this band would be a treat.

Playing in the Murphy marching band was sometimes rather boring and mundane. The halftime shows we prepared were good but somewhat bland. Not so with Moe. The formations we performed and the songs we played were original and always entertaining to the fans. Plus, he let me do a couple of solos.

The one I remember most is *Stormy Weather,* the great Lena Horne song of the 40's, while we formed an umbrella. I was the button at the top of the umbrella. Mr. T called me into his office one day after school and had me listen to a version played by one of the great trumpet players of all time, Maynard Ferguson. He told me, "Play it just like that." He let me take the recording home so I could play along with it. I never gave it back and he never said a word.

The second thing I remember is Prissy C. Her real name was Priscilla and she played clarinet. Unlike Murphy where all our football games were played at one of two stadiums: Grady or Cheney and you got to the game any way you could, SWD's away games meant that the band rode a school bus because they were sometimes out of town. I loved those bus rides home.

Prissy and I had become an item and we would always find our way to the back of the bus where the couples would situate themselves for a little lip-to-lip dialogue. The romance fizzled, however, when football season was over. I couldn't drive yet and an "older man", a Junior, came along and knocked me out of the picture. However, I got a little revenge back when a Junior girl, who happened to be a gorgeous majorette, came after me. She would drive us on our dates but would let me sit behind the wheel of the car when we "parked."

One of the things I did miss out on that year not going to Murphy was a banner football season. Murphy had put together a fantastic season and had won the City of Atlanta Championship in a game always referred to as the Milk Bowl. Why it was called that is beyond my scope of knowledge but my friend Tom would know, I'm sure.

Murphy played a powerhouse from Valdosta for the state title on a cold, wet night. Valdosta could probably hold up well against a lot of small colleges. Course, most of their players were college age. I went to the game with Kenny's family and at one point during the game went down to visit with the band. Mr. Sisk saw me and let me play one "charge" to get the fans worked up. It didn't help. Valdosta gave Murphy a good thrashing, 39-0.

I made a lot of new friends while there. Beautiful cheerleaders Peggy B. and Lynn A., majorettes Jennifer W. and Sherrie B., drummer Alan D., fellow trumpeter Mel P., next door neighbor Wesley T., Anna B., and many others. And remember that first kiss I told you about? Pam went there, too, but she had a boyfriend so there was no chance to duplicate that magical afternoon.

We were only three weeks away from starting a new school year which would be my Junior year. I would take over first chair in the band and the prospects for making the baseball team were good since I had had a good summer playing for a Glenwood Hills team managed by one of the school's football coaches who told me he would put in a good word for me.

The most surprising thing that had occurred during the summer, however, was the incredible growth spurt I experienced. In May of 1963, as the school year ended, I was measured at 5' 3". When I came back that Fall, I had grown to 5' 10". Seven inches in one three month period. That growth spurt would cause me some discomfort later because my bones couldn't keep up and I have joint discomfort in my knees to this day because of it.

My friend Alan and I had gone to Columbia Mall because I needed some new shirts and pants with cuffs that wouldn't be at my knees. He had driven that day and was dropping me off at my house. As we neared my driveway, I saw a sign posted in my front yard. "What's that?" he asked. When we got close enough I knew that Dad had done it again. It was a For Sale sign.

Later that night when he got home from work he explained that the commute each day was killing him, taxes were higher, and he just didn't like living outside the city. So, here we go again, I thought. Uprooted again after I had finally gotten to the point where I didn't constantly think of Murphy and all my friends there.

The good news, however, was that we were moving back to our old house on Memorial Drive and I would be going back to Murphy for my Junior year. Dad, it seems, had an idea that he wouldn't like it in the county, so he had rented our old house rather than selling it. I hated giving up that pool table since we had to sell it with the house, but as we pulled in to our old driveway, a big smile came over my face because I knew I was back home.

The morning of my history walk had started with a fine mist falling that was now turning into a steadier rain. The skies had turned as gray as the uniforms that the Confederate soldiers wore that morning 150 years ago. From the reports of that day, the skies had been clear and visibility was good but your senses still had to be keen because you had no idea what lurked behind the next tree.

I started back on my trek which now included a climb up a steep incline covered with pine straw making the footing slippery and treacherous for someone who was not as agile as they once were. For soldiers, carrying weapons and provisions, it must have been a very difficult climb. During my playing days here, some 50 years ago, the jaunt up this hill would have been nothing; now, it meant getting a good running start hoping my momentum would carry me up.

To add to the problem, I was wearing running shoes with rubber soles that provided no traction at all. I took a run at the hill and made it about two-thirds of the way before slipping. I caught my balance but had now lost impetus making the rest of the climb even more arduous. Persistence prevailed, however, and I finally made it to the top. I caught my breath, took a moment and continued through the woods that covered the top of the hill.

If I listened carefully, I could almost hear the voices of the men as they talked to each other that morning. Some of the conversation probably centered around the controversial decision that had been made just five days prior to replace the former commander, Gen. Joseph Johnston with Lt. Gen. John Bell Hood. Throughout the campaign that had begun in Chattanooga, Johnston had been a defensive-minded leader, retreating too often for Richmond's tastes. Hood was a more aggressive general and the march the men were taking that morning was an example of that "strike first" mentality.

Some of the talk was probably crude jokes that always seem to occur when men get together. But I'm sure most of the talk was about home and family. While the troops were made up of men from all over the south, it was primarily comprised of men from the state of Tennessee. Their official designation was Army of Tennessee, not to be confused with the designation of the Union forces which was the Army of the Tennessee, indicating the geographic location, in this case the Tennessee River, as opposed to the state or nearby town that the South used to identify specific battles. An example can be seen in the two different designations of the first major battle of the war. Confederates identified it as First Battle of Manassas while the Union called it the Battle of Bull Run.

For those who had survived this long ordeal, this was another day facing potential death. They knew that fighting was inevitable that day and the thought of never seeing loved ones weighed heavy on their minds. But loyalty for the cause reigned supreme and they marched ever forward, never once thinking about turning back.

I was saddened at the litter and debris that was strewn everywhere as I walked through those woods. I even came across a dirty blanket that someone, perhaps a homeless person, had used for a bed. Finally, after covering about 300 yards, I came to the opening and looked upon what were, to me, sacred grounds- the playing fields of Murphy High School. This open area contained the practice football field and the baseball diamond of my day. From reading personal diaries of soldiers of both sides who had fought here that day, the clearing was about the same then, just without the athletic fields. The soldiers described coming across an open area after marching through nothing but forests for miles. But things were different now.

Murphy High is now Crim Open Campus High School, a year-round vocational and secondary equivalent school enabling students who previously dropped out to return to school to obtain their GED's (General Educational Development). Since Crim no longer fields athletic teams, the open area where I spent so much time is now used for local recreational leagues. Where the football practice field was located in my day is now a baseball field and where the diamond was is now split into a softball field and a youth football gridiron.

But one thing remained. The "Hill". The hill was more dreaded by the football team than it was by the basketball or baseball players. For those of us who played those two sports, the hill was used for conditioning. The football coaches used the hill for conditioning, too but it was also used as a punishment tool for the football team. If a player was caught misbehaving or if they had missed an assignment or if the team, in general, had a lousy practice, up the hill they ran. I can still remember watching Curtis, our largest lineman, trudging up that hill. Most of the time smaller players had to get behind him and push him up.

The hill was a steeply graded rise of good old Georgia red clay leading up to the back of the school. The hill was probably about 60-80 feet from bottom to top. Getting up to the top of the hill was difficult enough in shorts or a baseball uniform but in full pads, it was damn near impossible, especially after a long grueling practice session.

But it's funny how time changes perspectives on things. When you are a young boy that hill looked like it was two miles high but today, it didn't seem to be all that intimidating. The second thing that had changed was that a stand of pine trees now covered the hill. I couldn't tell if they had been planted or had grown there naturally but there would be no way you could run a straight line up the hill now.

I think that it was at the top of that hill that Dad came to watch me play some of my baseball games. He could stand up there and be undetected. He never admitted seeing me play and he definitely never came to see me play basketball but I would catch him make a comment about something that had happened in a game that he would have no way of knowing unless he had seen it. I never let on what I suspected because, the truth was, I didn't really want him there anyway. In my earlier playing days I could have had a great day at the plate and all he wanted to talk about when we got home was the error I had made. It just seemed like he could never say anything constructive.

The rain had stopped falling by now and I turned around to the area that used to be the baseball diamond. Gone were the dugouts and stands but the memories of those great days lingered still. As opposed to basketball practices that were mentally and physically tough, baseball practices were always fun to me. I used to love shagging fly balls in the outfield; taking batting practice; and even infield and outfield practice was enjoyable. And they were made even better by the teaching skills of Coach Julian Mock.

I am fully convinced that we won most of our games during pre-game warmups. Coach Mock taught fundamentals and when he was finished with that, he taught fundamentals more. We were so precise and fluid in the infield that you could look over at the other dugout and see your opponents' jaws dropping with disbelief that we could be so good. Of course, it also helped to have pitchers like Bud, Butch, Jimmy, and Jim.

Let me give you a couple of examples about how fundamentally sound we were. For those of you who have played the game before, you will be familiar with the term "stepping in the bucket." That's when a batter pulls away from the pitch moving his lead leg to the left or right depending on how they batted. When a batter does this, their balance is thrown off and there is no way they can hit with any power or anything thrown on the outside corner of the plate because the bat naturally follows with the body. To keep a batter from getting into this bad habit, Coach Mock would, literally, put a bucket of water behind the batter's feet. If they moved their stance backwards and spilled any of the water in the bucket, they ran laps. Believe me, after a few times around the perimeter of a baseball field, those feet move toward the pitcher and the oncoming ball, not backwards.

The second coaching skill he delivered was base running and sliding techniques. He would stand us at first base with a Dixie Cup full of water in each hand and we would run to second and slide into the base. If we had water left in both cups when we got to second, we could quench our thirst and drink it. If we had run jarringly and hadn't slid smoothly enough and there was no water in the cups, we ran laps. Again, it didn't take long to develop the Coach Mock method of running although I don't remember Billy or Jerry ever getting a drink of water.

Of course, other memories flooded back as well. The day Ernie, our catcher, forgot his cup and got nailed with a foul tip right in his junk. The cruelty of young teenage boys was evident as we all laughed hysterically as he lay writhing on the ground in considerable pain. I can still remember Coach Mock leaning over him after he had finally gotten his breath back and it was evident he was going to be all right saying, "It's a shame it didn't hit you in the head, cause there ain't a damn thing up there to hurt!"

And there was always the standard hot balm pranks. There were two products that were generally used to relieve aches, pains, and muscle tightness; Icy Hot and Red Hot. You would put these on after practice and let them sit for awhile to soak in to help ease the discomfort. But if this clear, almost undetectable ointment was rubbed into, let's say, an athletic supporter and the unknowing individual wore it on the playing field and began to sweat, the resulting interaction of the two would cause an incredible burning sensation that was quite uncomfortable. I can still remember Lloyd, the prankster of the two twins, putting it into Dick's (now wasn't that appropriate) jock. When the ointment set in and began to do its thing, Dick M. could have set a world high jump record the way he was dancing around the infield.

I never got pranked in this manner but there was the time that I got left on the field tied up like a calf at a rodeo in nothing but my skivvies. If I had my guess it was probably Lloyd who was at the bottom of this also but it took five of them to haul me out of the locker room after practice one day.

The boys' gym area was segmented into what we called the cages with roughly eight individual stalls in each cage. On this particular day my back was to the door leading into the cage where my locker area was located and I never saw or heard the culprits come in. They grabbed me and carried me out to the field, tied me up, and left me to get untied and home the best way I could.

It took me over an hour to loosen the ropes enough to free myself (I would never be mistaken for an Indiana Jones in a difficult situation) and get back home. I got back into the locker area and found my stall completely empty of all my clothes. They had taken those with them. There was nothing else to do but start my walk back home. Anyway you looked at the prospects, it was going to prove to be an embarrassing situation because even though I lived nearby, I was going to have to travel down two major thoroughfares wearing nothing but my underwear and a smile unless I could come up with an alternate plan.

My idea was to try and make it across the street to some woods without being detected. Those same woods were directly across from my house so I felt like I could make it almost all the way home without being seen. Then it was just a matter of timing my dash across Memorial Drive when no cars would be coming by to get to our back door and into the house. There was just one problem: the cheerleaders were still practicing in the front of the gym and there was no way I could make it past them without being seen.

I thought that if there was a way to distract them long enough I could get past them without being detected. I snuck back up stairs to the entrance. I was going to tell them that Mr. Russell, our vice-principal, had just come over the intercom system telling them to report to his office. I would deal with the consequences of my leading them on this wild goose chase later. For now, my only thought was on getting home with a little bit of dignity.

Just as I was about to open one of the entrance doors enough to just stick my head out, I caught a reflection in the glass on the door. I turned around and there was Lucille, one of the cheerleaders. She had apparently gone inside to use the restroom.

This wasn't just any cheerleader either. Lucille C. was one of the most beautiful girls in the entire school. She was a stunningly gorgeous blonde who was just as sweet and beautiful inside as she was outside. She was special. Every boy wanted to be her boyfriend and every girl wanted to be her. She would go on to become our Homecoming Queen our Senior year.

We both just stood there for several seconds because she was just as shocked, I'm sure, to see me standing there as I was to have her seeing me in my underwear. To the best of my recollection, because I was so flummoxed I can't remember the moment in precise detail, the dialogue went something like this.

Me: "Hi, Lucille. Funny story."

Her: "I can't wait to hear it."

Me: "Some of the guys on the team tied me up and took my clothes and…."

Her: "Now you can't get home."

Me: "Yeah. I live just across on Memorial, you know."

Her: "You want me to drive you home?"

As I thought about this later, I should have said yes. What a feather in my cap it would have been for me to say, "I was in my underwear in Lucille's car." I would have conveniently left out the embarrassing part of the story. Instead, I said…

Me: "No, that's okay. Just help me get the girls away from the front of the gym so I can run across the street to the woods."

Her: "Sure. I'll make up something, but give me a few minutes to get them away."

Me: "Thanks, Lucille. And can you keep this a secret?"

Her: "I'll do my best. And Randy…."

Me: "Yeah."

Her: (with a little smile on her face) "You've got a really cute butt."

To her credit, she never laughed at me and I think she was true to her word that she wouldn't say anything because I never heard about the incident from any of the cheerleaders and this is the first time I've ever retold the story.

I went back downstairs and peeked around the corner of the building until the girls were gone. If one of the track coaches had seen me when I started running, he would have wanted me to run the 100 yd. dash because it was the fastest I had ever run in my life. I made it without being seen and started the painful walk through the woods. I was barefoot and I believe I found every rock in that section of the woods. Again, I dashed across Memorial and even if one of two drivers saw me, it was better than having the entire cheerleader squad giggling at my butt cheeks- cute or not.

I ran to the back door that was always left unlocked (different era when home safety was not the issue it is today). The guys had left my clothes on the back porch and since no one was home, the long ordeal was now over. For the first time in about 3 hours, I could finally breathe.

On July 9, 1982, PanAm flight #759, from New Orleans to Las Vegas, crashed shortly after takeoff killing all 145 passengers and 8 flight crew members plus several more on the ground. Lucille was a flight attendant on that flight. When the word began filtering around to all of us, we were crushed. She had been such an important part of our lives and now that beautiful woman had been taken from us. And she is not the only member of that graduating class that are now gone.

Dear Reader: please bear with me as I try to pay a simple tribute to those classmates I've lost. Some were closer to me than others but they are all important to me because of the common bond we shared. If you did not go to Murphy then I ask you to take a moment and reflect on those dear friends you've lost.

Murphy Class of 1965 Honor Roll

Phyllis A.	Trudy B.	John B.
Vicky B.	Larry B.	Linda C.
Lucille C.	Joe C.	Charles C.
Charles D.	Jerry F.	Heather G.
Jerry G.	Linda G.	Ernie G.
Sam G.	Ricky L.	Howard M.
Steve N.	Sandra P.	John V.

I continued my history walk by climbing up the "hill". Luckily, concrete steps had been added making the climb up the steep grade a little easier on this old body.

At the top of the hill was quite a different sight from the one I knew back in my school days. Behind the gym in those days was a basketball court. While I had a makeshift goal in my backyard nailed to one of the trees, it was less than satisfactory. The backboard consisted of some planks dad had nailed together and the goal was not set at regulation height. To make things even worse, the tree had a limb about five feet above the goal and if the ball ricocheted off it there was no telling where the ball would go. And dribbling off dirt is never easy either. So, my other alternative was to go to the school and practice my shooting there. Now, the goals had been removed and the entire area was paved over making a large parking area for faculty and students.

I took a quick little side trip to the wooded area behind the cars to see if I could locate the "log." This was the area where all the smokers would head between classes to catch a puff of their Luckies, Winstons, or Marlboro's. And the area got its name honestly because there was an actual log there for them to rest their butts or put out their butts, whichever suited them better.

This was also the area where all the fights took place. These fights had usually been preceded by the words, "Meet me after school" which had been uttered by one of the would-be combatants when his honor had been smudged for some reason.

I witnessed several good altercations at the "log", always from a safe viewing distance but the best fight that I remember took place between two girls. It was a good old-fashioned hair-pulling, eye-scratching, cat fight and they meant business. All the boys were hoping that blouses would be torn and skirts ripped but when that didn't happen, the next best thing was blood. We got that when one of the girls busted the others' nose with a good left hook. No fight between boys ever gave us that much entertainment.

I cut back through the parked cars and noticed that people were walking in one of the doors leading to the school itself. I had forgotten that even though it was July, this was a twelve-month school. So, while it was not a part of my original plans and itinerary, I decided to visit those sacred halls again. I opened the door and began………

CHAPTER 13

MY WALK THROUGH THE HALLS OF MURPHY

The physical configuration of the school is drastically different from how it was fifty years ago. The main difference is that the two buildings, one containing classrooms, cafeteria, and administration offices, and the other housing the gym and band practice room were now connected by a walkthrough hallway. The door I had entered took me in to this connecting hallway.

I didn't know if I was even allowed in the building with security issues being what they are in today's crazy world so, the first thing I did was to look for someone in a position of authority to see if my presence was acceptable. I hit pay dirt with the first person I saw. A very nicely dressed lady saw my inquisitive look and asked if she could help. I introduced myself and told her my background story- that I had gone here many years ago and had lived across the street. She volunteered to escort me up to the office to get a visitor's pass and along the way told me that she was the newly appointed principal of the school.

As we passed through the halls I pointed out certain rooms and what classes they had contained in my era. Once we arrived at the office, she introduced me to the secretary who had me sign in and get a visitors badge. As we walked back into the hall, she said, "Do you have a little time to show me around? I have only been here two weeks and I think it would be a valuable use of my time today to get the history of the building from someone who actually attended here."

I said, "Ma'am, I'm retired. I've got all the time in the world."

We walked down to one end of the school and I showed her where the library had been and told her some of the stories about Mrs. G, our school librarian. She was a no-nonsense lady who considered those books her own private property. Heaven forbid that you might bring back one of her books damaged in any way.

From there, we took the stairs and went up to the second floor. This floor held the labs for biology, physics, and chemistry. We had some real characters teaching those subjects. There was Mr. Bell, or "Ding Dong" as we called him and "Juicy Jaws" Graham. Mr. Graham had a lisp that caused him to spit a little as he talked. Truth be told, he spit a lot. If you had the misfortune to sit on the front row during one of his lectures, you had better bring a towel and non-smear writing paper.

But the real character was Mr. Bruner. His patience level on a scale of 1-10 was -1. The least disruption of one of his classes would bring out his famous, "Pick up your books and get out!" There's not a one of us that had him for chemistry that didn't hear that at least once during the year. I remember the day when two of our smartest and sweetest girls, Alice A. and Brenda F., even got thrown out.

As we continued our walk, I reflected on several other teachers that had made an impact on me during my days at Murphy. There was Mrs. King, one of the kindest people I've ever met in my life. I had her for Civics/Georgia History. It was especially gratifying to have the opportunity of knowing her after I had become an adult. One of my children, Brian, would also have her as a teacher and she insisted on being the teacher who got to present an award that my daughter would receive a few years later. If you look up the definition of teacher, you'll find her smiling face next to it. I'd like to think that Brian, now a 4th grade teacher himself, models his methods after her.

Mr. Evans taught me American History and he is responsible, in large part, for the interest I have in the Civil War I do today. He was gruff but he could make his subject interesting, at least to me, in ways I had never imagined from a teacher before. Another adjective I would use to describe him would be humorless. I'm not sure I ever saw him smile and he was not above making you pay in the most embarrassing ways if you ever disrupted his class.

The most famous Mr. Evans story involves a young girl who stood outside our classroom trying to get the attention of her boyfriend to give him a note she had for him. Mr. Evans spotted the boy mouthing silently something to her. He quietly moved to the door, opened it, and invited the girl into the class where he proceeded to make her read the note aloud to the entire class. It was rather personal and detailed and, needless to say, the girl left the room in tears. The boy, however, took it in stride and laughed at her predicament while she read the note. They broke up the next day.

Miss Hogan would wear a grass skirt over her dress and teach us the "Hukilau", an Hawaiian folk song about fishing. I'm betting that every Murphy student who had her for class could sing the song right now. And for our various English and Literature classes, we had Ms. Petty and Ms. Foley. I'm still not sure I understand the value of diagramming sentences but Ms. P made us do it anyway. And Ms. Foley certainly is partially responsible for my love of literature and grammar that I have today. I know she is smiling, knowing that I have had three children's books and several short stories published.

But, perhaps, the best teacher-related story from my days at Murphy involved the Spanish teacher, Mrs. Padgett. This lady always seemed frazzled. If you remember the character of Aunt Clara played by the adorable actress Marian Lorne from the television show *Bewitched*, then you can get a pretty good idea of how Mrs. Padgett was any day that ended in a "Y".

Her class was on the second floor and the culprits involved in the prank have changed over the years but the most common name associated with the incident is Freddy F. Freddy was our designated Class Clown. There is nothing that boy wouldn't do or say to get a laugh. He's just as crazy today as he was then. He was sitting on the sill of an open window one day as class was about to start. It was Springtime and rather warm so the window was allowed to be open to let some air in. No air conditioning then.

As she was arranging her desk to begin class, another pre-arranged student came to her door and told her she was needed in the office. When she left, Freddy ran downstairs and sprawled himself on top of one of the shrubs that lay underneath the window he had been sitting in making it appear that he had fallen out of the window.

The rest of the class gathered around the window and when Mrs. Padgett came back they all yelled, "Mrs. Padgett, Freddy fell out of the window!" She ran to the window, peered down, and saw Freddy's limp and apparently lifeless body. Her frantic screams cascaded throughout the halls and she ran back downstairs to get help. The class gave Freddy the signal and he scurried back up and sat, innocently, in his desk.

Mrs. Padgett and the principal, Mr. McCord, ran outside but found no one in the shrubs. When they got back to the class all the students were in their seats acting like little angels. Mr. McCord asked in a contrite deadpan manner, "Freddy, did you fall out the window?"

And in his best Spanish, Freddy replied, "No, senor. Y estado aqui." (No, sir. I have been right here.) Amazingly, he was not punished but there was no Spanish taught that day since the poor lady was too flustered to convey a coherent thought.

There was something missing from the halls, both upstairs and down, that had been a staple back then and that was the lockers that lined them. It was amazing but I could remember exactly where mine had been located. I pointed out the area where it would have been and also commented on how much brighter the walls were now than I remembered. I remember that they had been a rather dull gray that darkened the hallway even with the overhead lights on and the sunlight coming through the windows in the classrooms. Now, they had a yellowish tint to them that was noticeably cheerier.

And they seemed so much larger now than those days even though I knew they hadn't been widened. I think the perception was different because they weren't crammed tight with students trying to get to their next class. With no one in the hall except for the two of us, they seemed spacious and roomy.

We continued our walk and made our way to the building that held some of my fondest memories- some heartaches, a lot of sweat, and a treasure chest full of joyful times. How many hours had I spent here? Too many to even begin estimating. Basketball practices, pep rallies, assemblies, and band concerts all came flooding into my memory bank. I could still hear the cheers but most of all I heard Coach Davis giving us his instructions as he led us through our drills. The squeaks made by our black high-top Converse basketball shoes as we glided across that court still echoed in the rafters. We continued our tour with..........

CHAPTER 14

MY WALK TO THE GYM

I am amazed by the athleticism of today's athletes. And not just in basketball, but in all sports. The young men of today are bigger, stronger, faster, quicker; can jump higher, hit a baseball farther, and field a ground ball more effortlessly than we ever hoped of doing. But there is one thing that we had that is missing with many young athletes today- dedication to the team. For us, it was all about school and team. For them, from my perspective, it is all about me and that saddens me greatly because being a member of a team and winning as a team is one of the greatest experiences a young boy or girl can have.

I mentioned earlier that I loved baseball practice and while I loved playing the game, basketball practices were very tough- mentally and physically. I played in an era when it was unusual to see a high school player above 6'6" and if you did, he played center. Today, that is a routine height and they're guards who can handle the ball and shoot with all the skills imaginable of a smaller player.

The tallest player we had was Curtis W., who, at 6'2", was our center. The advantage he had over his counterparts was that

Curtis' weight in high school was around 230 or 240. He was our biggest lineman on the football team and while his vertical jumping capability was only about three inches off the ground, he still gobbled up most of the rebounds because he had the best boxing-out technique going. There was no getting around Curtis if you were the opponent. If you tried going around him, you'd have to get a bus ticket and if you attempted to go through or over him, you'd find yourself flat on your back on the court looking up.

While we didn't have great height, we did have speed and quickness. Coach Davis made sure of that. We ran a man-to-man defense the entire game. I can never remember us playing a zone-ever. We pressured the ball constantly with either a half-court or full-court press every time the opposition put the ball in play. That meant that we had to be in great shape and even though Coach Davis rotated seven or eight guys in the game, by the end of night you were exhausted. That meant that practices were run the same way- all out with very little time to recuperate between drills.

When I moved back to Murphy my Junior year after going to Southwest DeKalb the previous year, I had one goal in mind. I wanted, desperately, to make the basketball varsity. I thought I had a pretty good chance to do so now that I had added inches to my height and had improved my shooting skills but the day of tryouts found me nauseous and sick to my stomach due to the nervousness I felt. The other thing going for all of us Juniors who were trying out for the first time was that there were several open spots available. The previous team had been mostly Seniors who had now graduated so all of us that day were hoping to join Mike H., the only returning member of last year's team.

I knew that about seven of the spots were solidly entrenched with Mike and from my class Kenny, Floyd, Lloyd, Billy C., Curtis, and Dick. The other four or five roster spots would be up for grabs and the competition was keen. I, luckily, had a good day shooting and even played fairly decent defense (an area where I did not excel that I'll talk about later) and thought afterwards that I had made a good impression on the coach. Would it be enough, though? Others had looked pretty good, too.

I will admit that I didn't sleep very much that night thinking about my chances. The dreams of a young boy can be just as burdensome to them as those of an adult. And if those dreams are shattered, the devastation can be even worse.

I didn't get a chance to find out for myself the results because Kenny beat me to it. We had been told that Coach Davis wouldn't post the roster until after school but Kenny had seen the coach earlier and had weasled the information out of him. Kenny, being the friend he was, knew he was on the team because he had made it as a Sophomore. He was asking purely for me.

I saw him running down the hallway between 5th and 6th period towards me and I thought the excitement on his face was simply that he had made it. When he got near me he held out his hand and said, "Put er' there, teammate!"

In disbelief I asked, "Did I make it? Did I really make it?"

"Sure did #12. Coach has already assigned jersey numbers."

Trying to act cool I said coyly, "Aw, darn! I wanted #13!"

Thinking I was serious he said, "You still will be when we play away from home. Remember we wear an even-numbered jersey at home and odd-numbered jerseys away."

"I know, you big jerk. I'd wear any number he gave me."

He reminded me that we had our first meeting after school, said he'd see me there, and ran off to his class. I was so happy I couldn't move. When the second bell rang, however, I made a beeline for my class. It would not have set well with the coach if I had a detention on my first day as a Murphy War Eagle basketball player.

Practices were always physically tiresome because of the constant running but for me they also proved to be mentally tough because Coach Davis expected me to play defense, an art I never mastered. I had no trouble picking up the offense. We ran a system called either the Auburn shuffle or the wheel. It was named the Auburn shuffle because the man who developed it was an Auburn coach by the name of Joel Eaves. Eaves would gain later fame as the Athletic Director for the University of Georgia and as being the man who hired Vince Dooley to be Georgia's football coach in 1965. Eaves actually got his start in coaching as one of Murphy's first basketball coaches when the school originally opened.

It was rare that, as a young boy, I ever played against other boys. I usually just played alone in my backyard or at the school so, I never had the opportunity to defend anyone. All I did was shoot- free throws, layups, and jump shots over and over again. So, while I had developed a pretty good shooting eye, I didn't know defensive techniques at all. But I also discovered very quickly that you didn't get your name in the paper for having a good defensive game- you got it mentioned based on the number of points you had scored and being a kid who was hungry for attention, my emphasis was on scoring.

I was known as a "gunner" by my teammates and the students in the stands. A gunner is a player who shoots the ball whenever he gets the chance and that was certainly my motive. I never started but I usually got into the game fairly quickly since we rotated our players often. I always felt as if there was a lottery going on in the stands guessing how long it would take me to put up my first shot. Usually, the winner was the one that had the lowest time because, whether I made the shot or not, a cheer would go up in the crowd.

Coach Davis had other ideas and he was absolutely right because defense usually wins games. But no matter how hard I tried, I just couldn't grasp playing defense effectively. He had a nickname for me and it wasn't given warmly. He called me "The Matador." Get the picture. The matador stands in the middle of the bull ring waving his red cape to attract the attention of the bull. As the bull charges the matador calmly moves to the side and lets the bull charge by him. That was me on defense. The man I was guarding could usually glide right past me on his way to the bucket while you could imagine everyone in the stands shouting "Ole!"

When this would happen in practice, Coach Davis would yell, "That's two!" meaning laps around the gym after practice and if my player scored he'd say, "Add another!" I would hang my head as I watched our team manager, Dennis P., make a notation in the lap book. I usually had company running laps after practice but more likely than not, I ran the most.

There are several games that stand out as especially memorable from those days- some good, some bad, some ugly. The good was a game against North Fulton. As I look back on those years I would have to say that North Fulton was our biggest rival. They were the team that we battled in all sports for supremacy in our division. It was also a cultural rivalry as well. They were from the "rich" side of Atlanta. Their daddies were bankers, lawyers, and doctors while we were the more blue collar, hard-working type.

It was late in the season and, as usual, we were fighting for the top spot in our division. The game was nip-and-tuck all night but with 25 seconds left in the game, Kenny hit a 20 ft. jumper to put us ahead. Dick stole the ball and was fouled. He hit one of his free throws and then the same thing happened as Floyd stripped the ball and was fouled. He hit his free throw to seal the victory.

The bad was against our closest rival, geography-wise. East Atlanta was usually the basement-dweller in the division. Many of us, especially those of us who went to either Burgess Elementary or John B. Gordon, knew many of the students from EA because we had gone to grade school with them. EA had been built to help the overload that Murphy was experiencing and they were still a relatively young school. We had beaten them by almost 30 points just a week before but now they were coming to our gym and most of us on the team thought it would be another laugher.

There was no shot clock in play during those years so the EA coach used a stall tactic on us. Each time they got the ball they would deliberately pass the ball around with no real intent to score until they had run off a good portion of the clock. Since we were such a good offensive team with terrific scorers like Billy and Floyd, they wanted to keep the ball out of our hands. And it worked. The score was close, we trailed by one, going into the final seconds when we got possession of the ball under our own basket. One last chance to snatch a victory away. The basketball gods were not with us this night, however, as we turned the ball over and they held on to win. It was the first time EA had ever beaten one of our boys' team in any sport. Coach Wisener, who had taken over from Coach Davis for our Senior year, was so upset after the game that he slammed the door of his office so hard that he broke the glass out of the window in the door.

The final episode, the ugly, that immediately came to mind centered around a near-brawl that took place after a dirty play during a game with Roosevelt. Kenny was driving in for a layup and while in mid-air, a Roosevelt player undercut his legs flipping him over causing him to land on his head. He tore open a big gash in his head that would require stitches later on but the wound may have been made more extensive by the melee that immediately took place.

The action had taken place right under our goal near our bench. I don't know who the first players in the pile were from our team and who threw the first punch but I can tell you who the first players off the bench were. Lloyd and I. I had never been in a fight in my life but I didn't give a second thought to jumping in, throwing punches left and right. I was trying to defend a fallen teammate but, mainly, I was trying to defend a friend. I probably connected as many punches with Murphy players as I did Roosevelt because my eyes were probably closed as I flailed away. I just remember one of the refs pulling me off the pile and while he held me a Roosevelt player sucker punched me.

As was always the case in the various gyms we played, one set of fans sat in bleachers on one side of the gym and the other teams' fans sat opposite meaning that they couldn't get to each other because if that had happened it would have really been an ugly scene. Tensions ran pretty high the rest of the night among, not only the players, but the students in the stands as well. A couple of fights broke out in the lobby area where the concession stand was located and additional policemen were called in to protect both teams after the game. To make it even worse, they beat us.

There was one last area located in the gym that had a special place in my heart and that's the band room where we met for first period every day of the school year to practice. The principal and I then went down to where the old band room had been but it was no longer there. Since the school now had no band, the large practice area had been converted to classes. That did not stop my mind from recalling the wonderful music being made down here by a talented group of high school musicians.

I remember the beautiful tones coming from Mary Frances' oboe. I also remember the huge crush I had on this older (2 years) woman. Lynn K. and Charles C., who I had known since our East Atlanta Elementary Band days, on clarinet. Tim A. on trombone. Stephen C. and Terry H. on sousaphone. Tom on baritone. Peter S. on flute. And so many others. I was honored to have been elected Band President my Senior year and to represent these great girls and guys on the President's Council. I would give nothing for my band experiences. They are some of my best memories.

At some point during our tour I mentioned to the principal that I was now a writer and as we walked back to the office so I could turn in my visitor's badge, she turned to me and said, "I've got a great idea if you would consider it. We have a Creative Writing Class going on at this very moment and I know they would love to hear about your days here. Would you consider speaking to them and let them ask you some questions?"

Always eager to talk about those days, I told her okay. She took me in the class and after introducing me to the teacher, she excused herself and thanked me for my time. The teacher, even though her class had been interrupted by this stranger, was very gracious.

The class was a mixture of ethnicities and sexes and my guess was that the average age of the students was mid-twenties. These were young people trying to better themselves. There was probably a very good story behind each of the faces that sat in that class as to why they had originally quit school but were now fighting their way back. You had to admire them and I did.

A few routine questions about writing were thrown at me and then a young man stood and asked one of the best questions I've ever been asked: "What were some of the most important historical events that took place while you were going to school here?"

I didn't have to think long at all for my answer. There were two major events, one at the beginning of the school year in 1961 and the other in November, 1963 that shook the world and changed the course of events in our country forever. As I began my response, I remembered........

CHAPTER 15

MY WALK TO HOME ROOM

It was Wednesday, August 30, 1961- the first day of another school year. This was my ninth grade, or Freshman, year and I was anxious to get back to school where I could reconnect with all my old friends that I had not seen during the summer. But this was going to be a unique first day from any that I had ever experienced before.

We knew the day was coming but no one knew exactly what to expect or how to prepare. I woke up and opened the blinds shielding my room from the early morning sun. Since we lived within eyesight of the school I looked out the window and saw that there was considerable activity going on already. I spotted news teams from all three of the local television stations as well as vans sporting the name of our hometown newspaper. Photographers were setting up their tripods in places where they could get the best vantage points for their shots. And there must have been ten or more police cars directing traffic away from Clifton Avenue. No one was being allowed to enter the street in front of the school.

There were a few people, mostly men, milling around on the corner but they were doing nothing more than smoking and talking. Whether they meant to cause a disturbance later, the world would have to wait and see.

This first day was going to be different because two new students were entering Murphy today. Nothing special about that, right? The difference was that these two students, both girls, were black.

Nine black students, from all across the city, out of approximately 130 who had applied, were transferring from their previous all-black schools to four all-white schools. Murphy, along with Brown, Grady, and Northside High Schools, was one of the schools chosen to be the first to desegregate in the City of Atlanta. The nation had been asking itself for months since the decision had been made, can Atlanta, the largest city in the Deep South, keep this day peaceful or would it be disruptive and riotous like it had been in Little Rock and New Orleans?

I bathed and dressed and came out of my bedroom to the living room where I could always find Dad each morning. He was in his chair doing his morning crossword puzzle. He didn't acknowledge me but then he never did. Mom was in the kitchen so I went in to see her. She told me good morning and asked if I was ready for school. I told her yes. She looked at me and whispered, "Let's not say anything about school to your Dad. I don't think he's ready for what's happening today."

"Why?' I asked. "It doesn't affect him."

"Let's just be safe and not bring it up."

To be honest, I was a little surprised that he wasn't with those men I had seen standing on the sidewalk after what I had been hearing from him the past few weeks. He was not happy at all about the situation and he had not been quiet about expressing his views to anyone who would listen either.

The school had sent out letters asking that all students be inside the building by 8 am. First bell was usually 8:20 am but that's when the new students were scheduled to arrive and they wanted everybody inside, at their desks so there would be no additional commotion outside. I always got there early so I could take my trumpet to the band room so this was no problem for me.

As I headed out the door, the only words Dad said to me was, "Don't you speak to either one of them niggers!" I wanted to tell him that I'd have no reason to do so since they were both Juniors and we would not be having any classes together, but the consequences resulting from me talking back and getting him angry would not be worth it.

I began my 240 paces (I had counted off the number of steps from my front door to the main entrance before) to the school. I was attempting to do my regular routine of walking over to the gym but was stopped at the back door by Mr. Russell, our vice-principal. He told me that we had to stay in the main building until the new students were safely inside. There was nothing left to do but go to my home room and wait.

Several classmates were already there and the rest trickled in over the next few minutes. A few were missing and the rumor mill began swirling with "their parents are holding them out today" and other similar excuses.

Our home room teacher attempted to get us to take our seats but our natural inquisitiveness had us humming around the room like a swarm of bees. Around 8:25 am, activity started outside and all of us scurried to the windows to see what was going on. To this point, nothing much had happened except for a few shouts of protest or policeman yelling out orders.

At 8:27 am, a police car entered Clifton and roared down the street to the main entrance. One of the officers got out and opened the back door of the unit. The two passengers, arms loaded down with books, got out and started walking up the steps. One of the girls was wearing a red dress with brown loafers and bobby sox. The other was in an off-white, full flowing dress with black shoes.

They walked very erect and even in the midst of some rude catcalls from the onlookers, never looked at anything but the doors ahead of them. They entered the school and that was that.

The rest of the day was like any other school day. I never saw the girls again during the day and I didn't see them leave after the final bell had rung. I was told later that another police car came and got them but the next day, there was no such ceremony. How they got to school after that was none of my business. It was just another school day to me and I hope the two girls began having the same experience.

I never had any direct contact with the girls during the entire year as I had suspected but would see them in the halls each day. They smiled. I smiled. And we went our separate ways. I was told by those that did have classes with them that they were nice and very polite to the teachers. I'm not so naïve to think that nothing happened the entire year. I'm sure they got called names but, to the best of my understanding, there were no serious episodes involving them at any time during the entire school year. After the first few weeks, it was a non-event.

Rosalyn and Martha Ann, wherever you are, your courage in facing this difficult time has always been an inspiration to me. I know I would not have been strong enough to face what you did. The two of you, along with the seven other students who marched up the steps of a new school that day, are every much as pioneers as Lewis and Clark or Neil Armstrong.

I have always been exceedingly proud of the way our school and the entire city responded to this event. There were no reports of any disturbances at any of the three other schools that day and only a few isolated incidences the entire year. I believe this report from the September 8, 1961 issue of TIME MAGAZINE sums it up:

Last week the moral siege of Atlanta (pop. 487,455) ended in spectacular fashion with the smoothest token school integration ever seen in the Deep

South. Into four high schools marched nine Negro students without so much as a white catcall. Teachers were soon reporting "no hostility, no demonstrations, the most normal day we've ever had." In the lunchrooms, white children began introducing themselves to Negro children.

And the article goes on with its praise for our city .

We had a black boy, Grady, who made the basketball team during my Senior year. He became my teammate that year and through that relationship, he became my friend. There was never any thought of giving him special considerations. None were made for him or because of him. He showered with us, ate team meals with us, and practiced as hard as any of us.

We didn't stay in touch after high school but his race had nothing to do with that. There were many of my white classmates that I lost touch with after those years. I hope that he remembers our association as fondly as I do. We share a bond that cannot be broken. We both lived through an era of change- an era of transition. I know that the change made me more open-minded and more accepting. It would ultimately mold me into becoming a better person.

I never told Dad I had a Negro as a teammate, however. He wouldn't have been as accepting.

Then I told the class of..........

MY WALK TO AMERICAN HISTORY CLASS

At 7:30 am on the morning of November 22, 1963, in Fort Worth, Texas, the President of the United States, John Fitzgerald Kennedy, was awakened by his personal valet, George Thomas, with the words, "It's raining, Mr. President." A steady rain was coming down and the forecast called for it to continue throughout the day there and in Dallas where the President was scheduled to appear later in the day.

Why is this significant? Because if the rain had continued, the bubble top would have stayed on the President's Lincoln limousine and the subsequent events of that fateful day might not have happened. But the rain didn't continue. It stopped around 10:00 am and the decision was made by Roy Kellerman, the top Secret Service agent assigned to this leg of the trip, to remove the shield allowing President Kennedy more personal access to the adoring crowd already building on the streets of Dallas.

I have always loved trivia, especially American History trivia. I've always been intrigued and fascinated by little tidbits such as the above that turn an event in a totally different direction. Perhaps, my love for trivia began with Mr. Evans' American History class.

As I mentioned earlier, he was, easily, my favorite teacher in high school because he made, what could be, a boring and mundane subject filled with dates and documents into a subject that became interesting and fun. Yes, we were responsible for knowing significant dates in our country's history but he also told us the behind-the-story stories that livened up the subject.

For example, everyone who has ever picked up a history book knows that Abraham Lincoln was killed by John Wilkes Booth in April, 1865. But Mr. Evans made this fact more interesting by sharing with us the conspiracy plot that was going on at the same time; that not only was Lincoln targeted but the Vice President, Secretary of State, and Secretary of War were also to be slain that night by a group of Southern loyalists. Because of that seed of information planted by Mr. Evans, I've read dozens of books on this subject to help grow my knowledge of it.

Or did you know that America very nearly became a monarchy rather than a democracy and that George Washington almost became King rather than President? Betsy Ross didn't sew the first flag, Abner Doubleday didn't invent baseball, and Davy Crockett probably didn't die at the Alamo.

Those who know me well know that you do not call me on the phone- or if you do that I will not answer it- between 7: 30 and 8:00 pm. That is when *Jeopardy!* airs in my part of the world and I do not miss it under any circumstances. I believe that if the house caught on fire, I would find some way to make a call to get someone to DVD the episode for me.

I tried out for the show many years ago and was in the final 25 out of several hundred who went to the tryout that day but I never got the call to go to LA. I did make it to New York for *Who Wants to be a Millionaire* but didn't make it on stage.

My Junior year in high school had started out with a literal bang. Dad had, in an act totally out of character for him, let me borrow the family car, an almost brand new 1963 Pontiac Star Chief, to go to our first football game of the season. I had picked up my pal and fellow trumpeter, Alan P., and we had just watched Murphy defeat Southwest 21-0.

On the drive home, after stopping at Zesto's for a post-game burger and fries, I ran through a stop sign on Ormewood Avenue near Alan's home and was broad sided by an oncoming car. The impact was on the back seat driver's side but the collision caused my head to slam against the side window. Alan told me later that we spun around in the middle of the road several times before coming to rest. I don't remember because I was knocked unconscious and it took the rescue team about 40 minutes to revive me. I suffered a fairly bad concussion (is there a good one?) that would have a very definite effect on me later in my life. But I only lost a couple of days school, the only days I ever missed during my entire high school years, and September turned into October which blended smoothly into November.

Things were certainly different in 1963 than they are now with the most identifiable changes being in the cost of goods and services. Here are what some everyday items cost then:

Gallon of gas	.25¢
Postage stamp	.05¢
Pay phone (what is that?)	.10¢
Candy bar	.05¢
Magazine	.50¢

Minimum wage was $1.25/hour and average annual income was $5,623.

The Fugitive, The Patty Duke Show, and My Favorite Martian were some of tv's favorites. And a 6 year-old boy named Donny Osmond started singing with his brothers on *The Andy Williams Show.*

The first James Bond movie, *Dr. No,* premiered. *The Great Escape, The Birds, and It's a Mad, Mad, Mad, Mad World* were the box office hits.

Little Stevie Wonder, as he was first billed, releases *Fingertips-Pt. 2, Little Deuce Coupe* by the Beach Boys is a big hit, a song many thought contained obscene language *Louie, Louie* by the Kingsmen gains fame and a relatively unknown four-man group from England called The Beatles release *Please, Please Me* in the US.

The LA Dodgers won the World Series; Jack Nicklaus won The Masters; Southern Cal was the National Champion in football; the Boston Celtics were NBA champs; and Sonny Liston was Heavyweight champ. 1963 was also the year of the greatest sports trivia question of all time. Here it is- answer at the end of the chapter.

The MVP in the National League and American League in baseball, the National and American Conference in pro football, and the National Basketball Association all wore the same number. Who were the players and what was the number? No fair cheating and looking ahead until you've given up.

Michael Jordan, Johnny Depp, and Brad Pitt were born. Patsy Cline, Robert Frost, and John F. Kennedy died.

That day in 1963 was cloudy and overcast in Atlanta. It was the end of the football season and we, at Murphy, were all bummed out because we had been knocked out of the City Championship game, The Milk Bowl, the week before. The basketball team had been practicing for about two weeks to get ready for our first pre-season game which was scheduled for the following Tuesday. We had a practice session scheduled for that Friday afternoon.

The bell rang to end the fifth period and I was gathering my books from Ms. Foley's English class and was headed to Mr. Evans' American History Class. As I entered the hall, Bobbie, one of the prettiest girls in the school as well as being a cheerleader, smiled and said "hi" making my day a success in my book. Mr. McCord, the principal, came over the intercom saying, "Students. Get to your next class immediately. No loitering allowed. This is very important. Move quickly but safely."

You could hear by his tone that he meant business and so I hurriedly went to my class which was, luckily, just around the corner from where I was. The intercom was now playing a radio news report as I entered the room and took my seat. Mr. Evans sat at his desk with an even more serious expression than he normally had. There was no horseplay or unnecessary talking going on at all. Every student in the class could sense that something serious was taking place.

For most teenagers growing up in the early 60's, John F. Kennedy had become our idol. Very few of us were politically astute. We didn't know a Democrat from a Republican. We just knew that this handsome, charismatic young man from Massachusetts portrayed a different image from the man we had grown up calling President, the dour old general, Dwight Eisenhower.

Years later we would see that halo tarnished by the revelation of his marital infidelities and possible underworld connections, but in 1963, he was one of the top three men we looked up to in America. #1 was Elvis and #2 was John Wayne.

We were a country in a state of flux. Fighting in a little Southeast Asian country called Viet Nam had begun escalating.

The Civil Rights movement was in full swing. Organized crime and labor strikes made the headlines practically everyday. But in 1960, a wealthy Catholic from the Northeastern part of the country, a war hero with a beautiful high-society bride came on the scene telling us that he could fix all our woes. And as teenagers, we believed him. After all, look at the option we were given- a gruff, jowl-shaking Californian named Richard Nixon.

Kennedy had been elected, in spite of the negative factors such as his religious affiliation surrounding him, and had proven himself to be a very capable leader. He had faced Nikita Khrushchev down during the Cuban Missile Crisis; he, along with his Attorney General brother Robert, were battling the Mafia, and he quelled several potentially crippling labor strikes. He was doing what he said he would do. But he was also making enemies every step of the way.

Some of those enemies were Southern Democrats headed by his own Vice President, Lyndon Johnson. His trip to Dallas that day was an attempt to appease some of their concerns. Many in his staff, including his personal secretary, Evelyn Lincoln, had warned him not to go on this trip because of the possible trouble his presence might cause. He laughed this off telling his Secretary of Treasury and close personal friend, Robert McNamra, and referring to the underlying group of opposition in his own administration, "I'm more likely to get shot right here in the White House than I am in Dallas."

But the reports filtering back from the Secret Service agents on the streets were that the crowds seemed receptive and genuinely anxious to pay their respects to the President. At the same time, however, a troubled dissident named Lee Harvey Oswald planned to show his respects in a totally different manner.

At 11:40 am, CST, the President's plane arrived at Love Field after a short flight from Fort Worth. The President, along with his wife, Jackie, got in the limo, bubble top now off after the rain had stopped. Riding along in the same limo was Texas Governor John Connally and his wife.

The motorcade was to arrive at Dealey Plaza at 12:10 pm CST and travel to the Dallas Business and Trade Mart, where he would address the gathering crowd with a short speech. The motorcade was delayed, however, and was 15 minutes late in departing.

President Kennedy stopped the motorcade twice en route; once, to shake hands with some Catholic nuns and a second time to greet some schoolchildren. At 12: 29 pm CST, the limo entered Dealey Plaza after making a 90 degree right hand turn from Main

Street to Houston Street. Immediately on the right was the Texas School Book Depository. At 12: 30 pm CST, shots rang out and as the Zapruder film clearly shows, the President was struck several times, one being a brutally gruesome shot to the head.

At 2: 20 EST, a group of teenagers and one adult sat in a classroom listening to reports of the details of what was known at the time. The scene was similar throughout the school. We heard that Kennedy had been travelling in a motorcade in Dallas, Texas and that an unknown number of shots had been heard by those in attendance. Immediately after the gunfire was heard, the limousine sped off in the direction of Parkland General Hospital. President Kennedy had been rushed into surgery but the extent of his injuries was not known at that time.

At 2: 32 pm EST, the respected newsman, Walter Cronkite of CBS News, gave an unconfirmed report from the Dallas correspondent on the scene, a young Dan Rather, that the President had died but he stressed that, for the moment, the report was unconfirmed. Approximately 25 students and one teacher held their breath.

Then, at 2: 38 pm, Cronkite was silent for a moment. The only sound that could be heard was the rustling of some paper. Cronkite, his voice cracking with the emotion of an entire country said: "From Dallas, Texas, the flash, apparently official- President Kennedy died at 1:00 pm CST, 2:00 pm EST, some thirty-eight minutes ago." While we were listening to this from a radio, we've all seen the TV footage of his report hundreds of time. He removes his glasses, composes himself as best he can and continues: "Vice President Johnson has left the hospital in Dallas, but we do not know to where he has proceeded. Presumably, he will be taking the oath of office shortly and become the thirty-sixth president of the United States."

At 2: 39 pm EST in that classroom at Murphy High School in Atlanta, Georgia, there were very few dry eyes. We cried for ourselves, we cried for our country but, perhaps, we were also crying for our future. The hopes and dreams of a young generation putting all their trust in this one man had, seemingly, been snuffed out by a sniper's bullet. The dismissal bell rang at 3: 00 but the usual mad rush for the door, particularly on a Friday, did not take place. We had no idea what to do.

I slowly gathered my things and went to my locker to put up books I would not need for the weekend. I walked to the gym and down the steps to the locker room assuming we would still have practice. A couple of the guys were already there but the usual chatter that took place between us as we put on our workout gear was missing.

I went upstairs and grabbed a ball from the rack and began shooting. My concentration was non-existent, however, and I missed more than I made. When all of the guys arrived, we began doing some warm-up drills by forming a layup line. There was no spirit, no joy, and no effort. We were zombies, doing what we did everyday.

Coach Davis got there a few minutes later and called us together. We sat on the floor and listened as this big man poured his heart out to us telling us about the significance of what had happened to all of us that day. He never referred to basketball at all. This was not a basketball lesson- it was a life lesson. He told us to go home and be with our parents.

But I think the thing I remember most from that talk was that he told us not to hate. By that time, Oswald had been located while watching a movie and had been apprehended but only after killing a police officer as he attempted to escape. Coach Davis told us that the truth would come out and it would be up to us, the next generation, to make sure Kennedy's death did not destroy the country.

Fifty years later I'm not sure the entire truth has come out. I have devoured books on this subject and I still don't know much more than I did then. All I have are opinions. My family tells me I am an expert when it comes to opinions because I have so many of them and I am always so willing to share them with anyone who will listen. My mother-in-law gave me a sweat shirt for Christmas one year that read:

I'm not opinionated, I'm just always right!
She followed that up with a birthday present one year that read:
There are two opinions in the world
Mine and the wrong one.

But, for what it is worth, here is my opinion. I do not believe that Lee Harvey Oswald acted alone. I believe that there were multiple shooters and that they were located on what has come to be known as the Grassy Knoll. I do not know if they were working directly in conjunction with Oswald, that is, Oswald knew they were there, or if they were independent gunmen making sure that Oswald's assignment would be carried through and that he would be the fall guy. I believe that there was a conspiracy at work that day but I have no idea who or what was behind it. There were too many potential Kennedy-haters to be precise in this theory. Until someone directly involved with the assassination comes forward, this event will be one of the greatest mysteries in the history of the world, let alone the United States.

As many of us arrived home from church the following Sunday, the horrific weekend was taking another incredible turn. The nation would witness its first live murder.

After Dad had picked us up at church, I ran into the house to turn on the TV. I wanted to see what the latest developments were regarding Oswald. Just as the picture came on the tube, Oswald was being brought down a hallway in the basement of the Dallas Police Department's building. You've all seen the famous picture of the tall man dressed in a white suit in the big Stetson hat on Oswald's right recoiling as a small figure appears to Oswald's left. Shots ring out and Oswald slumps to the ground as screams and panic ensues. The camera picks up a scene of bedlam as men wrestle Jack Ruby, the shooter, to the floor.

There have certainly been other events during my life that have stunned the world: the attempt on Ronald Reagan, the Challenger explosion, the moon landing, 9/11 to name a few. The cumulative effect of those days have drained us all and taken their toll on our feelings of safety and security. The nation was stunned and as we watched the funeral ceremonies held the next day, we all mourned together. We mourned for Kennedy and his family but, mostly, we mourned for our country.

I finished my response to the young man's question and thanked the class for allowing me to come in. I went back to the office to turn in my visitor badge and told the secretary to let the principal know how much I had appreciated the chance to walk around those halls one more time. I walked out one of the side doors and continued.......

Answers:
They all wore #32

Sandy Koufax	National League (baseball)
Elston Howard	American League (baseball)
Jim Brown	National Conference (football)
"Cookie" Gilchrist	American Conference (football)
Jerry Lucas	National Basketball Association

CHAPTER 17

MY WALK THROUGH HISTORY (PART 3)

O ut of the school, I walked to the plaque, located at Memorial Drive and Clay Street, commemorating the first true shots of the Battle of Atlanta. On that morning one hundred fifty years ago, there had been some minor skirmishes earlier that morning but the real action was now taking place.

The day before, on July 21, 1864, the Union forces had established a defensive stronghold by acquiring a strategic location known as Bald Hill. After a staunch defense of the hill was made by Confederate troops under the leadership of Patrick Cleburne, they were finally overrun by the Union troops and the ridge was renamed Leggett's Hill. The actual landmark no longer exists but one can assume from its somewhat elevated locale that the hill, actually a rather long ridge, is located on what is present-day Moreland Avenue where I-20 crosses. From this vantage point, Sherman had an almost 360° view of the city and artillery could now easily reach the center of the city. Sherman also had an excellent view of the area where the fighting was taking place just to his east- the area where my boyhood home was located.

The fighting that morning consisted of individual skirmishes between companies from both sides rather than large-scale attacks. That is not to say that both sides did not have battle plans and objectives in mind, they were just not formulated into an all-out battle as yet.

From his vantage point on the ridge, Sherman witnessed large-scale troop and civilian movement within the city. Sherman mistook this movement as Hood's withdrawal from the city, indicating what he assumed would be a concession that would take place, in his words, "...before we sit down to supper tonight, boys!" This is when he ordered McPherson out to scout the lines. Sherman's mistake was compounded by McPherson's fatal mistake. McPherson noticed a gap in the lines and mistaking this for a Confederate retreat, rode right into the gap. Upon realizing his mistake, McPherson doffed his cap to a group of soldiers he thought were Union and rode back in the direction he had come from. In fact, these were Confederate soldiers who opened fire striking the general who fell from his horse mortally wounded.

An upraised cannon monument is located at the corner of McPherson Ave. and Monument Ave. near East Atlanta Village honoring this Union general. I have to admit that I have always wondered why there is a monument and a street named after a Union general in this very Southern city but later during my walk when I visited this monument, a fellow Civil War buff who was driving the area of the fighting that day told me that it had been erected by the Sons of the Union Army, an organization established to honor fallen Civil War heroes no matter where they died.

The left flank, or southern end of the Union forces, were pushed back by relentless pressure put on them by General Hardee's Corps and for a few minutes it appeared that the Confederates might win the battle.

The fighting continued the rest of the morning and early afternoon up what is now Memorial Drive, moving in a northwesterly direction towards a thoroughfare known as Boulevard Drive in my youth but renamed Hosea Williams Boulevard, after an Atlanta Civil Rights leader. Unaware that Union forces had stabilized their position, Hood launched a secondary attack around 4: 00 pm that afternoon near Decatur Street. The advancing Rebels overtook some of the artillery in the area and immediately fired on the retreating Yankees. But well-placed artillery coming from and directed by Sherman himself turned back the Confederates. Much of the cannon fire was directed towards an area known as Cabbagetown that now houses Oakland Cemetery and the once-prominent factory known as Fulton Bag & Cotton Mill, a location where both my mother and father worked for many years. The tenacity and the significant manpower advantage of the union troops finally formed and they were able to hold a line. With the reestablished Union line and with mounting losses, Hood calls off the attack and, for all intents and purposes, the Battle of Atlanta is over.

After reading the inscription on the plaque, I ventured back to the intersection of Clifton and Memorial. From there, I could see the boyhood home of, in this man's humble opinion, the best athlete ever to wear the royal blue and white of Murphy High School. Roy J. was a three-letter athlete; football, basketball, and baseball and if he had run track, played golf, or wrestled, he would have lettered in those sports, too. He would later play both football and baseball at Georgia Tech. Roy was two years older than me, so, we didn't hang out much then but we have become FaceBook friends and I stay in touch with him and his life in Colorado through that means.

The rain had completely stopped but the sky was still grey and overcast. The area across the street from my house was completely different from when I was a boy. What then were woods and open fields was now developed into a convenience store and a laundry on the corner. Next to the convenience store was a large open-air tent with racks and racks of clothes and tables set up with various knick-knacks for sale. Two older black men sat at the entrance. They watched me, somewhat suspiciously, for seeing a white face in this neighborhood now was as unusual as seeing a black face in the neighborhood in the 50's. I stood in front of the tent staring at my old home place because what I saw was devastating.

There was very little grass in the front yard of 1684 Memorial Drive. The shrubs Dad had planted himself at the front of the house were withered to nothing. The driveway was cracked and, virtually, inaccessible to any vehicle that wanted to keep its tires from being cut to pieces from the shards of asphalt. The front porch where the mailman would leave our mail in the box on the wall and where Mom would put the empty milk bottles on Monday, Wednesday, and Friday for the Mathis Dairy milkman to leave fresh ones (bottle up for sweet milk; bottle down for buttermilk) was still standing but the wrought iron railing was no longer there. But the real devastation was in the house itself. All of the windows on the front of the house were covered with plywood and there was a gaping hole in the roof covered by a huge blue tarp. The only evidence of any occupancy was a sign that read MADAME ROBERTA- FORTUNE TELLER AND HEALER.

It was apparent that the house had been gutted by a fire. I looked to my right and the house next to ours had suffered some damage but nothing as severe as what I saw from ours. The other two houses, the one where Angelo and Johanna H. lived, and the house on the corner were undamaged and it looked as if they were occupied.

The three houses to our left, the one where Laura S., Sharon, and Laura M. lived, had been gone even before I moved out. They had been torn down to make way for a service station during my college years and this, along with an ever-growing black movement in the area, was the final straw for dad. They sold the house this time and moved out to Lilburn, where they would stay until Dad's death.

The service station was long gone with the building being used now as what appeared to be a detail shop. It looked like it might be used for other purposes, not all legal, from the outward appearance of it. Over the top of the building I could see the massive back yard of Dianne and Miriam E. where many kick ball games were played.

I read the other day where some school officials are trying to determine if recess needs to be taken out of the daily curriculum for elementary age kids. That would be a shame. Heck, kids these days don't get enough exercise now as it is. It seems that today's kid comes home from school and immediately plops down in front of a computer screen. The only physical activity they get is the little they might achieve playing Wii.

My generation was all about playing outside. We ran, rode bikes, jumped rope, and played on jungle gyms all day long. I realize that it was a different generation but physical activity is so important in the development of a child. And I don't mean playing in different organized sports leagues, either. I mean playing.

I could do nothing but stare for the longest time. Finally, a voice behind me asked, "You lookin' for somethin' in particular?"

I turned around and walked toward the two men I had seen before. "Not really. I grew up in that house there (pointing to my old home) and I was just thinking about the past. My name is Randy Blalock" and I approached them and shook their hands.

They introduced themselves as Frank and Abner. "Do either of you know when the fire happened?" I inquired.

Frank immediately became the spokesman for the two and said, "Yeah- just last March." He offered no additional information other than that basic fact.

I asked if they lived in the area and, if so, how long? Again, the only info I got back was concise and cryptic. I explained what the area had looked like when I grew up there and they seemed interested in what I told them, asking a few questions themselves.

We talked back and forth for a few more minutes when I finally asked, "Do you think it would be okay if I went over and just looked around a little? I know I can't go inside but I'd just like to look at the old back yard one more time."

Frank again spoke up and said, "I cain't see that it'd be any harm but I better go over with ya'." He then verified what I suspected by saying, "I don't think them boys over there would take kindly to a white boy snooping around so, I'll go tells them whacha doin." I thanked him as he slowly peeled himself out of his chair to walk across the street with me. I told Abner it was good to meet him and Frank and I crossed the street to the house. He told me to wait at the side of the house while he went to talk to a man working on a car in the parking lot.

The man gave me a very definite scowl but nodded his head in agreement to whatever Frank was telling him. Frank then excused himself and went back across the street where he sat back down and continued his discussion with Abner as if nothing had interrupted his day.

It is amazing how your memories, especially as they relate to places, can become distorted over the years. Just like those halls of Murphy had seemed so small during my days there but were actually rather large, my backyard took on an opposite perspective. In my mind, my backyard was huge or at least it seemed that way when I was mowing the lawn on a hot summer day. Now, I was stunned by how small it looked.

The circular bricked structure was still there in the middle of the yard. Dad had originally built it as a wading pool for me but had filled it with dirt and converted it to a garden area once I had grown too big for its original purpose. Weeds and sticks were all that remained there now.

The building at the back of the lot that began as a covered patio area but later became Dad's darkroom and camera room for his business was falling down on itself. The chain link fence running along the left side and rear of the lot had been torn down a long time ago and the gate hung on a rusty post connected to nothing but air.

Regardless of the view I had now, all I could envision were the hours spent back here shooting hoops or throwing a tennis ball against the back steps of the house. I could see in my mind the activity of the twenty or so kids who attended my sixth birthday party, the only real party I ever had.

I stepped into the yard and stood looking at the big oak where the blue bird had perched before I shot and killed it. If you've ever seen the famous Andy Griffith episode where Opie accidentally kills a mama bird and how guilty he felt afterwards- the same thing happened to me. I had gotten a BB gun for my birthday and was shooting at birds not expecting to hit anything. But one fateful shot founds its mark and when that bird toppled out of the tree, my heart toppled with it. I felt so bad killing one of God's creatures that I swore I would never hunt animals when I became an adult. And I never have.

I could envision myself running around the back yard as a little boy in my Superman cape. Of course, it was nothing more than a towel wrapped around my neck secured by a safety pin, but with it on I became The Man of Steel. Then I saw a little boy wearing a coon skin Davy Crockett hat with Ole Betsy, a toy replica of his famous rifle, hunting for bears or fighting the Battle of the Alamo.

I was deep in thought when a voice from behind startled me out of my reverie.

"I didn't expect to find anybody back here." the lilting voice said.

"The man across the street said it would be okay for me to look around. You see, this was my home when I was a little boy."

"It was? Well, from the looks of you, you're not so little and you certainly ain't a boy anymore."

We both laughed and I replied, "You got that right! On both counts!" I told her my name and that's when I got a big surprise.

"Well, glad to meet ya, sugah. My name's Roberta. Madame Roberta, to be exact." I assumed that this must be the same Madame Roberta as advertised on the sign in the front yard.

She was a large woman, standing about 5'8" tall and tipping the scales at well over 200 lbs. She wore a flowing ruby red caftan trimmed with a gold belt. Her lips were painted bright red and she wore several bracelets on both arms and rings on practically every finger as well as a beautiful necklace around her neck. She had a turban on her head that matched her caftan exactly. But her most impressive feature was her broad smile. One look at this lady and you had a friend.

She almost glided as she moved towards me. I gave her some background on when I had lived there and what I was doing today and it was at that moment that I began..........

CHAPTER 18

MY WALK WITH MADAME ROBERTA

"So, you lived here when you was little."

"That's right! Mom told me we moved into this house just after it had been built. I was about eight months old when we moved in and I lived here until I moved out when I got married. That doesn't count the years I was in college or a couple of years when we moved away. We always came back to this place, though." I explained.

I continued by asking her, "Then I guess from the sign in the front yard that you lived here when the fire hit?"

A sad, woeful look came over her previous radiant face and she just nodded. There were a few seconds of silence as we both looked at the back of the house.

I interrupted the silence by asking her, "Are you originally from Atlanta?"

"Oh, no, honey. We moved here a few years ago after Katrina took our place in New Orleans. I'm a Dupree from a little town called Houma." I told her I knew exactly where she was talking about because I used to travel for my job and went to Houma a few times.

"New Orleans is one of my wife and my favorite places in the world to visit. We go there strictly to eat and maybe have a Hurricane or two from Pat O'Brien's. We love to have oysters and gumbo at Felix's, barbeque shrimp at Mr. B's, and crawfish etoufee at The Gumbo Shop. And when we want to dress up and get fancy there is no better place to go than Commander's Palace or the brunch at Court of Two Sisters."

I see you're one of them Georgia Bulldawgs." she continued, pointing to the cap I was wearing.

"Yes, ma'am. And proud of it." She laughed a big, hearty laugh when I said, "I'm Bulldog born and Bulldog bred and when I die I'll be Bulldog dead."

"My brother played football for LSU." She proudly added, "But I'm one of them 'Who Dat?' Saints fans.

"But, honey," she continued, "I can tell that your days here weren't always happy. You seem to me to be carrying a big old heavy weight around your shoulders." I didn't realize that it was that obvious but I've always been told that I wear my emotions on my coat sleeve for the whole world to see.

"Oh, there were good times but… there were some not-so-good times, too." The moment got the best of me, I suppose, and my eyes began tearing up as I thought back to my life here.

"Baby, Madame Roberta is a good listener and I got nothing but time. You tell me what it is that's hurtin' you so bad."

Why I felt so relaxed and so willing to open up my soul to this stranger that I met only a few minutes before, I don't know, but my feelings started spewing like an erupting volcano. I started with a few of the good memories.

I told her about the summer visits from my cousin, Donny, from Chattanooga. Donny was the youngest son of my dad's brother, Oather.

Donny was two years older than me and he came from a large family- three older brothers and an older sister. All of them were married with children of their own by the time we started swapping visitation weeks during our summer break from school. I was about 10 or 11 when the trips started.

I loved going to Chattanooga to stay and Donny loved coming down to visit with me. And the reasons both of us loved the visits were exactly opposite. Being an only child, I loved going to his house that was always filled with people. How my Aunt Eula handled all the noise and activity I'll never know. But she did and with the calmest demeanor of any human I've ever known. Nothing fazed her and whether it was a table for three or thirteen, she managed to always put on a delicious spread. But I've always felt that Donny loved coming to visit me for the peace and quiet.

Both of us loved baseball and we spent a good deal of time doing that in whichever location we were. Both of us had public swimming pools near us and you could find us there if we weren't at the baseball diamond.

Donny still teases me about a routine of mine that would happen every time he visited. As I mentioned earlier, we had a drive-in featuring ice cream concoctions near us called Atlanta Dairies. They were known for their milk shakes which went under the name of Wing-Dings. Never thought it was a particularly good marketing name but the shakes were fantastic. No matter how hard I tried to get Dad to take me there when it was just the three of us, I couldn't get him off his favorite recliner. But when Donny visited, well, that was a different story so I took full advantage of it. When the mood hit me, I'd say in my best pleading tone, "Let's getta Wing-Ding, Daddy!" Maybe it was the way I said it but we can't see each other today that Donny (now called the more mature Don Blalock) doesn't yell out those words. He even did it at his mother's funeral a few years back when he spotted me at the gravesite. He said it for everyone there to hear but also adding that I was Aunt Eula's favorite of all his other cousins.

There are two memorable events that took place during my visits to his house that stand out- one good and one that has sad overtones.

The good event involves a buddy of Donny's who had a paper route that included several of the ballplayers from Chattanooga's minor league team, the Lookouts. Reggie rode his bike over to the house one day all excited. He told us that he had been given some tickets for that night's game from a couple of the players but the real good news was that they told him we could ride to the game with them. Riding to the game with actual players. For three young boys it couldn't get any better than that.

The apartment complex where the players lived was nearby so the three of us met them there. Two huge men, in our eyes, walked out. In actuality, both men were just in there early 20's but to us they seemed like giants. They told us their names and one of these players, unbeknownst to us at the time, would go on to have a Hall of Fame career. His name was Harmon Killebrew.

One summer, most of Donny and my days were spent babysitting for his older brother, Chester's, two year-old son, Stevie. Both Chester and his wife, Alice, worked, and we kept him until Alice got home round 3: 00 each afternoon.

Stevie had a definite opinion on how he wanted things done even at that early age so one day, as I held him in my arms trying to get him to take a nap, he let me know in no uncertain terms that he was not in favor of that idea. Stevie bit down into my shoulder and took a hunk out of it. I still have the scar from that bite mark to this day.

A year later, however, we tragically lost Stevie. He and his mother were waiting to cross a busy street. Alice had him by his hand as they waited for the traffic to ebb. Stevie got impatient and jerked away from his mother. He stepped out into the oncoming traffic and was struck and killed by a pickup.

There is very little in life that we might have to experience that is more gut-wrenching than a funeral for a child. And for a 12 year-old boy, it became especially memorable. At one point during the service, being totally traumatized by the loss she had experienced, Alice ran up to the open casket and tried to pull the lifeless form of her son out. It took her husband and two funeral workers to, literally, carry her back to the pew. It took me a long time to get over that scene.

I finished telling that story to Roberta and as I did, she looked deeply into my eyes and said, "But your hurt is right here in this house." The way she said those words, it wasn't a question- it was a statement of fact.

A lot went on inside the walls of this house that none of my friends ever knew about. Even though he had no religious convictions to speak of, Dad never let me go trick or treating on Halloween. He said the day was evil and satanic. He would even short wire the front door bell so that kids coming up to ring the bell would get a small shock. And I've never been sure if I would have gotten anything from Santa if it had not been for Mom standing up to him. Dad was constantly verbally abusive to both Mom and I but the real pain would come when he lost his temper and went into one of his rages. There is one Saturday that stands out above all the rest.

The Madison Theater was the place to be on Saturday afternoons. It was the gathering place for all of us pre-teens who attended either Burgess or Gordon Elementary. And when you are 12 and have a girlfriend who would meet you there and sit on the back row with you, there was not a better place to be in the world. There was usually a double feature that would give you plenty of time to be with your girl. Mine that year was Alane. When the movie was over, you'd then cross the street to the Rexall Pharmacy or go up the street to Miss Georgia Ice Cream Parlor to end a perfect day.

The first feature would usually start about 11:00 am and it would be over around 2: 00 pm meaning I was expected home by 3: 00 since I had to walk from East Atlanta, about a 2 mile distance.

Dad was very particular about his deadlines. There was no room for leeway whatsoever. If he said 3: 00, it really meant that you better be walking in the door about five till.

I have no idea why I did what I did that day. I knew his rules and I knew what the consequences would be if I disregarded those rules. Yet, inexplicably, I stayed with some of the guys to see the first feature again. After all, I hadn't really paid a lot of attention to it the first time because my attention had been on Alane and it looked like it would be a really good Roy Rogers western.

When I finally said bye to the guys I saw that the clock in the lobby read 4:30. I started running as fast as I could. Along the way I tried to think of good excuses. I thought that maybe I could get home, sneak in my room and pretend that I had been there all along. I tried to think who I could live with after he kicked me out.

Roughly three or four blocks from home, I saw his car. I jumped in the bushes next to the road to hide from him. After he had passed by, I again started running. I got home and waited-waited for the inevitable. Mom was home and after scolding me for being so late she said that he was really angry.

Twenty minutes later the car pulled into the driveway. From my bedroom I heard him as he stormed in the door. "Allie, is he home yet?"

"Yes," she said, "but please don't whip him. He's knows he's worried us and he's sorry."

Not another word was spoken. The door to my room was flung open and in one fluid motion his belt came off and he began lashing at me with all his might. It was springtime and although I usually wore jeans I had worn shorts that day and had not thought ahead to change into pants that might have absorbed the blows better.

The pain was severe as the whipping became even more intense as his anger grew. My screams of anguish were drowned out by his yells of rage stirred by my disobedience mixed with the sound of the belt striking the bare flesh of my legs. Mom tried to intercede, not physically, but with her pleas of, "Horace, please stop! You're hurting him!"

He didn't stop. The whipping went on for a good five minutes and by the time he had spent all his venom, my legs were cut and blood spilled from the welts left by the leather belt. Mom immediately came to my rescue after he had left the room. She brought a damp cloth and patted the cuts attempting to ease the pain. She went to the medicine cabinet and brought some ointment and band-aids to close the worst of the cuts. All the time I sobbed uncontrollably thinking to myself, "I wish he were dead."

We didn't go to church the next day and I basically did nothing but lie face down on my bed, fearful to roll over on my back which would make my legs have contact with the sheet. Not going to school the following Monday, however, was out of the question. When I got to my class, I tried to sit down but I couldn't endure the pain. My teacher noticed my discomfort and called me up to his desk. I told him what had happened and he quietly, without alerting the class to my situation, took me to the nurse's office where I spent the rest of the day.

If this had happened in 2014, the nurse would have immediately notified DFACS and Dad would be punished in some form. But it was 1959 and things weren't handled the same way they are now. I was uncomfortable for several days afterwards but was at least able to sit at my desk the next day. I steered clear of Dad for many days, not wanting to anger him any further.

"You poor, poor baby." Roberta cooed. "Is he still with you?" she asked.

"No." I told her. "He died two years ago just 15 days short of being 100 years old. But Mom is still with me. I have her in a very nice retirement home in Winder, where I live, called Magnolia Estates. She'll turn 97 this December."

"My, my, my. You've got some mighty powerful genes going for you, don't you? Yo wife gonna have you around for a long time." Roberta chuckled.

"Yeah. Even though she's twelve years younger than me, she says I'm probably gonna out live her. Course, I tell her that life without her is not really living. Gets me a few brownie points with her, you know."

An inquisitive look crossed Roberta's face as she studied me intently. I couldn't tell what was going through her mind but she seemed to be looking straight into my soul.

"But you're not going to outlive her, are you?"

Trying to deflect the question I responded by asking, "What do you mean?"

"A lot of people don't believe in things like this but I've got powers and I see that something's inside you. Something that's eating away at you. The hurt you feel from the bad treatment you got from your daddy is not the only hurt you're dealing with."

I couldn't hold back any longer. The tears started flowing and in spite of my doubts regarding people who claimed to be able to read other people's minds, I had to admit that this woman was able to know things about me she had no ability to know.

I finally composed myself and looked at her. She smiled a big, wide grin, opened up her arms wide, and beckoned me with her fingers. "Come here, darlin'. You gotta let the hurt go. Come let Madame Roberta take <u>all</u> your hurt away."

I walked towards her and as I got close I felt a strange, almost magnetic, pull into her arms. Then, when she placed her arms around me, a tingling sensation shot through my body. She held me tight and it felt so warm, so comfortable, that I never wanted to leave her embrace. All I wanted to do was sink even deeper into her essence. But, after a few loving pats on my back, Madame

Roberta loosened her tight hold on me and said, "There, that should do it."

I backed away and thanked her for listening to my story. I looked at my watch and noticed that it had stopped. But from the sounds my stomach was making, it had to be after noon.

"Well, I guess I need to be moving on. I still have some places I want to visit before I head back home." I told her.

"I cain't tell you how wonderful it's been to get to meet you." Roberta said. "And don't you worry bout nothing. Everything's gonna be all right."

I smiled at her and walked out of my old back yard. Maybe for the last time. But as for today, there was more for me to see and remember. Familiar streets, buildings, old friends, old haunts and special places as I continued …………

CHAPTER 19

MY WALK DOWN
MEMORY LANE

I took a quick little detour about ¼ of a mile down Memorial to see the strip center that had been built during my teens. Before it was converted to a commercial retail complex, the property had been used as a golf driving range. But, then, the bulldozers came in and construction started on what I looked at now- a seemingly unoccupied and run down group of buildings in the middle of a virtually empty parking lot.

The main store in the center had been a retail store, along the lines of what we have now as Wal-Marts or Costcos, called Atlantic Discount. Most of us referred to it as Atlantic No Count because the merchandise they sold was pretty crappy. Several small retail outlets ran the length of the complex ending with a movie theater at the far end. A separate building ran perpendicular to the main complex. It housed Rinaldi's Bowling. I spent many hours there in my early teens trying to hone my skills. Never did get any good, though.

I walked back down in front of the house, waved to Frank and Abner and turned right on Clifton. I passed the school, the gym, and the athletic fields again before crossing over the bridge with I-20 traffic speeding by below. Then, on the corner of Clifton and Glenwood stood my old elementary school. It was no longer Burgess, but Burgess-Peterson Academy. In fact, the old building had been torn down some years before. Replacing it was a structure that was set up much like the design of the old school, but a good bit larger in scale.

I would have liked to walk those halls, too, but since it was not the same as in my days there and since I was getting very fatigued, I continued walking down Glenwood to the place where I had left my car. I took a few moments to catch my breath, ate a power bar, and hydrated myself with some water. I had had a good day, all in all, although I was still a bit mystified as to what had happened during my conversation with Roberta. There were still some things left to do before I headed back home. I wanted to drive down some of the streets where many of my good friends lived and relive the wonderful times I had spent going up and down those neighborhoods.

I pointed the car back up Glenwood in the direction of the Village passing by Clifton. I turned right onto Greencove Lane. This street was the home of several of my classmates: Bud M., Alan L., Ronny M., Brenda F., Leila C., and my sixth grade main squeeze that I spoke of earlier, Devon. The homes on the street were all well kept and, for the most part, looked like they did some fifty years ago.

Next was Maynard Terrace where Randy C. lived on the corner and Delores B. lived further down followed on the right by McWilliams. This street was home to Steve S., sisters Sheila and Sandy P., Teresa A., and my good buddy, Kenny and his brother Scott. Right behind Sandy's house on Paisley, the street running parallel to McWilliams, was Perry D.'s home. Haven't talked a lot about him to this point but he was one of my best pals.

Back on Glenwood I passed by the twins' house before I turned left on Blake. This was the demarcation point between Murphy and East Atlanta High. Most of the kids living on this side of Glenwood went to EA but I had gone to grammar school with many of them. I turned left on May Avenue and went by David R.'s house. I spent a lot of time at David's house as a young boy. Next to Kenny, he was probably my closest friend during my elementary years. A very pretty lady that I follow on FaceBook and that I see when we have some Burgess reunions, Debbie C., lived right next door to him. I rode down Newton where Joy C. (she would later marry Floyd), Ellen and Ben L., and Charlotte and Jimmy Y. lived. All of us knew where they lived because their mom was the School Patrol Lady that kept us all safe each day as we walked to Burgess. I also made a stop at the McPherson Monument where I met some fellow Civil War buffs who were retracing the battle that day in their own way.

Then, I made a quick drive through what is now called East Atlanta Village but to those of us who grew up here, it would always be just plain East Atlanta. It's hard to tell where the old theater was located as it looks today, because the marquee and box office are now gone, but I had no trouble in locating its doors. I passed by where the old A&P grocery store was located and turned left where the old branch of the Atlanta Public Library stood and passed a boarded-up John B. Gordon Elementary which had caught fire recently. Martha Brown Methodist stood on the corner facing Moreland Avenue and further down was Moreland Avenue Baptist. Kenny, as well as several other high school friends, were members here and I started going there when Brenda and I started dating.

I decided to drive out Glenwood and pick up I-285 for my drive home. I passed by East Lake Country Club and golf course on my left.

The club had its original roots in the late 1800's as the Atlanta Athletic Club. It moved into its present facility in 1908 and one of the people in attendance that day at the opening was a young

Bobby Jones who was there with his father, a charter member of the club. Bobby Jones, for the uninitiated, was one of the premier golfers of the first half of the 20th century and the first man to win all four major golfing tournaments in the same year.

East Lake Golf Course has seen its fair share of golf events over the years. It hosted the 1963 Ryder Cup and now is the permanent home of the Tour Championship event at the end of each golfing year. I can remember riding my bike and sneaking on the course as a young boy to see how many golf balls I could find in the woods or the shallow creeks that were found throughout the course. I'd then sell the balls back to the club house where they would use them as range balls. Needless to say, our family was not members of the club. In fact, the first time I ever got to step inside the main building was when we had one of our Murphy reunions there thanks to Archie W. who had gotten us in.

As I neared the intersection of Glenwood and Candler, I was reminded of all the great eating establishments we had to choose from to take our dates in the old days. Near that intersection was Pizza Paul's where I had my first slice of pizza and my first taste of beer. Loved the pizza- hated the beer. I rolled through the intersection where, if you turned left and traveled about ¼ of a mile, you'd find Lefty's Barbeque sitting directly across from Bill C.'s house. If you kept travelling on Candler and you went as far as the city of Decatur, you had another pizza choice- Pizza By Candlelight. This is where you took your date if you really wanted to impress her because they also served spaghetti and you sat at tables with red and white checkered tablecloths. And, yes, each table had candles for that romantic touch.

Just a bit south of Lefty's, Candler intersected with Memorial again. On previous trips down to my old stomping grounds I had ventured down Memorial which leads all the way to Stone Mountain. But before you got that far, you'd pass by two of the first shopping complexes built in Atlanta. The first one you came to was Belvedere Shopping Center. Its main attraction was Rich's, for those shoppers who didn't want to travel to downtown Atlanta or go all the way to Lenox Square.

Then, just a ½ mile on the left, was Columbia Mall. It held as its main anchor store a Davison's, which would later become Macy's. The most notable feature of this mall was that a grave was located in the middle of the parking lot. The family that sold the property to the developers of the project did not want to disturb the resting place of one of their ancestors so a walled monument was erected to protect it.

More good eating places could be found up and down this corridor. Directly across from the Columbia Mall was an Old Hickory BBQ. This was one of about six locations they had around the city. I still remember it to be some of the best BBQ I've ever had. Finally, there was Rio Vista, a fried seafood restaurant specializing in good old catfish, fries, and hush puppies. My mouth is watering just thinking about it.

Continuing with my drive home and farther out Glenwood was the Glenwood Drive-In. This was one of the few places we could ever get Dad to take us for entertainment when I was a boy. I guess the reason he'd consider going is that he wouldn't have to deal with people since you sat in your car, put the speaker in the window, and enjoyed the movie by yourself. I'd always spend my time sitting in the chairs located in front of the concession stand. I don't know why but two movies stand out that I vividly remember seeing there; *The Man in the Grey Flannel Suit* with Gregory Peck and John Wayne in *The High and the Mighty*. Later, as a teenager, I don't remember any of the movies that were showing when I took dates there. But on those evenings, the movies were never really the point.

The rest of the drive home continued to be filled with memories as my head raced with the emotions of the day, especially those experienced with Madame Roberta. Little did I know as I pulled into our garage that three days later I would take……..

CHAPTER 20

MY WALK TO THE BRINK

I would be coming home to an empty house. Cindy was off on one of her many business trips to Winston-Salem, North Carolina, the home office of the bank she works for. She was due back on Friday so, for the next two days, I had to make do for myself. In her numerous absences, however, I had become a pretty good cook. Nothing fancy, but I could fend for myself well enough.

That night, after making myself a pizza and talking to my girl on the phone, I lay in bed reliving my day. I still couldn't figure out how Madame Roberta knew or could figure out so much about me. I didn't have much time to worry about those things, however, because I was so tired from my long walk that I drifted off very quickly.

The next morning I woke myself up with a series of sneezes. "Great," I thought. "Another cold. That's what you get for walking in the rain, stupid!"

I had no energy at all and the sneezing became more regular plus I was beginning to get a sore throat as well. My head was stuffy and, like with any flu, all I wanted to do was sleep. Being a stubborn man who detests taking medicine of any type, I fought it as long as I could before succumbing to the necessity of doing so. Thursday turned into Friday and I was so glad that Cindy would be home that day.

When her car pulled into the carport late that afternoon I was still bundled up in a big blanket even though it was July and the outside temperature was in the 90's. I hadn't showered or shaved in a couple of days so I am sure that I was not a pleasant sight for her tired eyes. But being a loving wife, she forgot about being tired and started doting on me. That's really what a man wants when he's sick. He wants to be a little boy again and have his mommy wait on him hand and foot. Mommy is just replaced by a wife for those of us lucky enough to have one like I did. I was feeling so bad that I didn't even think about what this cold could be doing to my vulnerable system or the seriousness of what this simple cold could have on me.

Saturday was no better; in fact, I even felt worse. Cindy said my temperature was 103°. She called Dr. Joe, who, knowing what was going on with me, told her not to bother with bringing me to the office, he'd come to the house to see about me. While I still have not reconciled myself to living in a small town, this was one of its advantages. There is no way you could get a doctor in metro Atlanta to make a house call but here, in small-town America, it was not out of the question.

I had never felt so bad in my life. Even a bout with mononucleosis that I had experienced while in college was not this bad. When Dr. Joe arrived, he did the regular tests- temperature, blood pressure, pulse rate, etc. Cindy hovered over us all the while. When he finished with his tests, he asked Cindy if he could talk to me alone. A puzzled look came on her face questioning the need for this, but she did as he had requested, leaving us to have what I knew would not be a pleasant conversation. Dr. Joe closed the door after her.

"You've not told her anything, have you?" he asked.

I'm sure he could read the answer in my eyes.

"Randy, you're facing some serious stuff here and you need her to help you handle it. I have no idea how this illness might affect you but it can't be good based on how intolerant your system is to viruses and infections. You've got to promise me you'll tell her within the next few days or I'll be forced to tell her myself." he said sternly.

I nodded okay.

"Now, I'm going to give you some antibiotics and a sedative to help you sleep soundly but if this gets much worse, we'll have no alternative but to get you in a hospital." Dr. Joe told me.

He gave me a shot that I presume was the sedative because it took affect almost before he got out the door. My eyes became very heavy but I heard Dr. Joe and Cindy whispering through the door as I drifted off.

Most of my sleep was dreamless but the ones I did have were filled with anxiety. I had an on-going dream about playing in a basketball game. Every time I tried to pass the ball to a teammate, it would get intercepted by the other team and when the game came down to the final seconds, the last, game-winning shot would always come down to me... and I always missed.

I was constantly being chased by dogs in others and in the scariest of them, I climbed a steep hill and when I got to the top, I was at the edge of a cliff with no way down.

But when I was resting a little more comfortably, based on Cindy's details later, I'd dream of my mom.

Allie Arminda Noggle was born on December 19, 1917 in Copperhill, Tennessee. Her father was a mechanic for the Southern Railway and they moved to Atlanta when she was a baby. Mom didn't get to know her dad very well. He died from a bout with pneumonia when she was only 2 leaving Nanny to raise her by herself. The two of them moved in with one of Nanny's brothers to make ends meet.

Mom had a tough life. They barely got by and she was forced to drop out of school so she could help bring in additional money to help support the seven of them that were living under one roof. Mom had two half brothers, Richard "Red" Woods and Paul Noggle, from Nanny's first marriage, but they were both grown with families of their own. Paul had three daughters, Ruth, Helen, and AdaLee, who were more like sisters to Mom than nieces. It was very tough on Mom when the last of the three, Ruth, passed away just a few months ago. She felt like her entire family was gone and she was the only one left. Sadly, other than me, she's right.

Mom started working full time at the age of 15 at Fulton Bag & Cotton Mill. In 1936, at the age of nineteen, she met Lucille Dorsey, a vibrant, full of life woman from Calhoun, Georgia who had a brother named Horace that she wanted my mom to meet. Mom immediately fell in love with this handsome man who, many said, resembled Clark Gable and they married in 1937.

Mom was beautiful herself. She never had enough money to buy nice clothes but when she did dress up, she was a knockout. The Second World War came and went and in 1947, I came along.

To say that I was a mama's boy would be a big understatement. Mom doted on me and when Nanny moved in with us, it became even worse. I've always thought that Dad, perhaps, became jealous of all the attention I got and that was one of the reasons he was always so hard on the two of us.

I don't remember the exact year, but Mom left the mill and took a job with Rich's, the prominent department store in downtown Atlanta. None of the Rich's locations exists anymore after they were swallowed up in a corporate takeover some years back but for those of us who are Atlanta natives, there will always be a Rich's.

One of the most memorable events of the calendar year took place at Rich's each year on Thanksgiving- the Lighting of the

Great Tree. Rich's occupied two large city-block buildings right in the heart of downtown. One was the house wares area where you could find anything from tv's to dinnerware. The other building was the apparel store. Men's, women's, and children's clothes were available and at reasonable, affordable prices for those days. An annual trip to find clothes for the new school year was always on the agenda for Mom and I. And as a special treat, we'd always go up to the top floor where the Magnolia Room was located and have lunch where they served an incredible coconut cake.

The two buildings were connected by a three-story bridge with expansive windows instead of walls allowing you to shop and look down on the pedestrians and cars travelling underneath. On top of the bridge, however, was where the Great Tree could be found on Thanksgiving Night. Thousands would gather on Forsyth Street below to hear choirs sing until the moment arrived. When the lights came on the tree, there were collective oohs and ahs from all those watching this traditional beginning of the Christmas season.

Mom never learned to drive although she did take a week's worth of lessons one time. They didn't take. I think the only part of driving she grasped was where to put the key into the ignition. Because she didn't drive she was always dependent on Dad or one of her friends to take her where she needed to go if the bus line didn't satisfy her needs.

One thing mom did get to do, however, was travel. She would sign up to go along with church groups or, later, the Grandmother's Club she belonged to, allowing her to see a good part of the world. To Dad's credit, he never stood in her way of going. He told her that he didn't care where or how long she was gone as long as she didn't ask him to go with her. But, then, why should she? All he would have done is complain so there was no need to go anywhere for that to happen. She got enough of that at home.

Mom worked until she was 75 when they forced her to retire. She had become a little unsteady on her feet and she had had an accident and the company didn't want to take any chances. I couldn't blame them. I was beginning to worry about her, too.

Mom and I shared one common interest that bonded us throughout my entire childhood. Television. I am a couch potato today because that's what I grew up with. It was my babysitter in the afternoons and my entertainment at night. Every night after the dishes were finished- she washed, I dried- we would sit down to watch our favorite shows. Dad would usually go up to his bedroom upstairs around 8: 00 pm after watching the Huntley-Brinkley News Report and an episode of Amos & Andy, leaving the tv for Mom and I.

My morning routine when I got up and prepared for school each day included Captain Kangaroo, Mr. Greenjeans, Bunny Rabbit, and Grandfather Clock. But my favorite part of the show was the cartoon featuring Tom Terrific, "The Greatest Hero Ever", and Mighty Manfred the Wonder Dog. Tom could do anything or be anything once he put on his funnel-shaped "thinking cap." And when he faced his arch enemy, Crabby Appleton ("he's rotten to the core"), I cheered for him to save the day and he always did.

In the afternoon, I would hurry home from school and get my trumpet practice completed so that I could be finished by 4: 00. That's when the *Mickey Mouse Club* came on. A smile always crossed my face when those trumpets sounded their fanfare and Jimmy and Roy started singing:

Hey there, hi there, ho there
You're as welcome as can be
M-I-C-K-E-Y M-O-U-S-E

And it didn't matter if it was Special Guest Day or Talent Round Up Day as long as one Mouseketeer was featured- Annette. Oh, how I loved that girl! Cubby, Darlene, Mike, and Karen were all right but Annette was the dream of every boy in America. I could even tolerate Spin & Marty if Annette, who had a featured role on the series, was on that day's episode.

On Saturdays, it was a steady dose of *Roy Rogers, Sky King, The Adventures of Superman, Soupy Sales* and various cartoons. Then, in the afternoon I would watch the CBS Baseball Game of the Week featuring the dynamic broadcasting duo of Pee Wee Reese and Dizzy Dean. Dizzy fit his name perfectly because he had been one of the all-time characters in the game. After Dizzy, a pitcher, had gotten drilled by a line drive that hit him in the head, the local newspaper reported as their headline the next day *"Xrays of Dizzy's Head Reveal Nothing."*

Dizzy and Pee Wee were, by no means, the best baseball broadcasters but they could sure make the game fun with their antidotes from their many years in the game. Reese, a Southern boy from Kentucky, had been a Brooklyn Dodger and, as it has been documented in a recent film honoring Jackie Robinson for his contribution in breaking the color barrier in professional baseball, was one of the few on the Dodgers who befriended Robinson. Dean was a long-time member of the St. Louis Cardinals and a charter member of their famous Gas House Gang. Dean's biggest fan was himself and his Arkansas-born twang made for some funny stories.

Dean was responsible for one of the greatest tv bloopers of all time. One particular game the guys were calling had become lopsided and the boys were simply trying to fill time until the end of the game since all the suspense of the outcome had been taken away since the third inning. The camera spotted a young couple in the bleachers who were, obviously, enjoying their afternoon in the sun by making out in a fairly active manner. Dizzy, quick on his feet told Pee Wee: "See Pee Wee! That just proves what I've always said- there's nothing like fun at the old ball park. He's kissing her on the strikes and she's kissing him on the (BLEEP!)." The screen went blank and the technical difficulty screen came up as the censors took control. With what goes on and is said on tv today, this slip up seems rather tame, doesn't it?

The other famous, somewhat risqué, blooper that always gets a lot of attention is one made by the great Groucho Marx on his afternoon quiz show that he emceed called *You Bet Your Life.* Two contestants would vie for prizes by answering trivia questions but before they played the game, Groucho would interview them, inquiring about their lives. On one show a man was being interviewed and Groucho asked him if he had any children. The man proudly stated that he had 15 children. Without a moment's pause Groucho said, "I like a good cigar, but I take it out every now and then." He, too, got censored.

Wait! I've got one more. Red Skelton, one of the funniest men ever to grace this planet with his characters Freddie the Freeloader, Clem Kadiddlehopper, and San Fernando Red was doing a skit with the beautiful bombshell Jayne Mansfield as his guest. Red's character had his hands full with Christmas presents and Mansfield was digging in his pants pockets trying to find their car keys. After a few seconds of this, Mansfield says: "I feel so silly doing this." To which Skelton said: "If you dig a little lower, you'll feel nuts." OK, that's enough.

At night and depending on which night it was, Mom and I would watch our favorite shows. The programming changed over the years and favorites came and went but some of our favorites were:

The Red Skelton Show
The Milton Berle Show
This is Your Life
Perry Mason
Dobie Gillis
Wagon Train
Dick Van Dyke Show
Ed Sullivan/Toast of the Town
The Beverly Hillbillies
Green Acres

and after Dad bought us a color tv, there was no more need for us to say to each other, "I bet that is beautiful in color" each time *Bonanza* came on each Sunday night.

The dreams I had during my illness were usually on the positive side regarding Mom but, occasionally, they would dip into the reality of what I was experiencing with her now in her old age. Mom, who was never stubborn before, is becoming somewhat difficult to deal with, especially regarding health issues. This is not an unusual trait- I hear other children my age dealing with elderly parents' say the same thing.

When I originally moved her to her present home in April, 2012, she fought me tooth and nail. Dad was still alive then and in spite of what she had endured from him for over 75 years, she didn't want to leave him by himself. I had to stay firm in my resolve even though she was telling all those who would listen what a horrible son I had become and how I was mistreating her terribly. The words hurt but I knew they were being spoken more from fear of the unknown than actual spite towards me.

Eventually, she came around and began feeling more comfortable in her new surroundings and when Dad died later that year, her guilt at leaving him alone began to fade. She began enjoying having people to talk with and being waited on. Now, if I could just get her to wear her damn hearing aids so I didn't have to yell every time I visit her, things would be much better. But I don't see that happening in this lifetime.

I finally awoke fully Wednesday morning to see Cindy's smiling face. She had taken off from work, something she never does, to take care of me. And the best part was that I felt revived, energized, and rarin' to go. I felt no ill effects from what I had gone through. I felt like a new man.

Life went back to normal. I checked in with Dr. Joe who said he really hadn't expected me to fight off my illness that soon, if at all. I told him I was glad his diagnosis was wrong in this case.

I asked him if he thought we could still go on our annual trip to Fripp Island in late August and he said that if I continued progressing satisfactorily, he saw no reason I couldn't.

Fripp Island, on the South Carolina coast near Beaufort, South Carolina, is a special place in our lives. We had been vacationing there for over twenty-five years. It is a magical place where the worries and troubles of the world can be left behind for a few days once you drive through the gated entrance. The hard-packed beaches and hot August sun of this non-commercialized private island plus the fact that school is usually back in session by the time we go there, make it a veritable paradise for two people looking to get away from the rat race of life.

Cindy's parents had invested, along with three other couples from Winder, in a five bedroom house at Fripp just shortly after Cindy and I had been married. When the partnership was announced I didn't see how it could possibly work because of the diverse nature and personalities of the eight people involved. But through all the minor disagreements, the work got done to keep the place up, the payments and dues were made on time, and they spent many quality days down there together over the years until advancing age and even the death of two of them caused the partnership to dissolve with the subsequent sale of the house five years ago. We haven't let the house being sold stop us, however. We simply rent a condo for the week.

Each family would be allocated one week a month that was theirs. Cindy's parents were always kind enough to allow the two of us their week in August. Cindy went for the sun- I went for the food.

Cindy is a beach bum when she is there. She loves to sit for hours upon hours in her beach chair with a cooler filled with cold beer at her side and a trash novel on her lap. I think there is nothing more boring in the world than that so I would spend my time in my younger days running or cycling around the island, staying at the house in air conditioned comfort reading or playing my fantasy baseball game, Strat-O-Matic Baseball, or having myself a cold libation while riding around the island in our golf cart.

Cindy and I would get dressed up each night and select one of the many great restaurants within driving range to have our evening dinner. That was my favorite part. We could choose from the Bonita Boathouse (she crab soup and fried flounder), Johnson Creek Tavern (shrimp and grits), or the 11th Street Dockside Restaurant (fried seafood platter) and one night we would always choose to fix some fresh boiled shrimp that we had purchased that day from Gay's Fish Market. Man, that was good eatin'.

Actually, my favorite times were taking walks on the beach with Cindy. As I said earlier, I am a big romantic and these walks were very special times when there was no one else in the entire world but the two of us walking hand and hand in the surf.

Several times, when they were younger, my kids would go down there with us and those are some fantastic memories. But some of the best memories we have is remembering how our nephew, Chase, grew up down there. There were several times when all of Cindy's family, her parents and her sister and husband and both children, Chase and Sara Grace, would be there together. When Chase was a very little boy, I would often take him for bike rides on his special seat behind me. I can still remember how cute he looked with his little helmet on urging me to go faster.

One late afternoon, we were enjoying a ride when we stopped at a little lagoon to see if we could spot any fish jumping in the water. We got a bigger surprise when an alligator surfaced right before our eyes. "Unk!" Chase screamed. "Addigator! Addigator!" That was the battle cry for the rest of our stay. "Let's go see addigator!" I was exhausted by the end of our stay from toting that boy around trying to see that addigator again.

Cindy taught him a much more valuable lesson in the life of a little boy a few years later- how to blow on a beer bottle and make it whistle. Everyone needs to know how to do that, right? This was a talent that he shared later with some buddies at, of all places, church. Needless to say, when his mother discovered him doing this, she was mortified, blaming her sister for turning her son into a hoodlum.

Fripp was also the location where Chase and I held our secret lessons on how to grab your crotch and farmer blow when you step into the batter's box. He had just started playing Little League and I wanted him to look like a ballplayer even if he couldn't hit the ball at all. So, I spent a good deal of time teaching him how to, in order, knock the dirt out of your cleats with your bat, grab your crotch and pull as if you were adjusting your protective cup, and then, the coup de resistance, put your finger on the side of your nose holding one nostril down and blow. Sure enough, his first game he looked at me in the stands and went through the routine perfectly. I was so proud. His mother, on the other hand, was less so.

Now that I think about it, maybe his aunt and I haven't been really great influences on him. It is so hard to imagine that this little boy is now grown, married, and has a beautiful little girl, Ella Mae, of his own with his wife, Ashley. Where does the time go?

We had another wonderful stay and as an added bonus, Brian took a couple of days off from school and joined us the latter part of our week there. They tell me that I had a fun evening one of the nights as we just sat at the condo playing trivia games, having a few drinks, and enjoying each other's company.

Before I knew it, one of my most favorite times of the year was upon us- college football season. There is nothing like football in the South. Many of us, including me, take it way too seriously but, for me, there is nothing like sitting in Sanford Stadium, home of the Georgia Bulldogs, on a Saturday afternoon in the Fall with 98,000 of my closest friends watching the Dawgs play.

The anticipation of a new season was playing havoc on my nervous system as the days ticked off the calendar towards the opening game with Clemson. Would our defense be better this year with a new defensive coordinator? Would our quarterback be able to produce like his predecessor, Aaron Murray? At my age, would I be able to make the long walk back to the car up Lumpkin after the game, especially after the first few games of the season when it was still blistering hot? All those questions and many more raced through my head that Saturday morning of the game.

The game was being televised with kickoff at 4: 00 pm so we had a few more hours to prepare our tailgating gear than for a regular 1: 00 kickoff. As we left the house, I put in the same CD that I play in the car before each game. It's a collection of our various fight songs and anthems played by the Georgia Redcoat Band. It gets me fired up to hear the strains of "Glory, Glory", "Hail to Georgia", and "Let the Big Dawg Eat".

We pulled into the same parking space we've reserved for the last 15 years and after having a bite to eat, I was ready to take........

CHAPTER 21

MY WALK TO SANFORD STADIUM

I have always loved walking through the campus of the University of Georgia. Founded in 1785 as the nation's first state-chartered land grant institution, its rich history can be seen throughout the 759 acres it encompasses.

Cindy and I walked hand in hand making our way toward the stadium. From our parking space in the primary retail area of downtown Athens we passed by the many bars and restaurants along Clayton Street that would be filled with students after the game. Usually we walk down Lumpkin passing by fraternity houses and all the new construction going on but today I wanted to walk under the arch, for old times' sake.

I am a traditionalist and there are two such traditions pertaining to the campus that are not being observed as they were originally intended and, being a traditionalist, I get upset when I see and, in one case hear, them abused.

The first pertains to the hallowed arches. Tradition says that only graduates may walk under the arch. All others are supposed to walk around the arch. People no longer abide by this concept at all and it diminishes all the hard work put in by those who have earned their degrees. In spite of what Tech people think, they don't throw our diplomas through open car windows as we pass by. We've earned them.

The second concerns the Chapel Bell. Those of you who have ever attended a football game in Athens will know what I am talking about because you have, more than likely, heard its beautiful peal. Originally, the Chapel Bell was to be rung only after victories with Freshmen assigned to the task of ringing it with the number of points scored in the game. Ringing was to stop at midnight. However, the bell was to ring all night after defeating our arch rival, Georgia Tech. Now, sadly, the bell rings constantly on game day by little ones and not so little ones who don't know the sacred tradition.

Cindy and I walked down Broad Street and I passed under the arches to walk through the campus. It was a hot, sunny day but as with any game day, my nerves were frayed with anticipation of a new season. In spite of Dr. Joe's insistence during my recent close call, I still had not said anything to Cindy about my illness. I had just never found an appropriate time to do so. There probably is not an appropriate time though and I knew I had to do so soon, but I came from a family that kept secrets extremely well.

Cindy came from a totally different type of family environment from me. Where I had been raised by a loving mother but a father who had been an extremely strict disciplinarian who showed me very little affection, as has been depicted previously, Cindy's parents had showered her and her sister with nothing but massive amounts of love and praise.

Ambrose and Beverly Jackson had told their girls that they were special and that message had made them both confident, strong-willed, and strong-minded women. Cindy grew up in the town where we now lived, Winder, Georgia just twenty miles from Athens. She had been captain of the majorette squad in high school; very pretty and very popular. Many of her childhood friends never moved away so, when we moved to Winder in 1991, she was able to reconnect with many of them.

Cindy, like her father, never meets a stranger. Her warmth and smile win you over in a second. Cindy, like her mother, has a sense of love for family that surpasses all other emotions. There is absolutely nothing she wouldn't do for any of them.

But, if I am to be perfectly honest in this story, she, like her sister, were spoiled rotten. And the person to be held most responsible for this was her dad. He did everything and I mean everything for his girls. When Cindy first moved away from home to the big city of Atlanta, she would make a habit of leaving her gas tank almost empty and as she parked the car in the driveway, she would pop the hood. Her dad would give her a hug as she carried her dirty laundry inside for her mom to do several loads of wash. Then he would check her oil for her and take it to get it filled up with gas for her.

There were times, as I said during the eulogy that I gave for Brose at his funeral that I wanted to punch him in the nose for spoiling her so much. He certainly made my job tougher by his over indulgence of her. One of the first years we were married her auto car tag bill came in the mail. She handed it to me and said sweetly, "You're going to take care of this for me, aren't you?"

I looked at her with a puzzled expression and said, "What do you mean? The last I looked you had a brain and could do things for yourself. It's your car- your responsibility." I wasn't trying to be mean; I just wanted her to become more self-reliant.

Without one breath of hesitation she pouted and said, "Well, my daddy would do it for me."

To which I said, "Then, you better call him up and get him to do it." She did. He did.

Dealing with automobile issues has always been somewhat of a challenge for my girl. As a young driver, she didn't have the best driving record as it pertained to accidents. Never a problem with tickets or driving violations, just three or four fender benders before she got out of high school.

Brose always told this story about one of them. He travelled a good bit for his work and, as was his habit, he called home to check in. Cindy's mom answered and they chatted for a few moments before Cindy wrested the phone away from Beverly so that she could tell her dad the news of the day.

"Hey, daddy," she said in what I imagine was her sugary best. "I've got some good news and some bad news." Before he could reply she told him, "The bad news is I've had another accident. But, daddy, the good news is that this time it wasn't my fault!" God, I love this girl! Her vehicle-related accident proneness continued in her adult life, too. Within one 18-month span she had three, count em', three, deer run into her car causing some pretty good damage on all three occasions.

I was experiencing the same thing now in my life- good news and bad news. The bad news was that I had this cloud of impending illness which could result in me losing my life yet, I hadn't felt this good in a long time. I had resumed a regular walking regimen and was cutting back on my sugar and carb intake with the result being that I had lost almost fifteen much-needed pounds. I was sure that some of that weight loss had been due to my illness the previous month but I had been able to keep it off, which was good.

One of the other traits that separated my family from hers was the celebration of holidays. Dad did go to great pains to decorate the house at Christmas but the other holidays came and went without much fanfare. For the Jacksons', if it was as holiday, it was celebrated, and if it was celebrated, there were gifts, particularly at Christmas.

Christmas at the Jacksons' is a never-ending sea of gifts and it doesn't matter if the girls' have, let's say, received three sweaters already, they'll get two more at Christmas along with seven swans a swimming, six geese a laying, five golden rings. You get the picture. Over indulgence takes place, not just at the dinner table, but under the tree as well.

Cindy inherited many of her mother's qualities but one trait she definitely got was her love for shopping. They are both QVC addicts. I jokingly say that I know the names of both the Fed Ex and the UPS deliverymen because they stop by our house almost every day with a new "treasure" that she had to have.

I mentioned before that Cindy had reconnected with some of her past high school friends and reconnected, to her, in the best way possible- they shop together. Several years back, seven of them: Robin B., Vickie B., Pam W., Marsha B., Cindy C. Melissa S. and my Cindy had started going shopping together at Christmas. It started, initially, as an overnight thing but the getaway has now turned into a four-day shopping orgy. They even have a name for themselves- The Shopping Queens. They do get a lot of shopping done but I believe that the real intent now is to drink a little wine, gossip, drink a little wine, have lunch, drink a little wine, have dinner, gossip, and drink a little wine.

As we continued our walk toward, in my opinion, the best college football stadium in the country, I couldn't help but think about my days here on this campus. It was a long time ago, yet, it seemed like only yesterday that a scared kid arrived here to attend school and to, hopefully, play a little baseball.

I enrolled for the 1965 Fall Semester. After being accepted, my first concern was how I was going to afford the tuition. Dad had not offered to pay for any of my advanced schooling so it was up to me to find the way. Again, jealousy at my being able to do something that was utterly out of the question for him, having dropped out in the seventh grade, made him reluctant to help me succeed. I made several trips to Athens that summer arranging for jobs to help pay the way. I applied for every grant I could find and then I got a big assist from the Georgia baseball coach, Jim Whatley. He had seen me play while scouting several of Murphy's games and told me he was willing to have the school pay for my books and half of my board in Mell Hall for Spring Quarter, the time when baseball was being played. This was the most he could provide since the school did not give full scholarships to baseball players- they only went to football and basketball players.

At the time I was in college, freshmen could not play on the varsity team. We could practice with the varsity and we had a few games with other schools using varsity members who didn't get much playing time but, it didn't matter to me. I had that block G on my cap and I was in heaven. My grades were not.

While I had always done well in high school I had never really learned how to study. Things had come pretty easy so the science of studying had eluded me. Now, with the time constraints of classes, work, and, in the spring, baseball practice, I was just hanging on. But hang on I did because I had an additional incentive that many of my fellow classmates didn't. I was out to prove wrong the statement made to me that I wouldn't make it. The day I put on that cap and gown remains one of my proudest achievements.

After my first quarter, I skipped the Winter Quarter so I could go back home and work full time for a few months. I took an after hours job at Rich's and worked alongside my mother. Several days a week, I coached a grammar school's basketball team. That was how I met my first wife and how I would eventually get the job that would lead to my career choice.

The team I coached was Peterson Elementary. One of the little cheerleaders was a very cute blonde named Lynn whose sister, Brenda, would often bring the girls to our games. I noticed her sitting in the stands and thought she was very pretty. Lynn walked up to me one day after our game and said, "My sister, Brenda, wants you to call her." She handed me a slip of paper with her sister's name and their phone number. I thought to myself, "All right!" A few days later I screwed up my courage, called her, and we went out on our first date. I never dated anyone else after that.

I also became friends with the principal of the school. He was an athlete in his younger days having played football at Alabama and he would often hang around to watch our practices. After practice we would sit down and just chat. He found out that I wanted to get a business degree and wanted to find something in that area to do during the summer. He arranged for me to meet with one of the executives at Fulton National Bank, a downtown Atlanta financial institution, named Carl Floyd who was a good friend of his. Mr. Floyd told me to come back to see him during summer and he would find something for me to do. I worked each summer there as an intern and that led to my decision to make Finance my major.

Georgia has had some success with their baseball program in recent years, even winning the National Championship in 1990, but in those days of the late 60's, our teams weren't very good. We also played much fewer games than teams do now. Even though we couldn't play in the games, the five Freshmen who were on the squad dressed out and warmed up with the regulars for every home game. We didn't travel for away games except to go to Atlanta when we played Georgia Tech. This gave me a chance to catch up with a lot of my Murphy pals who had all decided to go there to play. The varsity went 12-10 that year with a 7-6 record in SEC play.

The next year was doubly special since we were moving in to a brand new stadium, Foley Field, on the campus and the fact that I might actually get to play was an extra bonus. I was not going to start but Coach Whatley said I would platoon against left handers and play left field. That opportunity came in just our fourth game of the season.

In one of the most ironic circumstances imaginable, my first start was coming against Georgia Tech and all my buddies. My nerves were shot because I wanted so badly to do well. Six of Tech's starters that day were Murphy alumni: my good friends Floyd and Lloyd, Randy C., Roy J. and Cleve F. were starting in the field. And to make matters even worse, their starting pitcher was also one of my former teammates from Murphy, Butch C. and if he faltered at all, there was Bud M., another Murphy grad, waiting to relieve him.

Butch was a hard-throwing lefty and the thought of facing him did not make for a promising day. I was scheduled to hit seventh in the lineup. In the top half of the first, we were playing the game in Athens, I made a nice running grab of a gapper hit by Randy C. As I look back, that was the highlight of my college baseball career. I had only had two at bats as a pinch hitter and had gone 0x2.

We put a man on in the bottom of the second and with one out, I came up to the plate. Butch was all business on the mound so I wiped the smile off my face and dug in. I had worked the count to 1 ball and 1 strike, just barely missing a hit down the third base line with a foul ball, as I waited for the next pitch. I guessed that Butch would give me a hard curve ball on my fists and so I was prepared for an off-speed pitch.

What Butch threw, however, was a high and tight fast ball that was meant to brush me back off the plate. I froze. The ball hit me in the head right above my left temple. We didn't wear hard protective helmets then so my felt baseball cap didn't absorb much of the force. I went down like the proverbial ton of bricks. I woke up three days later in an Athens hospital.

The first face I saw was Brenda's. She immediately called for the nurses who began cooing over me and then she called my mom to tell her I was awake. The doctor came in later and told me that I had been hit in the exact same spot where I had struck my head when I had my car accident. The bruise on my brain and the swelling were pretty severe and I would not be able to take another blow there. What he was really telling me was that my college baseball days were over. Of course, they had never really gotten started. I had so few plate appearances that year that my name doesn't even show on the roster for that year.

I stayed in the hospital for several more days but was elated when all of my buddies from Tech came by to visit the day after I woke up. Butch was almost in tears as he told me again and again how sorry he was. I told him it was okay. "It actually was my fault." I told him jokingly. "I knew your control was so good that you couldn't possibly throw a pitch that badly. But then you did, you big jerk!" To make it worse, however, they had to be sure and tell me that Tech had won the game to boot.

My fellow Bulldogs came to see me as well. Their visit was especially welcome because they brought Varsity hot dogs and fries with them. Only decent meal I had while in the hospital. The team that year went on to finish with an 8-19 overall record and a 5-12 SEC finish. But that year did have a very unique feat included in it. In March, 1967, the team was no-hit by a South Carolina pitcher but less than two weeks later, Buddy Copeland, our top pitcher from Atlanta, no hit Vanderbilt.

Cindy and I now sat in our seats, Press Box side, Section 133, Row 6, Seats 15 and 16 where we had called home for the last twenty or so years. I have a tradition of being in my seat at least one hour before kickoff. Brenda's dad had gotten me in that habit when I would go to games with him and it had stuck. I go to listen to the Redcoats fire up the fans with their pre-game music. I go to watch the teams warm up. But I also go to people watch as the fans file past my seat just outside the hallowed hedges that encircle the field.

Cindy is not always with me for the entire time, she's usually gone shopping at the Campus Book Store, but she is good to get there before the lone trumpeter plays those first fourteen notes of "Glory, Glory!" from their location in the upper deck. When we yell GO DAWGS! at the end, you can feel the excitement of game time.

I have one other pre-game tradition. When I enter the gate, I go to the same bathroom and I go to the same urinal. If someone is using it and others are available, I patiently wait my turn. I didn't follow this superstition one game several years ago and we wound up losing the game. That one's on me. If we lose now, it's on the team.

Football fans in the Southeastern Conference are truly fanatics. We take our football very seriously. Too seriously in some cases but there is a pride that surrounds our loyalties that is unmatched, I believe, in any other part of the country. And, without doubt, Georgia fans are at the head of the class regarding their love for their team.

There is the story of the woman who became the first female President of the United States. A few days after she had won the election, the president-elect calls her father and says, "So, Daddy, I assume you will be coming to my inauguration?"

He replies, "Oh, honey, I don't think so. It's a long drive and your mother isn't as young as she used to be and my arthritis is acting up again."

"Don't worry, Daddy. I'll send Air Force One to pick you up and take you home and I'll get a limousine to pick you up at your door."

"I don't know," he continued, "Everything will be so fancy. What would your mother wear?"

"I'll make sure that she has a wonderful gown custom made by the best designer in Washington." the president-elect countered.

"But you know I can't eat those rich foods you and friends like to eat." he complained.

"I'll take care of all of that with the caterer and we'll make sure that your meals are salt-free and meet your dietary conditions. Daddy, I really want you to come." she pleaded.

So, the father reluctantly agrees and on Inauguration Day his daughter, and a Georgian at that, is being sworn in as President of the United States. In the front row sits the new president's dad and mom and sitting next to them is the out-going President. Dad leans over to him and whispers, "You see that woman over there with her hand on the Bible becoming President?"

"Certainly!" he responds.

"Her brother played football for the Georgia Bulldogs!"

I have experienced many wonderful times in that stadium and I have experienced heartbreak and sorrow as my team, as hard as they might have tried, came out on the short end of a score. As far as I'm concerned, we never lose, we just run out of time.

But, without question, the best day I have ever experienced in Sanford Stadium was the day I took……..

CHAPTER 22

MY WALK WITH LARRY MUNSON

L arry Munson was the legendary voice of the Georgia Bulldogs from 1966 until health issues forced him away from his microphone in 2008. Georgia fans revered his play-calling style and would frequently turn down the audio of a tv broadcast and listen to his gravelly voice call the game from the radio even though there was often a time delay that you had to deal with.

Munson, originally from Minnesota, had been the Vanderbilt announcer but became one of the most loyal Bulldogs when he took the job. He also called Braves and Falcons games for awhile and even did Georgia basketball but he was in his realm sitting in that Sanford Stadium booth on football Saturdays. It is impossible to list all the great calls he made over the years but here are a few of the most notable.

Munson set the tone of the game vividly through his voice. He'd tell you to "Get the picture!" as he described the uniforms and the weather conditions for the day. There is no doubt that he was a "homer", a broadcaster who is obviously biased towards the team he represents, and Munson left no question that he lived and died with the Bulldogs.

Georgia has been blessed to have had many great players in its history but none greater than Herschel Walker. Walker would win the Heisman Trophy later in his career but on that hot, muggy night in Knoxville, Tennessee, he was a much-heralded, but un-proven freshman playing the first game of his college career.

Georgia was losing the game and Coach Vince Dooley, who never started freshmen, thought it was time to see what Walker could do. He inserts him in the game and on one of his first carries ever, with Georgia on the Tennessee 16 yard line threatening to score, Munson called the next play this way:

"They hand the ball to Herschel. There's a hole! He's got 5...10...12. He's running over people! Oh, you Herschel Walker! My God he just ran over people! He ran over two men! Touchdown Georgia!" Larry got into a little trouble with the religious left for using the Lord's name in vain but that's who he was- spontaneous and unabashed.

He asked the team *"to hunker down one more time"* when they faced a tense moment in Auburn. A victory would mean that we'd win the SEC title and go to the Sugar Bowl and when they did stop the Tigers or the War Eagles or whoever they are this week, he gave his listeners the best visual they could hope for: *"Look at the sugar falling from the sky. Look at the sugar falling from the sky."* And when we came back from certain defeat to beat Tennessee, again in Knoxville, on the last play of the game, he said, *"Georgia scores. Oh my God! Oh my God! Georgia scores from 5 yards out. We just stomped on their face with a hob-nailed boot and crushed their nose."*

But for any Georgia fan, the greatest call of all came in Jacksonville, Florida in the annual game against the Florida Gators billed as The World's Largest Cocktail Party. Alone, the play would have been stunning in that it became the game-winning touchdown but because of the greater implications the play would have on the Georgia season, it is historical.

Get the picture! Georgia trails Florida late in the game and we are backed up on our own eight yard line with time running out. Here's the way Larry called it:

"Florida in a standup 5, they may or may not blitz. They don't. Buck (Belue) back, 3ʳᵈ down on the eight. In trouble, gotta block behind him. Gonna throw on the run, complete to the 25, to the 30. Lindsay Scott 35, 40. Lindsay Scott 45, 50, 45, 40...Run Lindsay! 25, 20, 15, 10, 5! LINDSAY SCOTT! LINDSAY SCOTT! LINDSAY SCOTT!"

Did you notice something? While it was a foregone conclusion for all those listening, in his excitement, Larry never says it is a touchdown. In the bedlam that followed, both on the field and in the booth, Larry admits that he got so excited that he broke the metal chair he was sitting in. And then, making reference to all the Georgia fans/partyers who had rented condos in nearby St. Simon's and Jekyll Island and who would have something to celebrate that night, he said, *"Man, is there going to be some property destroyed tonight!"* I never heard Larry's call in person because I was actually at that game. It is one of only two Georgia-Florida games I've ever attended so, I was in the stands and couldn't hear the call in person but I've heard it hundreds of times since and it still gives me chills each time I relive that moment.

I enjoyed listening to Larry so much, as well as other great broadcasters: Vin Scully, Keith Jackson, Al Michaels that I thought I'd like to try my hand at it. I started doing press box announcing for a new high school that had been built here in Barrow County. I was good friends with the man who had been named head coach and he asked me if I would be interested in making announcements and giving play results and I told him sure. I did that for two years before our local AM radio station asked me to do play-by-play work for them.

I switched schools, however, and became the Voice of the Winder-Barrow Bulldoggs, a position I held for almost eight years.

One of the best parts about doing these games was getting to see our beautiful niece, Sara Grace, cheer on the sidelines. Not only did I call football but I also wound up doing basketball and baseball broadcasts. We weren't big productions like you see on tv by any comparison but I had a blast keeping in touch with the local sports scene. Even became a minor celebrity here in town with my own weekly sports show on our cable tv station. Well, maybe celebrity is stretching it but I did have two people recognize me once.

I modeled everything I did in the booth after Larry. I came up with my own catch phrases but style and my absolute homer attitude was all Larry.

At the end of each football season, the university puts on a big banquet to honor the seniors on the team. It is really a big to-do and for several years Cindy and I attended. Included in the festivities of the night are both a silent auction featuring a lot of Georgia memorabilia and an open auction where some very nice packages are offered for the highest bid.

We decided to go to the Gala in 2000. One of the feature items in the open auction was the opportunity to spend game day with Larry in the booth as he called the game. I lusted for that opportunity as badly as a hungry man lusts after a steak. As we walked into the banquet hall, Cindy said, "I'm going to bid on that day with Munson for you. It'll be one of your Christmas presents."

"Honey, do you realize how high you'll have to go to get that? It'll be worth three Christmas'." I told her. I had obviously forgotten her competitive spirit when it came to things like this. Put her on a tennis court and she could care less about the outcome. But put her in a bidding war and she is ruthless.

Not to bore you with the details of the auction, I'll keep it short. She won! I was going to get to spend the day with Larry Munson during one of the games the following season. We gathered all of the contact information I would need when the next season rolled around and I floated out of the building on cloud nine.

Fast forward to late summer, 2001. I got my information out and found the phone number I was supposed to call. They had not told me who it belonged to, just to call it. After a few rings, that unmistakable voice that I knew so well answered. It was Larry Munson himself.

I introduced myself and explained why I was calling. Larry could sometimes come across as gruff and ornery but, let me tell you, he was anything but. He was as gracious in scheduling our day together as he could be. I perceived in my mind that doing something like this, putting up with some guy on game day, was a nuisance for him but he never gave me that impression. We set the game I would be with him and he suggested that I call back the week of the game to make the precise arrangements. He asked for my number as well so we had a backup. I thought to myself, "No problem. I've got Larry Munson's home phone number and I'm in his personal phone book. How great is that?"

We had originally planned our game together to be against Houston, scheduled for September 15, 2001. I was going to give him a call on the Tuesday preceding that date. I never made that call because the world came to a standstill that day and the last thing on my mind, or anybody else's, that day was a football game.

Tuesday morning, September 11, 2001, two planes crashed into the twin towers of the World Trade Center, another tore into the Pentagon, and yet another crashed into a field in Pennsylvania. It was one of those days that you know exactly what you were doing when you heard the news.

I was working at a bank in Athens and was just organizing my day when I heard one of my fellow employees report that a plane had struck a building in New York. Not much more detail than that. I, initially, didn't give it much thought. Just a small private plane, I guessed. Probably not much damage, I surmised. I felt sorry for those who may have been hurt or maybe even killed in the crash, but then I went on with my work.

Minutes later there was more commotion outside my office as others started talking about the crash. It was more, maybe a lot more, than I originally thought. I joined them around a radio that had been turned on to listen to the coverage. More details were coming in. It wasn't a passenger plane but a commercial airliner. "Damn! How in the world could that happen?" I added to the other questions flying from all of us.

Then, when the second plane hit we all realized that there was much more to this than just an accidental crash. Someone ran home and got a portable tv and we all gathered around it to get more info. Worked stopped.

That historical day, for those of us who lived through it, is etched into everyone's mind and it will always be one of the most memorable days in my life. A couple of days later, Georgia announced that they were cancelling the scheduled game for Saturday and would announce when it would be played later. Most major events for the weekend were cancelled as well as major league baseball games and NFL football. The country was in no mood for entertainment. We were in mourning.

The next few weeks for our country were spent in recovery mode. President Bush roused the nation with his pledge to find the people responsible for this attack on our freedom and bring them to justice. Every person in America wanted to volunteer for the job of placing the noose around the necks of the terrorists who planned this evil plot.

The team had gotten off to a pretty good start at 4-1, losing only to South Carolina, under the direction of a new coach, Mark Richt. Richt was a young offensive-minded coach who had been responsible for much of Florida State's recent success as Offensive Coordinator for legendary coach, Bobby Bowdon. Georgia fans were hoping for great things from him after a few rather mundane, so-so years.

We were preparing for our game against Kentucky in which we would have to face their mammoth (6'6", 300 lb.) quarterback, Jared Lorenzen. I got home Wednesday of that week after work and saw that there was a message blinking on the phone. I pushed the button to listen and there was that voice again. Short and succinct, the voice said nothing more than, "Hey, Blalock. This is Munson. Give me a call."

I immediately got back in touch with him and he asked if I could make the game Saturday since our original game had been loused up by, his words, "those towel heads." I told him that I had season tickets and so our Saturdays were planned around Georgia football. He told me where and what time to meet him and gave me a little hint at what we'd be doing that day.

Knowing that Larry loved a good cigar and wanting to make a good impression, okay I was brown nosing, I went to several stores in Athens searching for his favorite brand. After making my purchase I was geared up for my day with him.

I was to meet him at 8: 00 am at a certain gate at the stadium. I got there about 7: 45 so that I wouldn't be late. The day promised to be a gorgeous fall day. Cindy had invited two of our friends, Heidi and Connie, to go to the game with her and they would arrive later.

Larry had a set routine that he followed each home game. After personal introductions, we went up to the radio booth to let him put some of the notes he had in a massive notebook down before we started walking around the stadium.

Larry was a huge movie buff. In fact, he had a weekly ritual where he would meet with a group of students, mostly coeds, on Sunday afternoons to watch one of the current movies out in theaters. Then, the following Monday on his radio talk show, he'd give a review of what they had seen. Instead of thumbs up or thumbs down, Larry would rate the movie on a scale of 1-5 bulldogs. Most of our early conversation centered around movies.

After a few minutes I gave him the cigar I had purchased and you would have thought I had given him the moon. The cigar was a hit and from that moment on, I was one of his best friends. Sanford Stadium, I might add, is a smoke-free building. Smoke-free to everyone except Larry Munson. We passed a guard who did nothing more than wave and say hi. We kept on walking and Larry kept on puffing.

Our tour of Sanford included a trip to the locker room. I was amazed at how huge it was. We went through a few corridors and back out into the sunshine and onto the field. As we passed by the stone bulldog where the team runs onto the field, I gave the statue a good luck pat. Larry still had his cigar going strong and when a few ashes fell on the 40 yard line, I looked around expecting someone to race onto the field at any moment and sweep up the debris.

We went back to the booth so that he could do a live pre-game report and that's when he told me that I would actually have an assignment that day. I would be the person responsible for feeding him scores from other games. He turned me over to one of the technicians who taught me how to operate the ticker. The only thing running through my mind was the same thought I had had since the man hammered down the gavel on Cindy's bid and said, "SOLD!" and that was "This is gonna be great!"

With kickoff scheduled for 1: 00 pm, we went to the get some lunch in the press room around 11: 30 am. These guys eat good. This was not a simple layout with a few sandwiches and hot dogs; it was a full buffet. We filled our plates and found a place to sit.

If this day wasn't great enough, what happened next was the icing. We were eating and Larry was asking some personal stuff about me. I told him about my short baseball career here and I looked up to see Vince Dooley, long time coach, and Buck Belue, the quarterback on our National Championship team, asking if they could join us. I tried to contain myself but inside I know my heart was racing like a little girl meeting Justin Beiber or the guys from One Direction. After that, the game was almost anti-climatic.

Things did not look good for us the first half. We could not stop their quarterback at all and Kentucky led at halftime. Sitting in the booth watching and listening to him work (I was given headphones so I could hear the broadcast), I couldn't help but chuckle with his references to their huge quarterback. Instead of calling him Lorenzen, Larry referred to him as Godzilla. "We can't bring Godzilla down. Godzilla got that pass off with three Dawgs hanging all over him."

As fans, all we hear is Larry's voice and the occasional comments of the color commentator, Scott Howard, or the sideline reports of Loran Smith, but what goes on behind the scenes is mind-boggling. First of all, there are eight men in that booth and I made nine that day. Along with Larry, there was Scott, two spotters, one sitting on each side of Larry, and four technicians. The spotters job was particularly interesting.

The man on Larry's left had a big board with every Kentucky player listed on it by position. One side was offense and the other defense. The spotter on his right held Georgia's board. After each play, Kentucky's spotter would be pointing to one of the names and the Georgia spotter would be doing the same. In this way they would be telling Larry who ran the ball, who made the tackle, or who made the catch, depending on which team was on offense. They even had hand signals notifying Larry of penalties or other necessary information the listener needed to know. It was fascinating.

Larry, like me, is a world class pessimist with regards to the Dawgs. I have given up on many games only to see them come back and pull it out. As we lamented during the halftime break, both of us thought we were in for a long afternoon. Our offense was not playing particularly well and neither of us could see how we could stop them from scoring more. But then came the second half.

The defense rose up and finally sacked Godzilla several times and intercepted two of his passes. The offense came to life and our quarterback, lefty David Greene, connected on two long touchdown passes to freshman Fred Gibson. Georgia pulled away and won 43-29.

Towards the end of the game when it finally looked like we would pull it out, I handed Larry some scores to report. He looked at them and said on the air, "Well, Blalock and I had given up at halftime. You had, too. Here are some scores from around the conference that Blalock's just handed me." Larry Munson said my name on the radio. I know it's silly but how many of you can say that?

After the game, Larry gets out of there as quickly as he can so the goodbyes were short. But, along with my photos of he and I in the booth together and my autographed press pass, I have some wonderful memories of a most gracious and cordial man.

Above my desk in my home office where I am writing this hangs a large painting of Larry with some of his most famous quotes and calls framing his face. He is wearing his headphones and his black with red striped tie that he wore to every game. It is titled "The 12th Man." Pardon us, Texas A&M, the first to use this phrase as an honor to someone who provides above and beyond support to the team, but, in this case, it applies to Larry.

Larry Munson passed away on November 20, 2011 and the entire Bulldog Nation shed a tear. I shed several. Fans of other teams all think that their announcers are the best but I have no doubt that if there is ever a Mount Rushmore of college football announcers, Larry Munson will be one of the four faces shining down on us.

———&—

Cindy and I walked back to the car after the game feeling good. After a close first half, Georgia pulled away in the second half to beat Clemson so, all was right with the world.

While watching some of the games that night, a promo for a special was shown. The special was going to be on the life and career of the comic genius, Robin Williams, who had died in an apparent suicide just a few weeks earlier. Saddened by his death, I reflected back on a time when I was part of a group that had the chance to talk with him, or rather, he talked with us some years before.

I've actually had the chance to meet directly, not just be in the same room, but actually talk to several other stars in my life so I thought back on ………

MY WALK WITH CELEBRITY

Celebrity, like beauty as the old saying goes, in the eye of the beholder. Someone who may be construed in one person's opinion as a celebrity is just a nobody to someone else. I wouldn't give you a dime to meet any of the brainless Kardashians, Paris Hilton, or Miley Cyrus even if they showed me their bare butts, yet, they continue to occupy the headlines and airwaves. Someone, then, must think they are interesting. Webster defines a celebrity as "someone with fame or renown" and I think that definition fits for those individuals I have had the chance to meet in person.

Jerry Clower was a comedian, or as his website calls him, "a rural observationalist." However you describe him, he was funny. His down home stories about the people in and around his home town of Liberty, Mississippi, especially the Ledbetter family, will keep you in stitches.

When Cindy and I moved to our present home in Winder, Georgia so that I could become the President of one of the local banks, I felt it necessary to get involved with several of the local civic groups. I'm not really a "club' person but it was good business

211

for the president of the bank to be seen around town, so I made the personal sacrifice. One of the organizations I joined was the Barrow County Chamber of Commerce.

My first official position as an officer was to organize the annual banquet. I would need to find a suitable location for the event to be held as well as make arrangements for the entertainment, or guest speaker, for the night.

I was having some difficulty in finding a speaker but while listening to a country music radio station one morning, I got inspired. The show was interviewing Clower and he was telling one funny story after the other. At the end of the interview, he gave information on how to reach him to schedule an appearance. I jotted the phone number down and said to myself, what the heck, it's worth a shot even though I was doubtful I could pull it off. I had a rather limited budget and I guessed he would be too expensive.

I dialed the number later that day and spoke to his manager. After telling him what the event was and where we were located, the manager said, "We're actually doing a show close to you on Friday night so, I just may be able to work something out if you'll agree to let us record the event for an upcoming album."

I checked with several other officers and we all thought it was a great idea. When I got back with the manager to work out the arrangements he told me that they had already come up with a great name for the album- Sidewinder, incorporating the name of our town which would give us some great PR. When word got out around town that Jerry Clower was going to be the guest speaker, ticket sales went through the roof. I, of course, was a hero and would have the honor of introducing him that night as well as sit next to him during dinner.

The evening was a continuous string of hilarious episodes about his life in Mississippi. Many of his stories deal with his neighbors the Ledbetter's; Marcelle, Claude, Nujean, and Uncle Versie Ledbetter. Clower told one story about visiting the family one Sunday afternoon. Suppertime was long over but when he got to their house, the entire family was still sitting around the table staring at the last remaining piece of fried chicken left on the plate in the center of the table.

There is a certain code of conduct when it comes to meals in the South which says that it is rude and impolite to take the last piece of chicken and the Ledbetter's were obviously honoring this code. But at the same time, all of them were hankerin', in Jerry's words, for that last piece. Afraid that if they left the table another family member would take it, all of them refused to move. There they sat, none of them saying a word, just staring at the plate until dark.

The Ledbetter's didn't have electricity so as dusk fell, no one lit the candles for illumination because no one wanted to leave that table. Jerry relates that it was so dark you could not see your own hand in front of your face, yet, no one moved from that table. Suddenly, a scream of pain rings out from one of them. Jerry finds a candle and lights it. The scream had come from Uncle Versie who had four forks sticking out of his hand that was tightly grasped around that piece of chicken.

My other favorite story from that night concerns the great evangelist, Billy Graham. Graham came into the Atlanta airport for a speaking engagement. He was met at baggage claim by a chauffeur assigned to take him to his destination. They picked up Graham's luggage and went to pick up the car. When Graham saw the stretch limo he told the driver, "I've always wanted to drive one of these luxury cars. Why don't we switch roles? You sit in the back and I'll drive." Who was the driver to argue with Billy Graham? He did as he was told.

Graham heads down the interstate and begins to really let the limo loose. He had the car travelling well over the speed limit when a state patrolman spots the speeding vehicle and pulls them over. He lumbers up to the driver's window and Graham lowers the window. The patrolman immediately recognizes that the driver is Billy Graham, excuses himself for a moment and calls his captain back at the station.

"Sir, this is Officer Blake and I think we have a problem."

"What kind of a problem, Officer Blake?"

"Well, sir, I think I have just pulled over a dignitary and I'm not exactly sure I know what to do, sir."

"Officer, you know that we don't make exceptions for dignitaries. If they have broken the law, then they are written up just like anyone else."

"With all due respect, sir, I don't think it is as simple as that. I think this is someone very special."

"Who is it, son? Is it the mayor?"

"Oh, no, sir. It's someone bigger than that."

"Then is it the governor?"

"Negative, Captain! Much bigger than that. Maybe the most important ever!"

"Son, you're trying my patience. Who is it?"

"All I can say Captain, is that, whoever it is, he's got Billy Graham as a chauffeur."

I've also gotten to play tennis with Jimmy Connors. What possessed me to volunteer one year to be a linesman at a tennis tournament being played in Atlanta, I'll never know. That experience was one of the most stressful things I've ever done in my life. The pros involved in the tourney could be very hateful towards us lowly lines people if we happened to miss a call. One particular player even had the nickname of Nasty, Romanian Ilie Nastase. Luckily, I never had a run-in with him or any of the other pros but I was constantly on pins and needles worrying about missing a call.

Between matches, we were allowed to wander around and could watch the guys warming up. Usually, they would hit balls with each other or a practice partner that travelled with them but on one occasion I saw Connors stretching before taking to the court and wished him good luck in that night's match. He was one of my favorite players at the time and I wasn't calling his match so I didn't think speaking to him was out of line.

Connors smiled and asked if I'd like to hit with him since his partner was occupied with something else. He offered me one of his spare racquets and we volleyed together for about thirty minutes talking all the time.

Connors had the reputation of being somewhat of a brat himself on the court but he was very cordial to me. He was dating Chris Evert at the time and I admitted that I had a crush on her and thought she was very pretty. Evert's on court style was so focused that she was called "The Ice Queen." Connors winked when he told me that she was not that cold off the court- a fact I've never disclosed until now. My appreciation for her after that was now based on a whole new set of parameters.

Then, after winning a local radio station contest, I was able to meet the three members of the singing group, The Lettermen. My name was drawn and I won ten tickets to their upcoming concert. The Lettermen were a singing trio who were extremely popular in the 60's and 70's with hits like *"Theme from A Summer Place"*, *"The Way You Look Tonight"*, *"Can't Take My Eyes Off of You"* and many, many others. Their harmonies were always perfect.

The added bonus was that the prize winner would get to meet them at a special reception after the concert. The concert was at The Fabulous Fox Theater in Atlanta, one of the most beautiful theaters in the entire country.

My group was escorted to the reception area where a lavish display of finger foods was laid out. The three of them: Tony Batula, Jim Pike, and Bob Engemann spent considerable time with us. We had the required pictures made and they gave me a signed greatest hits album that I still have.

While not in the same one-on-one setting that the other celebs gave me, I did get the chance to shake the hand and have my picture made with my boyhood baseball idol, Eddie Matthews. Eddie was doing an autograph signing session nearby making my opportunity to meet him in person after watching him play on tv more feasible.

Cindy and I went to the signing site and she patiently waited in line with me. As we neared the table where he was set up to do the signings, one thing was clear- the years had taken their toll on his physique. Cindy looked at me and whispered, "That's your hero? He's just a balding, chain-smoking, pot-bellied, middle aged man."

"Yes," I replied. "But he's MY balding, chain-smoking, pot-bellied, middle aged man. It doesn't matter what he looks like now or what he looks like to you. My eyes see the young third baseman who could tear the cover off the ball." She nodded understandingly and we moved closer. The picture of him shaking my hand is one of my most prized possessions.

But the most memorable celebrity I've had the chance to meet in person was, without a doubt, Robin Williams. From his days as Mork from Ork to his great standup routines seen on the Comic Relief specials he did with Billy Crystal and Whoopi Goldberg, he has made this nation laugh. And I've always thought that he was a fabulous dramatic actor as well.

I was in Chicago for a banking convention with my gang and three of the Four R's were there. We had decided to go to a club just outside downtown Chicago called *Chicago City Limits*. The club was a combination comedy club and dance bar. A comedian would come on and do a set and then there would be thirty minutes or so of dance music played by a deejay. When word got out of our plans, several others asked if they could go with us so we wound up with a group of ten or so.

The club was situated in a strip mall and we had been there for about an hour when we saw and heard a commotion going on at the front door. One member of our group went to see what was going on and came back to report that a big limo had pulled up. The door opened at the front of the club and a huge cheer went up. When the crowd dispersed a little, there stood Robin Williams with a lovely escort on each arm.

Stood may not be the proper definition because it was all he could do to stand and stay upright. The girls were great eye candy but I believe their real purpose was to hold him up. It was obvious that he was as high as a kite. I don't know what he was on but whatever it was, it was working very effectively on him. His speech was slurred as he greeted those near him. He tottered as he tried to walk. And his eyes were half-drawn like window shades trying to keep the bright light of the sun out.

He took a few steps inside the club and for some reason he targeted our group and our table. Perhaps, because we had a relatively large table he wanted the attention of some of his adoring fans. Maybe he saw some of the attractive ladies sitting there. Or the best guess is that it was the only one he felt like he could make it to without falling on his face.

As we have come to learn later about Williams' life, this was the period when he was battling substance abuse difficulties. And he was losing those battles on a daily basis. Yet, he was at the top of his game professionally having major success with *Mork and Mindy* and his first feature film, *Popeye.*

He came over to the table and never really asked if he could join us but what were we going to say? Were we going to refuse Robin Williams? Certainly not! R4, always the host of the group, asked him if he could buy him a drink and Robin looked at him like he was an alien at the absurdity of that question. I believe this may have been his first taste of Wild Turkey and water but it could have been motor oil and Williams would have drunk it.

Pleasantries were made around the table and then Robin shouted, "Wait a minute! Wait a minute! I've got a joke for you."

His stand up routines did not usually consist of jokes, per se. He was more known for his ad lib, improvisational characters but, again, when he spoke you listened.

"There was a white guy and a black guy who were best of friends going all the way back to childhood. Both were good at everything they did, but the white guy always seemed to come out just a little bit ahead."

"When they were in Little League, the black kid hit .440, the white kid hit .446. In high school, the black kid was an all-region running back, the white kid was an all-state quarterback. They went to college where the black guy had a 3.8 grade point and the white kid had a 4.0. It was the same in marriage; they got married on the same day. The black guy married Miss New York and the white guy married Miss America."

"They went on joint honeymoons and after checking into their hotel, the guys went to the bar to have a drink. The black guy said to his friend, 'Listen! You've beaten me in everything we have ever done but I know there's one thing that black guys can do better than white guys. I'll bet you a hundred bucks that I can make love to my wife more times tonight than you can.'

"The white guy took the challenge but asked, 'How are we going to know who's made love the most?'

'Simple. Just write the number of times on your bathroom mirror with a piece of soap and we'll compare them in the morning.'

"The two friends finished their cocktails and joined their brides in their respective rooms. The white guy had a wonderful in-room dinner with his bride and then they consummated their marriage by making wild and passionate love. He then went to the bathroom and made a mark on the mirror with the bar of soap. He returned to the bedroom where they made love a second time, again making a mark on the mirror. After a third session, he proudly notched his third mark and feeling confident about himself, drifted off to sleep."

"The next morning, the two pals let their wives sleep while they had breakfast together.

'I know I got you this time!' said the black guy. There is no way you could have outdone my performance.'

'Don't be too certain.' the white guy replied.

'Did you keep score?'

'Yep! Just like we said.'

"They went up to the white guys room and crept into the bathroom so they wouldn't disturb the sleeping wife. The black guy said, 'Damn! I don't believe it! You've beaten me again!'

"The white guy asked, 'By how much?'

" The black guy looked at the mirror and answered, 'One hundred eleven to thirty-eight.' "

Robin was still at the table when the owner came over to him and asked him if he would get on stage and entertain. Let me reiterate that all the time at the table, Williams showed no signs of coherency at all. He appeared, and was, stoned and he had lit up and continued drinking all the time he had spent with us. But he agreed and walked toward the stage literally stumbling as he climbed up the steps.

But the moment he took to that stage and the spotlight hit him and he heard the cheers and applause of the crowd gathered around him, there was a remarkable transformation. He became as coherent and as clear as a pastor in a pulpit. Everything he did that evening from then on was totally ad lib and off the cuff but it was a hysterical performance. He was on a roll and couldn't be stopped. He performed for over an hour and barely took a breath between his impersonations and his characterizations.

When he finally stopped and stepped off the stage, he went right back into his stupor. He stumbled as he walked, held up by his friends on each arm. He made his way to the entrance, turned around to wave to the crowd, and left.

I will never forget the comic genius I saw that night. But I will also never forget the sad look in his eyes as he tried to escape the trials of life through outside means. Robin Williams fought depression all his life and even though he was more successful than any of us can ever hope to be, financially, he didn't have happiness. His death, like those of so many other celebrities who face these problems, have taught me that there is no greater gift in life than the gift of happiness.

Has life had its ups and downs for me? Sure- whose life hasn't? We're not promised anything but I also know that those who wallow in self-pity will never find that elusive butterfly of happiness. You have to make your happiness by making each day just a little bit better than the day before. I try to live by an old adage that I heard many years ago. I wish I knew who the original author was- I'd give them the credit they deserve for coming up with it, but it's just one of those little quotes that can grab your heart and never let go. It says:

You cannot become what you need to be
By remaining what you are

Never stop growing. Never stop learning. Never stop loving. This illness was not going to take anything away from me. I planned to live out whatever days I had remaining before my illness ate away at my body with the same philosophy that the fine coach and even greater motivational speaker, Jim Valvano once gave. "Do three things each day. Laugh. Think. Cry. If you do those things, you'll have a full day. Cancer (and in my case, this mysterious infection inside me) can take away all my physical abilities but it cannot take away my mind, my heart, or my soul. Don't give up. Don't ever give up."

Meeting celebrities is always thrilling but it is even better when you have the chance to be one, even for just a short, insignificant moment. Believe me, it was a very fleeting moment when I took........

CHAPTER 24

MY WALK AS A NEAR CELEBRITY

I spent over thirty years in the banking industry and most of those were spent with one bank. I started working during the summers while I was in college, as I've said before, with Fulton National Bank. In 1979, the bank changed its name to Bank South to incorporate a more regional presence than the identification as a locally owned Atlanta financial institution the old bank had maintained.

After receiving my degree, I became a Management Trainee. These were the employees who were designated to be the new blood of the bank and those who would eventually become officers. Because of my summer experience, I was put on a fast track and my trainee term was shortened considerably.

After finishing my trainee period, I was sent out to work at one of the bank's retail branches. Unless the trainee had a specialty like accounting or marketing, the branch system was where everyone got their start. At the branch you did everything from run a teller window to opening new accounts. Sometimes you even swept the sidewalks and picked up trash around the parking lot. The fine print of your job description read "You will do anything required of you by the branch manager." So, rule #1 in working at a branch, get on the good side of the boss.

I became an assistant branch manager a year later and was elected an officer by the Board of Directors a few months later. Like Methodist ministers, we rotated from branch to branch fairly regularly and it was during one of these assignments that I got my first chance to be a B level celebrity.

I had been assigned to our Luckie Street branch and it was here that I met Mike Thevis, who held the Atlanta nickname of the "Scarface of Porn". In the mid to late 70's, Atlanta had become one of the largest producers and distribution centers for the porn industry, making more films every year than even California. And Thevis' "studio" made more than anyone.

But even porn filmmakers have to have banking relationships and his was with that particular branch. And, as new guy on the block, I inherited his account in my portfolio. Thevis was an imposing figure- not from a size standpoint, but from the way that he controlled a room just by his mere presence. When he sat down at your desk, you stopped everything else you were doing and listened to his every word.

I had been working with him on a loan request. Why he needed a loan, I'm really not sure. I'm absolutely positive that most of his dealings in his business were cash-only basis transactions and that he reported very little of his "income" to the government but, nevertheless, here we were negotiating loan rates and terms.

We were in the final stages of that negotiation and in an effort to get a better interest rate on the loan, he made me an offer that no one before him had ever offered. He told me that if I would lower the rate by just .5%, he would put me in one of his movies. He assured me that no one would ever see my face so I didn't have to worry about my career. He even pulled out pictures of potential "co-stars" for me to select from. I wish I could tell you that if you rent "*Long John Banker*" you could see me in action but I politely turned his offer down.

Throughout my banking career I had the chance to work with a lot of great people. The list of my closest pals from those days is very long but a few who stand out in my mind are: Bill H., Don S., Charlie B., Don P., Chuck B., Bucky K., Charlie C., and Bill G.

I will never forget the lunchtime walks up Peachtree Street with Don P., Chuck, and Bill G. The primary purpose of our walks was not discussing banking practices, bank policies, or regulations. It was to gaze upon the beautiful girls of Atlanta. But as I eulogized at his funeral a few years back, I think that three of us, not bad looking guys ourselves, spent our time watching the girls ogle Bill G.

There was a certain presence Bill had that caught your attention immediately. A strikingly handsome man, he was once called by a fellow female worker, a black Robert Redford. I will never forget Bill's advice to me given during a time when I thought my career wasn't progressing quite as rapidly as I thought it should. He said, "Randy, you've got as good technical skills as any of us. You're one of the best business developers in the whole bank. You're just too laid back. You need more fire in your belly." That phrase has stuck with me and since then I became more outspoken and more confident in myself. If shown in the right way, confidence is a person's most important quality.

Some of the people I worked with over the years were, how do I say this gently, characters. One of the most memorable characters was George in our Recovery Collections Department.

When loans go bad, as they sometimes do, the bank has to repossess the collateral that has been used to secure the loan. The cardinal rule was that you should never make a loan solely on the collateral available but on the customer's ability to repay but "the best laid plans" sometimes go awry and we have to collect our collateral and sell it to, hopefully, receive enough from the sale so that the loan can be paid.

George was the head of the RC, as we called it, and he could be a little eccentric. George was a mid-40's bachelor who lived with his mother and his pet cat. If that was not enough, George hated the color yellow. I told you he was eccentric. He had an unnatural fear of it and chastised you severely if he ever saw you wearing a yellow tie. In fact, if he saw you coming in his direction wearing anything yellow, he would turn and walk the other way.

A group of ten or twelve of us were sent to Birmingham, Alabama on one occasion to pick up some autos from a used car dealership that had gone under. George went along. When we arrived at the lot, we saw that there was one lone VW beetle. It was the brightest canary yellow you had ever seen. All we had to do was look at each other and the game was afoot. On signal, each of us ran as fast as we could to one of the vehicles, jumped in, started the engine, and started driving back to Atlanta. One car was left for George to drive. You guessed it- the yellow VW bug.

The story started circulating the next day about what had happened to George. He had called in from Birmingham that morning telling the secretary that he wouldn't be in until later in the day. He had to wait on the first bus to leave from Birmingham going back to Atlanta. He told her he was not driving that VW back under any circumstances and if it cost him his job, well, so be it. He told her to send someone over to get it. By lunchtime, those of us who had been involved in the prank were having a good laugh and George was somewhere between Birmingham and Atlanta on a Greyhound Bus.

After my Luckie Street experience, I was assigned to the largest branch in our system- the Buckhead branch. Buckhead is one of the most prominent and affluent areas in the city, and it was particularly so in the late 70's. It was here that I got the opportunity to make what has turned out to be the most significant loan I ever made in my career and meet the entrepreneurs who would give me a chance at celebrity a few years later.

Much of a banker's time is spent in locating new business opportunities. The existing book of business you carried in your customer list was important, but you were always looking for more. New business was the lifeblood of growth and that was what the corporate home office was looking for. If you weren't out on the streets calling on prospects, you were back in your office dialing for dollars.

So, when two gentlemen walk into your office with a very formalized strategic business plan on the start up of a new business, in this case a new restaurant, you are taken off your feet. That's what happened when Pano Karatossas and Paul Albrecht were introduced to me by our receptionist.

Pano and Paul had run a restaurant for a resort complex in the Midwest but Pano, who was originally from Savannah, wanted to come back south to open an upscale dining experience in the heart of Buckhead. Pano was the business side of the team and Paul was the classically-trained chef who was the mastermind of the great food they would present.

They had found their location and now just needed some capital for the interior design, marketing, and all of the other necessary aspects of a restaurant. Really important things like tables, chairs, and, oh yeah, food.

The loan was approved and a few months later, one of the best restaurants to ever grace this city, was opened. Pano's & Paul's became the place to experience a fine dining experience. That initial restaurant has grown into the corporate entity called the Buckhead Life Group which consists of nine restaurants in Atlanta with three others in south Florida. The day-to-day operations of the restaurants has been turned over to others but Pano still has his hand in making sure everything is up to standards by visiting the restaurants daily. And he continues to show why he was the best host in town.

Cindy and I had planned to celebrate Valentine's Day at one of his restaurants, The Fish Market, earlier this year. We were waiting, along with many other patrons, at the bar for our table to be ready. Pano walks in and greets and is greeted by several of those "regulars" that he recognizes. He looks across the bar, spots me, and I can tell that even after ten years, he recognizes me.

We do the usual "great to see you" routine and he snaps his fingers and one of the hostesses' hurries over. He tells her, "Get this man a table and his dinner is on me." I told him that wasn't necessary but, and this was what made banking enjoyable, he looked at Cindy and said, "This is the man who put me in business. He made all this possible. It's the least I can do." That one statement made all those years worthwhile because I'd like to think that there are others that we, as bankers, help that feel the same way.

One more branch banking story before I tell you about my other near-celebrity status. After my Buckhead assignment I was promoted to Branch Manager of our Ponce de Leon Plaza office. This particular area of town had gone through a variety of changes over the years and through them all had attained a reputation as an eclectic hybrid of interesting residents. We lovingly referred to that branch located in an area known as Virginia-Highlands as the Granola Branch because the customers that weren't fruits or nuts were flakes.

We had the "parrot lady" who always came into the branch with her pet parrot on her shoulder. The lady would walk up to the teller's window and the parrot would say "Stick em up! This is a hold up!" Always a hilarious thing to hear in a bank. Usually, the parrot would then make a deposit of its own right on the carpet.

But the biggest flake of them all and the most interesting loan request I had in my entire career was by a guy who calmly walked into my office one day and requested a loan, not a handout mind you but a loan, in the amount of $2.25. I was intrigued so I played along.

"And what is the purpose of your loan?" I inquired.

"I need to get my uniform cleaned." he said.

"What type of uniform would that be?"

"Why, my Confederate uniform naturally."

Naturally, I thought to myself.

He continued, "You see, General Lee is coming for inspection tomorrow and I want to look good for him."

I wanted to say 'Wouldn't a white jacket look better?' but I didn't.

I was so tempted to continue this interview by asking him what type of collateral he had to secure the loan but at the same time I wanted to get him out of the bank as quickly as I could. I tried to explain that the bank didn't make loans that small so we wouldn't be able to help him. I even thought about just giving him the money but that just might encourage him to come back some other time so, I politely led him to the door. I was hoping that would be the last of it. No such luck.

The next day we were conducting business as usual when I looked outside and to my surprise saw my Confederate friend picketing the front of the bank with a sign reading This Bank UNFAIR to Rebel Soldiers. He paced back and forth in front of the branch for about an hour. Getting no sympathy from any of the passer bys on the street or any of the customers walking in the branch, he finally left. I hope he wasn't court-martialed for his unkempt uniform.

I spent a little over a year at that branch before getting my biggest break of my career. I was called on to join the bank's Correspondent Banking Department, one of the most prestigious groups in the bank. I was asked to fill a newly created job calling on banks all over the southeastern portion of the US. Its primary goal was to solicit these banks to form an alliance with our bank enabling us to make bigger loans. This would allow us to grow and have a bigger presence in the competitive Atlanta market.

For the next seven years I spent a lot of time in airports travelling to Birmingham, Mobile, New Orleans, Memphis, Nashville, and Jackson, Mississippi as well as smaller southern cities establishing what we called the "Dixie Banking Mafia". Because of these relationships, the bank was able to achieve what it was trying to do and our area was greatly responsible for that success.

While working in that area my phone rang one day and it was Pano. He asked me if I'd like to be an extra in a movie scene that was being shot in his restaurant and I, of course, said sure. Brenda and I got all dressed up and drove to the restaurant. Shooting of the scene wasn't going to begin until about 10: 00 pm but Pano had said come hungry cause we'd get fed that night as well.

Let me tell you about the movie. It turned out to be one of the worst movies ever made. It starred Michael O'Keefe who had brilliantly played the oldest son in *The Great Santini* and later won acclaim as Danny O'Keefe in *Caddyshack* and Rebecca DeMornay, Tom Cruise's hooker friend from *Risky Business*. The movie's title was *The Slugger's Wife*. The plot, what little there was, centered around a baseball player's pursuit at a home run record and the conflict the pursuit of that record was having on his marriage. Real compelling, huh?

Our scene was a simple one. The couple, played by the stars, was having dinner one evening at this swanky restaurant discussing their situation. Brenda and I, along with five or six other couples, were patrons in the backdrop enjoying our meals. The director told us to whisper to each other to make it look like we were talking but absolutely no laughing, coughing, or other sounds were to be made. He said nothing about the gagging that might result from listening to the insipid dialogue that the actors were uttering but I managed to hold that back as well. In spite of the fact that I had had no theatrical training, I figured I was good to go with those instructions. One of the other ladies acting as an extra in the scene actually had the nerve to ask the director if she could move to the other side of the table from her husband because the light was casting a shadow on her face. He shrugged and said, "What the hell do I care."

The entire scene only lasted a few minutes on screen but we were there for over six hours. I lost count on the seventeenth take.

When the movie came out in the theater we were excited to go see it. Here it came- our big chance at stardom.

Needless to say, no movie scouts came busting down our doors after our magnificent portrayal of "couple dining in restaurant." No award nominations came our way even though I had my acceptance speech prepared. We weren't even listed in the credits. If you blink your eyes, you miss the two quick flashes where the camera catches our images. In fact, we're pretty much focus-blurred unrecognizable. Imagine the gall of honing in on DeMornay's face instead of ours. Brenda can be seen fairly clearly in one shot if you look over DeMornay's left shoulder.

So, that was my shot at near celebrity on a big scale. My movie career, like the movie itself, thudded back down to earth. Of course, if I had taken up Thevis' offer, you never know. Maybe that would have opened the door to superstardom.

Fall always goes by so quickly. Between the football games and the preparation for the holiday season, the days of the calendar fall off rapidly. I still had said nothing to Cindy. I was still feeling good so I just didn't see the need in worrying her during this busy time.

I was watching my morning sports show, Mike & Mike on ESPN 2, and the headlines were still being filled with the misbehavior of today's athletes. The current headlines were not for less critical acts like taking steroids or other Performance Enhancing Drugs or signing memorabilia items for money, however. These were far more serious acts like child and spousal abuse and even a case of murder.

I went out for my morning walk and was deep in thought, thinking about these athletes. "What are they thinking?" I asked myself. "They have the whole world in front of them. Their future is filled with positive hopes and dreams. The professional players are making more money than they can spend in five lifetimes and the college players have that same potential. And, yet, they do something stupid and throw it all away." Then I realized that they weren't thinking. They think they're bullet-proof; that nothing can harm them; that they are above the law because they're athletes.

And the sad thing is that, for the most part, they're right. They get themselves into these predicaments and the respective leagues that they play for do nothing more than give them a slap on the wrist. They serve a short suspension of a few games, pay a fine that is a mere pittance to them, and they are right back on the playing field to the cheers of the fans in the stands.

Maybe it's the fans who should take most of the responsibility in these situations. I remember when a baseball player named Ryan Bruan came back from his suspension to play for the Milwaukee Brewers. He had cheated the game by taking illegal substances that he knew were banned; lied to the fans and the media when he said he had never taken anything illegal; and then when he was caught his excuse was that "everyone else in the game was doing it." Yet, the day he came back and his name was announced, the fans stood and cheered him like a hero. I will never understand that mentality.

The ones I am really sorry for are the young people of today. What kind of role models are these athletes being to the kids? They see these people do something wrong with little penalty and they think that will be the same for them.

As I continued my exercise, my internal dialogue continued as well. "I'm glad I never did anything stupid when I was younger. I'm glad that I thought out every action I ever took with a systematic approach concluded by logic and good reasoning."

"Wait a minute!" I remembered. "Maybe I was a stupid kid once or twice. Maybe I acted more on impulse than rational thinking a few times myself and did something that I know now I shouldn't have done. Just a harmless little prank. No harm could come from that, could it? Now, it's a little clearer than when I took..........

CHAPTER 25

MY WALK ON THE WILD SIDE

I think the statute of limitations is up on this so I can confess to breaking some windows in various buildings when I was a young boy. And I can own up to the fact that I pilfered some comic books, or were they Playboy Magazines, from the drug store. But I never even considered anything more serious than that because of the absolute wrath I would receive from my dad if I had ever been caught.

I could never begin to tempt fate like the two little boys who, one morning at breakfast, decided they were old enough to start cussing. When their mother asked them what they wanted that morning the oldest boy said, "I think I'll have me some of them damn Cheerios." His mother grabbed him up from the table, whacked him on the bottom and sent him to his room. She glared at the other boy and asked, "Now, what do you want?" Without hesitation the little boy said, "Well, you can bet your sweet ass it ain't Cheerios."

The three episodes I'll choose to disclose now were more of the mischievous variety. They weren't meant to be mean-spirited or harmful, yet, as I look back on one in particular, I'm surprised the lady involved even speaks to me or the other culprits. What all three had in common was that they were stupid. What were we thinking?

As I mentioned earlier, my senior year I was elected president of the band. That would mean I would be a member of the President's Council. To this day I don't know what our purpose was or even if we met to make any decisions at all, but it looked good on your senior picture resume that appeared in the yearbook to show that you were a member.

I was joining a pretty good group of people so, I was excited about my inclusion. Of course, every club was included so that meant the presidents of such organizations as the Latin Club, Future Homemaker's of America, and the Good Reader's Club were also in the council so maybe it wasn't so prestigious after all.

I was approached one day at school by three guys who I admired who were also members of the council. Don M. played football and was ultimately voted Best All Around in the Senior Superlatives. Tommy F. was the highest ranking officer in our ROTC (Reserve Officers' Training Corps) program and also played football along with being one of the smartest individuals I've ever met. It turned out to be quite fitting for Tom to be the leader of ROTC since he went on to have a very distinguished career in the Air Force. And the third member of this illustrious group was no less than the President of the Student Council and a long-time friend from our early church days, Wayne H.

They told me that as the newest member of the council they wanted to welcome me by inviting me to go grab some burgers that night at Krystal so we could talk about plans for the council. That part turned out to be a big ruse since, as I said before, the council never really did anything.

Now, before I go on with the story, please tell me you know what Krystal hamburgers are. In some parts of the country a similar chain called White Castle, made famous by Harold and Kumar's search, with a similar slice of heaven is served. But here in the South we lay claim to Krystal as being right up there with Krispy Kreme doughnuts in southern supremacy.

Wayne picked us up and during the ride to the nearest Krystal location on Moreland Avenue, the guys told me the real purpose of the evening. I was being included, not because of my affiliation with the President's Council, but because I had been chosen to be a member of an off-campus, unauthorized organization called the Varsity Club and this was the initiation.

The VC had been established years before and the tradition continued into the 70's, I'm told. I guess we could have chosen a better nickname for ourselves in light of what was going on in Southeast Asia but that was how we referred to ourselves. It was an exclusive male only group made up exclusively of lettermen from the various sports. There was a teacher who nominated the names based on athletic and scholastic performance but his identity was an absolute secret and to this day I don't know who he was. He would give the name to a letterman who had already graduated who, in turn, would let the Chairman of the club know the name of the nominee. It was our responsibility to make sure that things went smoothly around the school- to self-discipline any male student who got out of line by having a friendly conversation with them. Kind of a secret police, you might say, without the Gestapo tactics.

The initiation consisted of us performing a "gulp and go" with me being the last individual to leave. This prank also goes under the name of a "dine and dash" but, essentially, it is simply going into a fast food restaurant, ordering a large amount of food, and running out without paying. If I got caught, I would have to pay the entire bill. You couldn't get away with this now because you pay when you order but in the 60's you could actually order, eat, and then pay if you were dining in.

I had to make this work because I only had about $3 in my pocket-just enough to pay for my food. We approached the counter and even though Krystal's were only $.10 each in those days, the three of them ordered enough burgers, along with fries and drinks, to feed a small army; well over the amount I had on me. At least it wasn't like the eating challenge we gave Curtis one night after a basketball game.

We were celebrating a big victory over Dykes High and we challenged the big guy to see how many of the little burgers he could put down. It was sorta like the egg-eating contest from the movie, *Cool Hand Luke.* He gulped down 21 that night along with a large soft drink. We were in awe.

It was my turn to order and after doing the mental math of what the total bill would be if I got caught and realizing it was much more than the $3 I had, I said to myself, "What the heck! If I get caught at least I'll be well fed." and ordered myself a big order.

As we sat there enjoying our food, we made our plans for the dash. One by one the other three would leave and go to the car. On the signal of the flashing headlight, they would drive around to the other side. I would wait 30 seconds and make a run for it. All systems go. Synchronize your watches.

Tom went first. Then Don. Then Wayne. I was there all by myself. I kept waiting for the lights to flash but the car just sat there. The longer I waited, the more I perspired.

I heard a voice from the counter ask, "Where did your buddies go?"

"I guess they all went to the bathroom." I responded meekly.

Finally, a flash of light came through the window. I got up quickly, yelled back "Sorry, Ruby!" and made a dash for the door. I ran to the other side of the building expecting a big guy with a meat cleaver to come after me at any minute. The car was not there.

I was frantic. Do I make a run for it? Do I go back in and take my punishment? I peeked around the corner and much to my surprise, the guys were still there, sitting calmly in the car laughing their heads off. I raced up to the car, yanked the back door open and screamed, "C'mon, let's get outta here!"

"What's the rush?" Don asked.

"Are you kidding me, you idiots? Let's go! I don't have enough money to pay for all that food!" I pleaded.

"Relax." Tom replied. "I took care of it on my way out. That's part of the initiation; to see if you are willing to do what the club needs and, buddy, you passed with flying colors."

"You mean it was all a set up?" I asked.

"That's right." Wayne chimed in. "We've all had the same thing done to us in different ways. It's why we always have three of us involved so the last two can distract you while the first guy pays for it. By the way, the newest guy has to pay next time so save up your money- it's your turn."

A few months later I gladly paid when we admitted Jerry O. into the VC.

My second walk on the wild side also had club overtones. At Murphy, there were two predominant civic organizations. One was the Junior Civitan Club, which was co-ed and the second was a male only club called the Key Club. The Key Club was affiliated with the Kiwanis Club and we teamed up with the local adult chapter for most of our projects but we also did some on our own.

I had been nominated to join Key Club as a junior and since that was the club where all my closest buddies were, I readily accepted my nomination. Had I known about the initiation, I might have declined.

East Lake Park was the site of our cookout/initiation. It started out innocently enough with us grilling some burgers and hot dogs.

Some of the moms had made some potato salad and desserts for us and there was some genial goofing around while we ate. Then the fun began.

As I recall, there were four other inductees that night, Archie W., Jamie M., Tommy M., and Perry D. and we were called on to stand up and face the other members. I thought we'd probably have to recite a few things, pledge our loyalty to the club, and that would be it. We did have to go through those rituals but then I understood why we were told to wear old clothes.

Each one of us had a member assigned to us and as we stood there, quietly and unflinchingly, the member, and mine was Dick M., began the torture by cracking about a half dozen eggs over our heads. Then, they poured honey over us and I can still feel the gooey substance trickling down my back. If you think honey in your butt crack is a good thing, then you're just a pervert.

Now that it had something to cling to, a 5 pound sack of flour was thrown at us. By this time you could not see a thing so you couldn't really tell what was coming anyway. Then, so that we could all feel like Dairy Queen sundaes, chocolate syrup and whipped crème were added to the concoction. The final phase was a walk across the street where all the members were gathered on the top of a big hill. At the bottom of the hill was an ice cold, especially in October when this took place, spring-fed lake. We were instructed to get on our hands and knees before several members each grabbed our arms and legs and threw us down the hill. We couldn't have stopped our momentum even if we had tried so the ultimate result was that we splashed into the icy cold water which made all the other stuff cling to us even more.

Shivering and miserable from the combination of sticky substances all over me, I wondered if this was worth it. But getting the handshakes, the smiles, and welcome from the guys dispelled those thoughts immediately. It's always a great feeling to be included in something special and these guys were that to me. I was now one of them- "the mischievous trumpeter who knew all the tunes" as my senior picture described me, was now a Key Clubber. I couldn't wait for next year so I could be on the other end of the initiation.

The JC's (Junior Civitans) and us had a rivalry as to which club could win the most honors, raise the most money, or have the best service project of the year. But our real competition came with our efforts to disrupt each others' meetings. We had kept the date and time of the initiation quiet so that they wouldn't try anything that night. They didn't keep their next meeting quiet so, we were ready to wreak havoc on them.

We got word that they were holding a meeting at Alice's house so we went to the grocery store and loaded up on eggs. We drove our caravan consisting of about six cars with three to four guys in each car and parked a few blocks away so that we could sneak up on the house. We made a pact that only the cars would be egged since we all liked Alice so much that we didn't want her to get into trouble if her house was egged.

The attack began and we had made a successful salvo on many of the cars before anyone inside even knew what was going on. When the doors flew open, we scattered and made our way back to the car. For some reason, I turned and hurled one more egg and caught Jonnie P. right between the eyes. But right before the egg hit, he yelled, "I see ya, Blalock! I can guess who the others are but I see ya!"

A little known fact about eggs on cars is that if you don't wash them off immediately and the sun gets to them, they can chip paint off of a car. Jonnie, apparently, did not check the surface of his little VW well enough because the next day, which turned out to be a bright, sunny day, did just that. His blue car now had little polka dot spots of yellow on its roof. He also had not looked into the back seat to see several well-thrown broken eggs back there either. The heat got to them as well the next day and the aroma could not have been pleasant.

Now, I have no idea if I had been the one to hit his car or to find his open windows, but being the only one he had seen and recognized, he blamed me for the damage for quite awhile. He even made a comment about it when he signed my annual the following year. He said, "I held a grudge for quite some time when you egged my car but I am over it now." I am certainly glad he forgave me because Jonnie, or Judge Jon P. as he would later become, could have caused me a lot of problems if I had ever appeared before him in his courtroom.

My last walk on the wild side is definitely the one I regret the most. This will be the section where you female readers will become truly disgusted with me. But, ladies, I was not alone and remember- we were stupid. I am just the only one willing to write about it. As I said, why the young lady who was involved ever speaks to any of us is a mystery to me.

East Lake Park was not only the location where we gathered for cookouts and other club activities, it was the make out spot we would head to on date nights. I was dating Cathy regularly during our senior year and Lloyd was dating Renee G. on a steady basis. The other guys were still playing the field.

I cannot remember who came up with the plan but I do remember that all five of us thought it was a great idea and one that would be absolutely hilarious. Wrong on all counts.

The plan was that the other four would cover our faces and sneak up on Lloyd and Renee while in their car occupied in lip locks, pull Lloyd out of the car, and proceed to fake beat the crap out of him. We rehearsed our fight scene down to the last punch. We orchestrated each blow with sound effects and dramatic emphasis. Stop groaning, ladies. That ain't the worst part. Floyd, who had a starter's pistol that, of course, fired blanks, suggested we even fake shoot Lloyd. Won't that be a trip! All right, now you can really groan.

The big night came. The four of us skulked down the hill to where Lloyd's car was parked. On signal, we ran to the car and started beating on it yelling for him to get out. Renee, bless her heart, was terrified. We yelled at him saying that we were from a rival school and we meant to beat him up. Lloyd, never afraid to mix it up even though it was mostly with his brother, got out of the car and with all the bravado he could muster shouted back at us to bring it on. We pored in and started raining fake punches at his body and face.

I, along with the other three, was so wrapped up in our production that we couldn't see the shocked and terrified look on Renee's face. The final scene was supposed to act out like this. Lloyd was going to get in a good punch on Floyd who, while on the ground, would pull out the pistol and fire at Lloyd. We would then pull off our masks, which were hose that we had stolen from our respective mom's dressers, and laugh and say "Surprise!" The best laid plans of stupid kids oft go awry.

When the gun went off, Renee, who now must have feared for her life, ran screaming from the car across the open fields of the park. She lived only a few blocks from the park and she was trying to get home to call for help. While the five of us stood there laughing hysterically, Renee was sprinting toward home.

When realization hit us, we charged after her yelling her name. Renee, seeing five crazed maniacs running after her, now surmised that she was going to get raped or shot herself so she ran even faster. Being the fastest, I got to her first and literally tackled her to the ground. Like the moron I was, I still had the hose pulled down over my head so that even though I was telling her who it was, she was fighting, clawing, and scratching with everything she had. And she had plenty, let me tell you.

After a few seconds of being brutally beaten by this firecracker, the other guys got there. It took all five of us to pin her down and calm her down enough for her to recognize who we were. When she finally composed and gathered herself enough, she simply got off the ground, brushed the grass off her dress, turned around and walked straight home. Lloyd pleaded with her but she was having none of his apologies. I think it was about a month before she agreed to go out with Lloyd again but I can assure you they never went to East Lake Park after a date again.

So, as I think back about these three episodes, I don't guess I should ever ridicule anyone for their own stupid actions. All of mine were, in my mind, harmless at the time but each of them could have had some serious repercussions. Thank God my dad never found out about any of them.

Thanksgiving was now approaching and I was scheduled for a follow up visit with Dr. Joe during the week after the holiday. But to prepare for that appointment, I had to go to the hospital on the Monday before to have some blood work done. Dr. Joe wanted to see if my white blood cell count had deteriorated more to determine if any additional medicines or treatments were necessary.

I'm not sure that any of us like hospitals but during this period in my life, I had come to really dislike them. Entering the doors always brought me back to the reality of what was going on with me. I tried to escape from it and, for the most part, had been successful in not dwelling on the finality of what might happen but the sights and sounds of the place always reminded me of the prospects of my illness.

There were four times in my life when a hospital brought joy, however. Those four are named Brian, Jessica, Brendan, and Patrick- my son, daughter, and my two grandsons. Thinking of them reminded me of...........

CHAPTER 26

MY WALKS TO THE HOSPITAL

I guess I have more of my dad's characteristics than I'd like to admit because when Brenda and I got married, we decided, much like my mom and dad had, that we would not start a family until (a) we finished school and got our degrees and (b) had enough money to put a down payment on a house and move out of the apartment we called our first home. I was still working part-time for the bank and knew that I would stay with them after I obtained my degree, but I would only be making about $15,000 a year and it took a long time to save up enough to even consider looking for a house.

We would travel around the suburbs on weekends looking for potential places to live. We thought we'd have to look for a resale but on one of our excursions we came across a nice little 3-bedroom with a full basement and a spacious back yard that was in the final stages of completion. We pulled into the driveway and were greeted by the son of the builder who was there doing some trim-out work in the kitchen. As soon as he told me his name, I realized that I had actually gone to school with him the one year I went to Southwest DeKalb. We introduced ourselves and he remembered me as well.

To give you the Reader's Digest version, we bought the house for the whopping sum of $32,500 and moved in to Hanarry Estates subdivision in Gwinnett County during February, 1972. One of the first purchases I made was a pool table for the basement. Brenda was in charge of the practical things like linens for the new beds, dining room furniture, etc. Her mom and dad bought us a new piano for the living room since Brenda, being an accomplished pianist, had missed not being able to play while we were in the apartment. We were all set for suburbia.

During the month of October, 1972, I received two phone calls that changed my life. The first was made by the gentleman who was in charge of the branches for the bank. He was a gruff and rather severe man who could be very intimidating. I had been made the assistant branch manager of one of our locations in Decatur and when the phone rang and the secretary told me it was Mr. Johnson, my throat went dry and my hands began to shake. "Oh, Lord!" I thought. "What have I done?" I picked up the phone and in the best professional voice I could muster said, "Yes, Mr. Johnson, what can I do for you today?"

Without a moment's hesitation he said, "Well, for one thing you can tell me why you're signing your letters wrong!"

"I don't understand." I stammered. "What do you mean I'm signing my letters wrong?"

"Son, do you take me for a fool? How are you signing them now?" he asked.

"I sign them with my name, sir."

"And what title do you put under your name?" he continued.

I was terrified now and thought that he would fire me at any moment for what was, apparently, a non-forgiving, grievous indiscretion. "Sir, I don't really have a title other than assistant branch manager. Is that what you mean?"

"Damn right, that's what I mean!" and I could hear the beginning traces of a little chuckle in his voice. "You're signing them wrong because today the Board of Directors elected you to be an officer of the bank. Congratulations, Randy. You are now an Assistant Vice President!"

I sat there stunned, not knowing what to say but relieved that I still had a job. Breathing a huge sigh of relief I said, "Thanks, Mr. Johnson. I am very excited."

"AVP's get to call me Bob. Keep up the good work and, speaking of that, get back to it. Somebody will be in touch with you soon to talk to you about the press release and your new business cards."

I immediately dialed Brenda at her workplace to share the good news. She was equally elated and we decided to go out and treat ourselves to a celebration dinner that night. My excitement got dampened a little by my next phone call. I called my parents.

Dad picked up and after sharing the news with him, he said, "Well, aren't you just the big shot now? You've always been a little too big for your britches but now you'll have an excuse, I guess." Leave it to him to take the air out of my sails.

The second phone call happened just a few days later. Brenda initiated it and it was even more exciting than the first. I was pulling some late hours preparing a loan presentation. I was all alone in the branch and it was dark outside when the ring of the phone startled me out of my study of some financial statements.

Knowing it had to be Brenda checking on me I answered, "Hey, hon! Should be home soon."

Her reply was "Hey, Daddy!"

I misheard her and said, "Hey, baby yourself."

"No." she corrected me. "I said hey, Daddy!"

In that instant I put two and two together and actually came up with the right number. "You mean?"

"That's right, Daddy. After what Mr. Johnson did to you last week I wanted to make sure you knew your new name. I got the results today from the doctor. We're due early June."

The rest of the conversation was filled with the usual questions and when I hung up the phone, the numbers I had been staring at had no meaning at all so I closed up the branch and raced home. Brenda's parents were ecstatic and her dad even started talking about what sports the boy would play. We told him that we didn't know, of course, what the gender was but he was sure it was a boy. "I've got two beautiful girls but God likes to even things out so I know it's a boy." he explained.

My mom was jumping for joy with the prospects of a potential little girl and, for once, Dad didn't ruin the news and actually seemed happy at the idea of being a PaPaw.

I received some additional good news early in 1973 when it was announced that Elvis (no last name needed) would be coming to Atlanta to perform a series of concerts in late June at the Omni. Now, there are much bigger fans of Elvis than me, I'm sure, but the prospects of seeing him in person were too much to pass up. After all, how many of his fans could list, in order, his movies? There was just one problem- the birth of our first child was expected in June so how would we work this out?

Brenda's original due date was June 5th and the concerts were scheduled for Thursday, June 21, with two more following on the succeeding days. We figured that we would have had the baby by the 21st and she'd be feeling good enough for her to get out for the first time. Her mom could keep the baby and we could enjoy his concert together. We sent in the order form and a week or so later the two tickets arrived. Now, it was just up to the baby to co-operate. It didn't.

The first few days of June came and went with no baby nor even any signs of its eminent arrival. My birthday (June 9th) passed and no baby. Another week went by. No baby. June 19th came and went. No baby. Then, early on the morning of Wednesday, June 20th, Brenda woke me and said she was having contractions. We called her doctor who told us to come in.

During the ride to the doctor's office we listened to the radio in an attempt to fill the silence and to take our minds off all the things we'd be responsible for now as parents. For Brenda, it was more an effort to take her mind off the pains that would hit her every 4-5 minutes. *Kodachrome* by Paul Simon was the #1 song at the time and we talked about all the pictures we would take. Brenda had just read *Jonathan Livingston Seagull,* which was on the Best Seller's list and we talked about vacations at the beach we would take. Anything to occupy our minds.

After examining Brenda, the doctor said that it would be soon but it was too soon to send her to the hospital. Just go back home, he said, and wait until the contractions got even closer and call him again. Living in Gwinnett County as we did, we were about 40 miles from the hospital so I suggested that we first go to my parents' house, my boyhood home, which was only 5 miles away to see what would happen over the next few hours. Of course, this meant spending the day with my father but Brenda could also see the logic in being closer so she was a big sport and agreed.

When we got to the house we told Dad what was going on and for the next few hours we stared at each other. The two men, not knowing what to do, and poor Brenda having to put up with our lame attempts in keeping her comfortable. Around 2:00 pm she had had enough and demanded that we go home in spite of the circumstances.

The next few hours were more of the same. Waiting. Waiting. Waiting. Then, about 9: 30 when the pains became much more intense and much more regular we knew the wait was over. We knew that this was definitely it so we called the doctor once again who told us to meet him at the hospital. Before leaving, we called Brenda's parents who said they'd meet us there as well.

Brenda and I still had no idea if it was a girl or a boy. This was years before sonograms came into practice so we were as in the dark as anyone. We had not officially decided on names but were leaning towards Brian Jeffrey for a boy and Stephanie Lynn for a girl. The name "Brian" had come from a recent popular movie called *Brian's Song,* the story of the relationship between two football players named Brian Piccolo and the great Hall of Fame running back, Gayle Sayers. If you believe in fate and destiny then you won't be surprised when I tell you that the song playing on the radio as we pulled into the hospital parking deck was the theme to that same movie. I knew right then that we were having a boy and that his name would be Brian.

As I filled out the massive amount of forms to check us in, a nurse came and took Brenda to the maternity ward and told me I could find her in the labor room. On my way there, I ran into her parents and brought them up to speed with what was going on. I think her dad was every bit as nervous as I was but now that my own daughter has given birth to two children, I know what he was experiencing as a potential grandparent.

I learned a valuable lesson as I sat or stood next to the gurney Brenda was on holding her hand. Do not wear rings on any of your fingers. Trying to comfort her through the painful contractions became almost as painful for me. With each contraction Brenda would squeeze my hand so tightly that the rings, my college ring on one hand and my wedding ring on the other, actually cut through the skin on my fingers. I know what you ladies are saying. "Poor baby. We feel so bad for you going through all that nasty pain." Ease off, ladies. You know us guys are wimps.

Brenda had decided to be sedated through the delivery process so when they came to give her the medicine to put her to sleep, I had to leave. I was not allowed in the delivery room nor did I want to be. I had barely made it through the films we had to watch. N.T. and Janelle were there waiting on me. Janelle told me she had called my mother and I said a little private prayer that the phone call, since it was now past midnight, had not woken up my dad. That would not have made for a pleasant scene.

While Dad had shown some excitement about the arrival of his new grandchild, he would not have wanted his sleep disturbed for any reason. Luckily, I was born in the afternoon but, nonetheless, he was not at the hospital when I finally arrived. On that day, he had taken mom to Crawford Long Hospital and had waited with her for a couple of hours. But when I was slow in arriving he told her he was going to work because he had already lost several hours.

There were several other fathers waiting along with me and one by one their names were called until I was the only one left. But about 1:45 am on Thursday, June 21, 1973, a nurse came and told me we had a boy. The three of us hugged and the nurse took me to the recovery room where Brenda had been taken. Her doctor was there checking on her. We shook hands heartily and he shared with me the fact that Brenda had said some very unkind things about me during delivery. He said, "I thought you had parents but from what she called you she must have the opinion that you were born out of wedlock. And I hate to be the one to tell you, but I don't think you're ever having sex again."

I held Brian Jeffrey Blalock for the first time about 3 am and it was a sensation I will never forget. Words can't express it. Tears don't explain it. Emotions won't define it.

Brenda finally came out of her fog and we shared the joy together. She was taken to her room and after I helped with his first bottle she told me to go home and get some fresh clothes on. I think her exact words were, "You stink!" I obeyed like any dutiful husband would.

I got back to the hospital early that afternoon with my arms full of the obligatory daddy gifts for the two of them- mom and baby boy. There were balloons, a stuffed animal (a Georgia bulldog, of course), flowers for her, and candy (mostly for me). We shared in the multiple feeding duties all afternoon. We laughed and we cried over this new joy in our lives.

Brenda had come through the delivery and recovery in good shape. She was feeling great, her words, and so, when the clock on the wall struck 6: 00 pm she looked at me and said, "You want to go to that concert, don't you?"

Honestly, I can't say that I had totally forgotten about the two tickets to the Elvis concert that would start in a few hours since they were in my coat pocket. But my real intent was to give them away or try to sell them. I had no thought of going myself. But, ladies, give me a break. It was her idea. I had her permission.

"Are you sure you wouldn't mind?" I asked meekly.

"No, go on. There's nothing else you can do tonight. The nurses won't let me bathe him yet and I can handle the feeding myself. All he's doing is sleeping and you've seen him do plenty of that. Go on. Have fun."

I hesitated awhile longer- the angel on one shoulder and the devil on the other pulling me in both directions. The angel was about to win until Brenda said, "Maybe he'll sing *Blue Hawaii*." She had tempted me with my favorite Elvis song. I asked her one more time if she really minded and when she assured me she didn't, I kissed her, got my car, and drove to the Omni.

That's how I came to be in the audience that night with an empty seat next to me. I passed out cigars to all the guys around me and got evil looks from all the women. I didn't care because the only vote that mattered was Brenda's. Maybe she really wanted me to stay with her that night but, to this day, I don't think so. I think she really wanted me to make this day extra special, if it could be more special than it already was. And to top it all off, Brenda was right. When the first notes went up and he sang, "Night and you and Blue Hawaii" I knew what I needed to do. I drove back to the hospital that night after Elvis had left the building, opened the door to her room, kissed her on the forehead so I wouldn't wake her, and laid the Elvis scarf I had bought her at the souvenir stand on her chest so it would be the first thing she saw when she woke up.

The arrival of our daughter, Jessica, and my walk to the hospital was no less exciting three years later.

Actually, there was another trip to the hospital even before that one. A few days after his second birthday, we had to rush Brian to the hospital with a broken leg. We had gotten him one of those cheap plastic wading pools for his birthday. He was playing in it one afternoon under Brenda's supervision but the slippery surface caused his leg to slide out from under him. He hyper-extended his leg and that caused a spiral fracture of his left leg.

He was laid up in a cast the entire summer that year but I do believe his incapacitation provided one big benefit. All the little guy could do was lie on the sofa and watch tv- but the main show he wanted to watch was <u>Sesame Street.</u> By the end of the summer, he had seen every episode so even at the age of 2, he knew his alphabet, could count to 100, and was doing some light reading. Oh, and he could sing the entire *Rubber Ducky* song by heart.

After our experience with our first child being a late baby, we were convinced that the second would arrive more on schedule. Brenda's due date was set at, ironically, June 21. Since that was Brian's birth date we wanted a day or two leverage one way or the other, so they wouldn't have to share their special day, but we had no idea the leverage we would get would be so dramatic.

As before, her due date came and went with no baby in sight. 1976 was this nation's Bicentennial year so the entire country was celebrating on July 4th of that year. Wouldn't it be great if the baby came that day we thought? It didn't. I have wonderful home movies of Brenda pulling 3 year-old Brian sitting in a little red wagon decorated in red, white, and blue ribbon in the neighborhood parade.

We had tried all the old wives' tales to hasten the birth to no avail. None of the special drinks or diets, riding over railroad tracks, or any other suggestion had proven successful and now it was July 16th, almost a full month after her original due date.

On her weekly visit the week before, the doctor that had seen Brenda had told her to come the following week prepared to go straight to the hospital where they would induce labor. Great, we thought. We can make arrangements for Gran to keep Brian, I can take the day off from work, and we can leisurely drive to the doctor's office which was located conveniently across the street from the hospital.

We arrived at the office, suitcase in hand, and waited for her name to be called. Brenda's OBGYN was a group of doctors, not just one so, the doctor who examined her this week was not the same one who had seen her the previous week. When she came out crying, I knew something was wrong.

This doctor did not have the same opinion as the other. He did not feel that inducement was warranted so he sent her home. I will admit, I was furious. How could they do that? Didn't they know what we had already been through with the prolonged anticipation we had already gone through? That anger obviously transferred to Brenda and mixed with her disappointment and frustration created a bubbling cauldron of emotion.

I am absolutely certain that Brenda self-induced herself that day because just as Johnny Carson was finishing his monologue, Brenda woke me up where I had fallen asleep on the sofa and said, "Let's go!"

We made it just in time. We pulled up to the emergency ramp at 12: 30 am and Jessica Lynn Blalock, all 9.5 pounds of her, was born a little after 1 am on Saturday, July 17, 1976.

I have witnessed these two grow into adults that any father would be proud to call his. Brian is a 4th grade teacher in Gwinnett County. I know I am prejudiced but he is excellent in what he does. The reason is that he cares for his students. It took him a little while to find his career but when he did, he found the right one. And Jessica became a nurse specializing in neo-natal care. After being a practicing nurse for several years she is now in the administrative side of nursing but her heart is where it should be- with the children.

Brenda and I divorced when they were 13 and 10 respectively. I was not there with them day-to-day after that and there will always be a part of me that regrets that. But I never shirked my responsibilities, financially or otherwise, and I think they know that. Unlike my dad with me, I have always tried to let them know that I love them. I tell them often.

They both have many of my personality traits- some good, some bad. Brian doesn't like to be told that he looks a lot like me. But he does. One thing that he and I definitely have in common is a love of North Carolina basketball. And Jessica is organized and punctual to a fault- just like her old man but she hates it when I get on one of my soapboxes and start pontificating. But more importantly, they are their own free-thinking, free-willed people. Our politics, religion, and priority-choices don't always match but if they were puppets of me, they wouldn't be Brian and Jessica. I can't bear the thought of being separated from them.

Cindy and I have made two more trips to the hospital. One for the birth of Brendan and one for Patrick, our two grandsons. Jessica was the absolute opposite of her mother in her pregnancies. While Brenda was late on both occasions, Jessica was 2-3 weeks early.

I was holding out hope that Brendan would be born on my birthday so that he and I could share the same birth date just like his mom had been able to share her birth date with her grandfather, Brenda's dad. But, alas, June 9th came and went with no Brendan. We got the call from Jessica's husband the following day that her water had broken and they were going to the hospital.

Cindy scurried home from work and we drove to the Athens hospital where Jessica would be.

We got to the hospital and sat. And sat. And sat. And sat some more. Brenda would come out to the sitting area from time to time with reports but the main news was that the baby was not ready to appear quite yet. Finally, some 20 hours after going into labor, Brendan was born on June 11, 2005. He is now a sweet, 9 year-old marvel who can tell you the nickname of every major college team in the country as well as being his class leader.

Patrick almost shared his birth date with his mom and great-grandfather but was born two days later on July, 19, 2009. There were a few minor complications with Patrick that concerned us for a few days. Being born a few weeks too soon, he had liquid in his lungs that made it hard for him to breathe so he was under pretty close watch causing him to have to stay in the hospital for about a week longer than mom and dad liked. But like his brother, he is now a robust 5 year-old who absolutely adores his CiCi. That's his name for Cindy, who dotes on both of them like any grandmother would. I love my two boys dearly and they love their Pops.

When we are young and thinking about our future, I don't think that many of us fantasize what being a grandparent will be like. We think about getting married, having children of our own, what our careers might be, and the places we'd like to visit one day but we don't consider the great joys surrounding being a grandparent. I know I didn't. That's just too far down the road. I see pictures of my high school friends holding their grandchildren and I ask, "who are those older people holding those babies?"

But now that I have two grandsons of my own, I can tell you that there is no sweeter sound in the world than hearing them say my name. Pops. I can't be a Pops. I'm still that young kid shooting hoops or shagging fly balls. At worse, I'm that guy in the office putting together loan packages. But Pops I am and there's nothing like it in the world.

Then, about seven years ago, Cindy and I were blessed to have two others added to our grandparental list. Hannah and Spencer Smith adopted us as grandparents and we could not ask for two better children/young people to have calling us Pops and CiCi.

Hannah was in the third grade, as I recall, and Grandparent's Day was coming up at her school. Since her paternal and maternal grandparents' lived out of town, she approached me one day at church and invited me to come to her class that day and be her adopted granddad. With watery eyes I accepted and they have called us Pops and CiCi ever since. Later, I was Hannah's Confirmation Mentor and I was honored to be a part of that time in her life.

They are both great students, competitive swimmers, and two of the most polite and considerate individuals I've ever known. Some of that comes from their Perfectly Polished training but most of it is because of the parenting skills of Steven and Kim. There is never a time when they see us that they don't give us big hug. Hannah is now in the 10th grade and she is becoming a beautiful young lady and Spencer is, well, he's my buddy. We'll be seeing him swim in the Olympics one day if he keeps improving at the rate he is going. Let me tell you a little story about how big his heart is.

My birthday in 2014 fell on a Monday. Sunday afternoon the phone rang and it was Spence. "Pops, would you take me out tomorrow and play some baseball with me? We can just play catch and hit a few flies and grounders. I need the practice." There was just one problem with that statement- Spence doesn't play organized baseball, but he knew that would be something I would like to do on my birthday. It was his way of giving me one of my best presents last year.

I felt literally drained coming out of the hospital. They had drawn enough blood to fuel Red Cross needs for a month it seemed. I tried to focus on the feast that awaited the family on

Thursday. One thing had not disappeared during my illness and that was my appetite. I could still put my groceries away and I certainly meant to do some damage Thanksgiving Day.

Cindy gets her cooking ability from her mother and along with all the great food, there would be someone new at the table to be thankful for this Thanksgiving. As I mentioned earlier, my nephew Chase and his beautiful wife, Ashley, had had a baby girl the previous April. Ella Mae, who had already stolen my heart, would be joining us for her first Thanksgiving.

The only thing to do after that was wait for.......

CHAPTER 27

MY WALK TO DISCOVERY (PART 3)

It was the Tuesday of the week after Thanksgiving and I sat in Dr. Joe's waiting area listening for my name to be called. I had experienced several sleepless nights leading up to this visit. Many prayers had been lifted. I knew I couldn't do anything about the results I would be receiving in a few minutes but I could ask for strength in handling whatever I would hear. And, mostly, I prayed for courage to tell Cindy. I could no longer keep her in the dark about this. She deserved to know and I needed her to help me through the trials I would be experiencing if Dr. Joe told me my illness was getting worse.

I had not shared my illness information with anyone, not even my pastor from the church, or any of my old high school or banking buddies that I kept in touch with. A few comments in passing had been made to me regarding some weight loss I had experienced, but I shrugged those off giving credit to an increased exercise and diet regimen. I was actually being truthful with that since Dr. Joe had disclosed to me during one of my earlier visits that, on top of everything else, I had become a Type 2 diabetic. Upon discovering this bit of news I had told him, in one of my dark humor moods, "I've always said, if there are no Snickers or ice cream in heaven, I'm not sure I really want to go."

I had brought my lap top with me so I could do some research and make some notes for my annual Christmas Eve Candlelighting message I'd be giving at our church. This would be the tenth year I would have the honor of doing this and I wanted to make this one a special message since I would be delivering the message at all three services that night and because I also faced the sobering fact that it might be the last time I would get to do this.

There is no service during the year that moves me as much as that 11: 00 pm Christmas Eve service. It is our tradition that we sing *Silent Night* in a darkened sanctuary as we light our candles and on the last verse of the hymn, the congregation holds their candles high in the air. Believe me, there is no more meaningful sight in the world than viewing several hundred candles held aloft to glorify the birth of Our Savior. Then, there is an extra special feeling you get as you walk out of the church and it is the first moments of Christmas morning. I have experienced a lot of wonderful moments in my life but few compare to that feeling.

I also, from time to time, fill in for our pastor on Sunday mornings presiding over the morning services. I do this because of one man, Don W.

Don approached me one Sunday morning about twelve years ago asking me to consider being the Lay Speaker on Laity Sunday. One week in October in the United Methodist Church, lay people take over all the regular assignments of the pastor and his staff and Don, as Lay Leader of the church, thought I would be a good candidate for the lead speaker that year. I had been teaching an adult Sunday School class for several years but I had never considered for one moment ever standing in the pulpit to preach. Years later, I still don't consider what I do preaching or giving a sermon. I'm nowhere near qualified to do that. I simply deliver a message.

After that wonderful experience, me and the Lord took it a step forward and I took classes and became a Certified Lay Speaker. This designation allows me to fill in at other churches in our district and I have done this on many occasions. To stand in a pulpit and speak before hundreds of people is certainly a distinct change from the scared creature I used to be, a person who was terrified to speak in front of people.

The number one fear that most people have is speaking in public and I certainly had that fear as a child and most of my adult life. I would do anything to keep from standing in front of the class and give a presentation. I'd slink down low in my seat and try and hide behind the person in front of me. I'd avert my eyes and not make eye contact with the teacher. I'd even take on more difficult assignments like lengthy papers to keep from speaking.

This fear extended into my banking career, too. When it was time for me to make a loan presentation before the senior officers of the bank so that it could get approved, I would get physically sick the night before with stress and worry. I couldn't wait for that ordeal to be over and on those Fridays when I had been successful enough in persuading the Loan Committee to approve the loan, the rest of the day was a breeze.

I guess the main reason I always feared these meetings was because you made your presentation in front of your peers and you didn't want to look like a bumbling fool in front of them. Of course, the primary people you wanted to impress were the three significant voters of the committee: Frank B., President of the Bank; Arnold J., Senior Credit Officer; and Bill H., Executive VP of Commercial Lending. Monday through Thursday these men were close friends and lunch companions. Friday mornings they could cut you to the quick with their questions and if you were not prepared, well, heaven forbid.

I don't have Cindy's skill of thinking on my feet quickly and saying what needs to be said in a tactful, yet decisive, manner. When I let my mouth start talking before my brain has had a chance to filter my words, I get in trouble. But there was one day in Loan Committee when I out did myself.

In my job in Correspondent Banking I travelled around the Southeastern part of the country calling on banks, working with them in getting loans to larger companies made that were too large for them to fund by themselves. One such situation occurred when we were called in to assist a bank in Jacksonville, Florida in making a large loan to one of their better clients- a large auto hauling company headquartered there. These are the trucks you see up and down the highways with several vehicles attached in double-deck fashion transporting these vehicles to automobile dealerships.

Our President, a man I had known since my first days with the bank, chaired the committee and one of his absolute no-no's, for some reason, was companies that used acronyms as names. He hated them and if you presented a loan for a company using an acronym, it usually didn't have much of a chance in getting approved. The name of the company I was presenting this particular morning was, I kid you not as Jack Paar used to say, S.H.A.F.T.

I was scheduled to make my presentation that morning but before it was my turn, one of the other loan officers made a presentation that got ripped to shreds. He was just not as prepared as he should have been and the committee declined the loan as the officer slunk back to his seat. Frank and the rest of the men were now in very bad moods. The committee secretary called my name and I knew I was dead meat once I uttered the name of the company.

What was I going to do? I was nervous enough without this additional stress. Could I endure this humiliation I was about to experience? The owner of the company I was presenting was named Shaffer so, in the most shiningly brilliant moment I ever had as a banker, I said….

"Frank, I know how you hate acronyms so let me tell you right off that the name of the company I'd like to present this morning is an acronym for simplicity sake only because it would cost too much money to paint <u>S</u>haffer <u>H</u>auling <u>A</u>nd <u>F</u>reight <u>T</u>ransfer on all their trucks." Frank looked at the other two men and began laughing as hard as I had ever seen him laugh. Of course, when Caesar laughs, everyone laughs and the room was now filled with that beautiful sound. It eased my nerves and I was able, once the laughter died down, to complete my presentation. I can now tell the truth. I have no idea what those letters stood for. I totally made the name up. By the way, the loan got approved.

Over the years, my terrifying fear of speaking in public has lessened and I am now able to proudly deliver these spiritual messages as well as make talks in front of youth groups without too much difficulty. I realize that it was God's hand in this because He had a job for me to do. My main goal each time I stand before a congregation is to give Him the glory and to give back to Him just a small portion of all that He has blessed me with. It's the very least I can do.

While I cannot say that I have totally conquered my fear of speaking in public, it has diminished somewhat over the years. I cannot say the same for my fear of snakes and dentists. I had always been told that the way to defeat your fear of public speaking is to force yourself to do it. Eventually, they said, your fear would go away. Using this same logic, defeating your fear of snakes would be equivalent to jumping into a pit of them like Indiana Jones did or getting over your fear of dentists would just mean you have all the painful dental work you can so it becomes more natural and, therefore, less scary. Ain't gonna happen on either account!

I was intently reading some good resource material so I didn't hear when Mary Ann called me the first time. She finally got my attention and I stood and walked with her to the examination room. She went through the usual process; took my temp and blood pressure, weighed me, and measured me and told me Dr. Joe would be in shortly.

Once again I prayed, *"Lord, please be with me not just in the next few moments but in the days to come. Let me be aware of your presence and give me strength to accept whatever may come."*

The door opened and Dr. Joe entered. He didn't give anything away by his facial expression and although I was on the proverbial pins and needles, I waited patiently for him to get to the results of the tests and blood work that had been done the previous week.

"Randy, there is no easy way to tell you this. There is no scientific explanation. There is no medical rationale. But..." He paused as he opened up my personal file and the short delay was excruciatingly long.

"....you appear to be totally cured."

He continued, "Your blood work shows no signs of the virus and your blood cell counts are absolutely normal. I don't often get to relate good news but this is one time I can. We'll do a follow up in about three months just to make sure, but as for today, congratulations, you are virus and illness-free."

"I actually started seeing a slight turnaround," Dr. Joe continued, "when you got sick this past July. Some very strange things were going on with your system that I couldn't explain. It was as if your body was doing everything it could to get rid of the virus and that's unusual since it is normally the virus that wins out in these situations."

"What do you think happened in July? Did my sickness trigger this reaction?" I asked.

"I really have no idea, Randy. Something sparked the change, though. Can you think of anything you did out of the norm?"

I told him no and he was already aware of my history walk that I had taken right before I had gotten sick but what could that have done unless the extra exertion was the cause for the change. Then, I remembered the sensation I felt when Madame Roberta hugged me- the strange, tingling feeling that went through me at her touch. I didn't really believe in healers but maybe I had not given them enough credence. Maybe there was something to it. Whether she had anything to do with it or not, my curiosity was now high and I made myself a mental note to go seek her out again and talk to her about it. The week after we got back from our upcoming trip, I would make the drive back to my old stomping grounds and try to find where she lived and go see her.

We could have turned the lights out in the room and it would have still been adequately illuminated just from the smile on my face. I'd do a more adequate job of thanking later but, for now, I just quickly closed my eyes and uttered a simple, "Thank you!" to God.

Dr. Joe went over some other matters but they glossed by me without too much impact. I had just heard the sweetest words I had heard in a long time.

One of the things he had told me was to maintain some dietary restraints and to try to lose a few more pounds. I'll do that tomorrow, I decided. Right now, I'm going to DQ and get me a large Blizzard to celebrate. For today, Type 2 be damned!

I had the afternoon to myself until Cindy got home from work. I devised several ways of telling her the good news, but in telling her the good news I realized I would have to admit that I had kept a secret from her for several months. I didn't think she'd be happy about that.

Maybe, I thought, the best time to tell her might be during our trip to Charleston, South Carolina scheduled for the week after next. She would be shopping which meant she would be in a good mood. Perhaps, she'd be more receptive then.

The next few days were spent in an euphoric state. The cloud that had been hanging over me had disappeared. I looked forward to going off and spending time with my girl.

Cindy and I had made a habit of taking a long weekend during the Christmas season to visit other cities to see their light displays and enjoy the festive time each place offered. We had been to Nashville and stayed at the Opryland Hotel. We'd been to Ashville, North Carolina and stayed at the Grove Park Inn and, of course, visited the beautifully decorated Biltmore House and Gardens. Savannah, New Orleans, Memphis, and even New York had been previous destinations.

I am not a big fan of New York at any time, but especially at Christmas. There are just too many people. I enjoy our nights at the theater while there but the rest of the times are not my favorite experiences. Cindy, on the other hand, is in heaven. She loves the hustle and bustle. What she really loves is Macy's, Bloomingdale's, the craft vendors at Grand Central Station, and all the other shopping opportunities.

A very unique thing happens to Cindy when in New York- she can suddenly tell direction. Drop her on Broadway and 7th and she knows which way Central Park is. If she is on 42nd Street, she knows exactly which direction to turn to get to the Empire State Building. Why is this so unique, you ask? Because anywhere else in the world, she has no sense of direction at all. She has difficulty remembering which way the elevator is when we're in hotels.

An excellent example of this is the story we often tell of our visit to St. Paul's Cathedral in London. The latest version of this architectural masterpiece of Christopher Wren was built between 1675 and 1710 and sits on the highest elevated point in London. The interior of the building containing the famous High Altar where royal weddings and crownings have taken place is beautiful but the most famous location in the church is the famous Whispering Gallery located in the domed rotunda of the main building.

The gallery is located some 30 metres from the cathedral floor and you have to climb almost 300 steps to get to it. No elevator access at all. The gallery contains some beautiful paintings located around its circular walkway looking down on the cathedral floor and up to the dome ceiling. The remarkable aspect of this gallery is not the artwork, however, it is the acoustical features found there.

Legend has it that one person can face the wall on one side of the gallery and whisper something into the wall and the person on the other side of the gallery, some 80-1oo yards away, can hear what they said clearly and distinctly. During our visit, Cindy and I thought we'd try the experiment out.

I told Cindy that I'd stay where I was and she should walk around to the point where she would be directly opposite me. Simple enough, right? Cindy starts out walking. She walks and she walks and she keeps walking. When she gets to the point I want her to stop, she keeps walking. I couldn't yell at her to stop. That would cause too much of a scene. This was a church, after all. Besides, I'm amused at this point and am curious to see just how far she'll walk.

She has now walked full circle and is within five feet of where I am standing. She has no idea I am standing that close to her. She turns to face the wall and whispers, "Randy, can you hear me?"

I sneak up behind her and say, "Yes, very well since I'm right behind you."

I am bent over with laughter as I tell her that I haven't moved one inch. She, on the other hand, has walked the entire circumference of the gallery and has come back to where she started. I so love my blonde who then said, "I thought it was a long way." But, like I said, put her on 5th Avenue in New York and she can get anywhere in the city she wants to go.

We had been to Charleston a few years prior and really enjoyed the city. Marion Square is lit up beautifully and the food is great there. We also had discovered a Christmas show put on by a couple with former Broadway experience that is just as good as anything you'd see in New York. Brad and Jennifer Morantz stage a family production with singing, dancing, and comedy that features some of the best talent we've ever heard.

The drive to Charleston takes only about five hours from our house but I still have to have something to occupy the tedium, so Cindy always reads me trivia questions to pass the time. I am always on the lookout for good trivia books for this purpose and had found one that would satisfy my needs.

Where my love for trivia came from I cannot say. I've always been an avid reader but I like to take my reading material much farther than just the basic facts being presented. I enjoy getting inside the situation and learning about the little known facts that caused the event to happen. Here are a few examples of what I mean:

- The reason men have buttons on their coat sleeves was begun by Napoleon Bonaparte. He got tired of his soldiers wiping their noses with their sleeves during the bitter Russian winters so, he had brass buttons sewn on all the coats. In the bitter cold, the soldiers who still did this would freeze their noses to the buttons.
- The kiss that is given by the bride to the groom at the end of the wedding ceremony originates from very early times when the couple would actually make love for the first time under the watchful eyes of the rest of the village.
- Rome, Italy was the first city to reach a population of 1,000,000.
- Ronald Reagan was the first choice to play Rick in *Casablanca* rather than Humphrey Bogart.
- Bugs Bunny was going to be called Happy Rabbit. Mickey Mouse was to be called Mortimer.

- Chocolate syrup was used as a substitute for blood in the famous shower scene in *Psycho*. And one more
- Americans eat more bananas (11 billion a year) than any other fruit

We arrived in Charleston and after checking into our hotel we went to our first stop to get some lunch. One of our favorite restaurants there is called Fleet Landing and if you are a fan of shrimp and grits, you have to check them out. The rest of the afternoon was spent shopping in the old Slave Market that has been converted to numerous craft vendors. Then, we walked up and down King Street checking out all the retail shops located there.

The weather that day was gorgeous. Temperatures were in the high 60's with not a cloud in the sky. We went back to our room, which had a nice balcony area overlooking the city, where we could enjoy some wine, cheese, and summer sausage that we had bought. The sun filtered through the buildings casting beams of sunlight making the scene almost surreal. I thought that this would be an ideal time for me to confess to all that had been going on with me the past few months. But also to share the wonderful news I had received.

I didn't know how upset Cindy might get with me withholding news this serious from her even though it had a happy ending and I couldn't really blame her if she was furious. I thought I would try to lighten things up a bit by telling her a joke I had heard recently. We were relaxing on the balcony and I jumped right in.

Miss Beatrice was the church organist. She was in her eighties but had never been married. She was known for her sweetness and kindness to all. One day the pastor visited her in her home and she showed him to her quaint sitting room and told him to have a seat while she went to prepare some tea.

As he sat facing her old pump organ he noticed a glass bowl on top of the organ filled with water. Something seemed to be floating in the water and when he went to take a closer look, the pastor was stunned to see that it was a condom. When she returned with the tea and finger sandwiches, the pastor tried to stifle his curiosity regarding the bowl but finally it got the best of him and he asked her, "Miss Beatrice, I wonder if you would tell me about this." The old lady smiled and said, "Yes. Isn't it wonderful? I was walking through the park a few months ago and found that little package. The directions on it said to place it on the organ, keep it wet, and that it would prevent the spread of disease. And do you know that I haven't had the flu all winter."

She groaned but from her smile I could tell that she thought it was funny. I had now reached my point of no return and so I began.

"Honey, I have something to tell you about what's been going on with me for the past few months and I'm sorry that I haven't had the courage to say anything before but I just couldn't face talking to you about it. The reason I've been going in for so many tests to Dr. Joe's office and the hospital is because……"

And before I could finish the sentence, she interrupted me by saying, "It's okay, sweetie. I've known for quite awhile. I confronted Joe when you were sick last July and made him tell me what was going on. I knew something wasn't right and I wanted to know what to do to help you."

"That's okay. I've actually been keeping something from you as well. Even though you woke up at home, you were actually in the hospital for several days. After Joe came by and we talked, we transported you so a close watch could be kept on you. Your temperature wouldn't break and they had to start your heart with the paddles one time. On Tuesday your vitals started getting better and he thought it would be okay to send you back home. That's why you woke up at home. But, honey, it was really touch and go for awhile."

I got up from my chair with tears in my eyes and put my arms around her and said, "I'm so sorry I didn't tell you before."

"Well, I can't say that I'm happy with you for keeping something as important as that away from me but I figured you would tell me in your own sweet time." she said with tears in her eyes. "What am I going to do when you get sicker? I don't want to be in a world without my Randy."

"Then you don't know the most recent news?" I asked.

"What do you mean, recent news?"

"I met with Dr. Joe last week and I'm cured. The virus has disappeared and he gave me a clean bill of health. You're gonna be stuck with me for a long time."

I'm sure the people on the street below us thought there was a murder taking place from the sound of the scream that came out from Cindy's mouth. We embraced and jumped with the joy of a little child coming down the stairs to see what Santa has left for them. This was easily the best pre-Christmas present either of us could hope for.

When we settled down we went back out to the balcony and I said, "But I want to tell you about something that happened back when I took my history walk and see what you think."

I went through the whole story of that day- the historical part of the walk and my meeting with the principal and my discussion with the class. But what I was really leading up to was my encounter with Madame Roberta. I went through the whole event, the entire conversation as I recalled it. I then related the strange feelings I received when she touched me with her embrace. I asked her if she believed in faith healers and did she think there was anything to my questioning of whether she had anything to do with my cure or not.

She confessed that she was not sure what she believed since she had never had anything like my situation happen to her directly or to anyone she had ever known. "But I can tell you that Dr. Joe said he had never seen someone be so sick and, yet, recover as quickly as you did in the hospital. He even said himself that it was like something took a hold of your system that was beyond the scope of medicine. If she had anything to do with that, well, you're just going to have to answer that question for yourself."

I told her that I planned to go back to my old house and neighborhood after we got back from Charleston to try and find Madame Roberta so I could ask her some questions and Cindy agreed that was the only way I could satisfy my curiosity.

The rest of the trip was fantastic. The music that night at the show was more uplifting, the food we ate was more delicious, and there were other parts that were darn good also. Modesty keeps me from discussing those in detail, however. The drive back home went by quickly because I was focused on how to seek Madame Roberta out.

My first thought was to go see if Frank and Abner were still holding down the fort at their open-air store across the street from the old house. They might have some clues as to how I might find Madame Roberta. Talking to her would be the only way I could continue with……..

CHAPTER 28

MY WALK TO THE TRUTH

We got back from Charleston on Monday and after taking care of a few errands the next couple of days, I decided I would drive to the old house on Friday. I was anxious to get there because the questions I had for Frank and, eventually, Madame Roberta were boiling away in my head.

I drove out of Winder to Hwy. 11 which takes you to the city of Monroe, Georgia. Once there I take Hwy. 138 and travel to Conyers where I pick up I-20 that takes me to my old neighborhood.

I had crossed under I-285 and was coming up to Candler Road. On my left was Columbia Mall, the site of another time when Dad had let me down.

One of the anchor stores in the mall when it was originally built was Sear's. One of my favorite baseball players and the greatest hitter of all time, in my opinion, was Ted Williams of the Boston Red Sox who also served as a spokesperson for the fishing gear they carried.

Williams interrupted his baseball career on two occasions during his prime playing years to serve his country in both World War

II and the Korean War causing him to lose, in total, four years of playing time. If he had been playing during that time, his statistics would have probably been the greatest of all time.

Williams, personally, was not a likeable fellow. He detested the press and rarely gave interviews. When he did, his answers were curt and they could be laced with profanities that the writer would, naturally, have to edit before he printed what Williams had said. He worked extremely hard at his craft, however, and took exceptional pride in his hitting ability.

Long after his playing days were over, he was once asked by a reporter if he thought he would be a good hitter in that era facing the pitchers of today. He quickly responded that he thought he could be a .320 to .330 hitter. Since he had maintained a .344 lifetime batting average, the reporter thought this was Ted's way of saying that the pitchers of today were better than the ones he faced and that they would be able to get him out more frequently.

When approached with that theory, Ted said, "Hell no, son. They're not better. I'd only be able to hit .320 cause I'm 74 years old."

I had opened the paper one morning when I was around the age of 14 and read where Williams was going to make a personal appearance at all of the Sear's locations in Atlanta including the Columbia Mall location near us. I begged Dad to take me to go see him and he said that he would. I was excited beyond measure with the chance of seeing this great player. Williams was going to be there from 3 pm until 6 pm so, Dad said he'd take off from work early and come pick me up.

I hurried home from school that day and waited patiently for the car to pull in the driveway. I had my autograph book and Ted's baseball card ready for signing. I was all set.

The minutes ticked by as I peered out the big picture window looking for the car. Minutes turned into hours. It was absolutely forbidden for me to call Dad at his work place unless it was an emergency and while this certainly qualified as one for me, I knew it wasn't for him.

At 6 pm I knew he wasn't showing and that I had missed my chance to shake the hand of Ted Williams. At 6: 15, the car pulled in and I ran out the front door to the car.

"Dad, did you forget what we were supposed to do today?"

"Naw, I didn't forget. I just decided I didn't want to go and get in the middle of all those people."

That was the only explanation I got. No words of consolation about letting me down. No words saying he was sorry. You see, in his mind, Dad never had to do that. You didn't warrant an explanation because you were just a kid. It was not necessary for him to console because you were supposed to be tough. And he definitely never apologized for anything. A man didn't ever have to apologize.

I took the exit ramp off the expressway on Glenwood and turned right on Clifton. When I came to the intersection with Memorial, I turned into the parking lot of the convenience store on the corner and was glad to see that the tent with all the merchandise for sale underneath it was still there. And, sure enough, there was Frank in his chair waiting for potential customers.

I looked across the street at my old house and the sign was still there proclaiming Madame Roberta's talents as well as the board-ed up windows. Nothing had changed in the five months since I was last here.

I approached the tent and said hi to Frank. He didn't seem to recognize me so I reminded him of our previous meeting.

"You may remember me from when I was here a few months back. You took me across the street so I could get a better look at the old house where I grew up."

"Yeah. It's coming back to me now. You were taking some kind of hike, weren't you?"

"That's right. I'm a Civil War buff and I was walking the path that the soldiers took at the start of the Battle of Atlanta."

He asked, "How'd that turn out?" and for a moment, based on his expressionless face, I couldn't be sure if he was asking about my walk or the Civil War. So I gave him an answer to both.

"The walk turned out fine but sometimes I'm not sure that the war solved anything. Seems like our problems are just as bad as they were then based on the way things are still happening in this country."

With a slight nod of his head he said, "You got that right, fella!"

"Look, I was wondering if you could help me with something that happened here when you took me to look at my house."

"Do what I can. I wondered what was going on over there since you stayed there as long as you did."

"Well, the reason I stayed so long is what I need your help with. You see, while I was looking around the back yard a very nice lady and I talked for quite awhile and I'm trying to locate her again. I think she helped me with a big problem I was having and I just want to thank her. Maybe you know how to get in touch with her."

"A lady? What she look like?" he inquired.

I described Madame Roberta but added, "I can do better than describe her. She told me her name. Well, not her name exactly but she said she was the same Madame Roberta as the one on the sign and that she used to live here."

Frank's head popped around and he looked me square in the eyes as he asked, "You say you talked to this woman?"

"That's right, Frank. For a long time. She wanted to hear all about my life when I lived here and she was able to know things about me that she couldn't really know. I'm never really been a believer in psychic powers but, well, I can't explain what happened that day. But something that I can't explain did, I'm sure of it."

"Son, I don't know what you're trying to pull but what you're saying happened couldn't possibly have happened."

"Frank, I'm not pulling anything. I'm serious. I think Roberta cured me of a disease that I had when I was here before. She touched me and now it is totally gone."

A tear started rolling down the man's cheek. The last thing I wanted to do was upset him but it was obvious that something I had said had bothered him.

"Frank, I'm sorry. What's wrong?"

It took him a moment to compose himself but finally he said, "I'm not sure what you saw that day but it couldn't have been Roberta."

"Well, that's who she said she was."

"It just couldn't have been." he muttered as he shook his head.

"Why, Frank?"

"Because Roberta was my wife and she died in the fire! I was away at work and she got trapped in the house and couldn't get out. The firemen got to her before the flames got her but she died from the smoke. She looked just like you described her- a big woman and her lungs just couldn't take it."

My natural reaction was to ask him if he was sure but I caught myself before the silly words came out. Of course he would be sure.

We stood there looking at each other. Neither of us knew what to say next. Frank sighed and then said, "I guess I can finally let her go cause now I know she's still doing good in the world. And I can forgive myself. The fire started because I had left a burning cigarette in the trash. She always told me that you gotta let the hurt go- no matter what it is. I can now let go and forgive."

"She told me the same thing." There was only one thing I could do. I took him in my arms and gave him a big man hug. Right there, with traffic speeding by, a white man and black man embraced. And it felt right. But at that exact same moment, I felt the same strange tingling sensation that I felt when Roberta hugged me. Frank could feel it, too. It was as if the power that

Roberta had placed in me, the power that defeated my illness, was being transferred to Frank so that he could get rid of his hurt.

"I think it was her, Frank." I told him.

"It was her." he softly replied.

As the traffic flowed past us we just stood and stared at the house for several minutes without saying a word. Frank was lost in his memories and I was lost in mine. I could only imagine what was going through Frank's mind but I was reliving almost twenty years of experiences in one brief moment. They say that your life flashes before your eyes right before you die and I guess I was having those visions myself at the realization of what I had just discovered.

I saw Christmas lights on the house.

I saw a little boy playing football by himself in his make-believe world.

I saw that same little boy cutting the grass.

I saw my Mom holding my hand as she walked her toddler down the front steps.

I saw a young boy coming out the front door on his way to baseball practice.

I saw a teenager driving in the driveway after a date with Cathy.

I saw a boy crying on the front steps because he didn't get to go to the circus.

I saw a young man dressed in a tux heading for his wedding.

I saw Madame Roberta blowing me a kiss.

Strange as it would be to explain, I now had my answers. I now knew the truth. Frank forgave himself. Now, it was time for me to do the same. Frank and I said goodbye and I crossed the street so that I could take.........

CHAPTER 29

MY WALK TO FORGIVENESS

The man I grew up with and called Dad died on December 6, 2012, just 15 days shy of his 100th birthday. He had been born in Adairsville, Georgia in 1912 to Thomas Monroe and Rosalee Blalock. His parents had participated in the 1889 Oklahoma Land Rush but had found their way back to Georgia where most of dad's siblings had been born.

I actually think he started dying the previous April when I had moved Mom out of the house and into the retirement center where she is now. His verbal abuse of her had gotten worse and worse and she just couldn't take it anymore. She called me one day telling me she had to leave him. I told her I would make some arrangements but for her to pack her things- I would come get her that Friday. While I carted out her tv and her clothes to my car, he lay in his recliner sleeping. Actually, I was glad he was sleeping because I really didn't want any confrontations with him. Mother insisted on saying goodbye to him, however. She gently woke him up and told him she was leaving. The confused look on his face told me that he didn't really comprehend what was going on. After 75 years of marriage, she kissed him on the forehead and walked out the door. She only saw him one more time and that was in the hospital before he died.

He had started slipping away mentally some time before. There were several occasions when he had taken his truck out to run an errand and had gotten lost. One time was pretty serious. Mom called me about 5 pm one day saying that he had been gone since 9 that morning and she was, rightfully so, worried that he had gotten lost again. I asked if she knew where he had been going and she told me that it was Thursday so that was Big Lots day.

Big Lots was his favorite store. Dad was a hoarder. He just couldn't pass up a good deal. It didn't matter to him that they already had 10 liter bottles of Pepsi in the house, if they were on sale he'd buy more. I think growing up in the Depression made him understand and appreciate the importance of "things" and once he had a little money his philosophy was "if one is good, then more of them is even better."

When I was cleaning the house out after his death I came across an unbelievable amount of stuff that he had amassed over the years. Desk drawers were filled with AA and AAA batteries, all with expired dates on them. He had bought over twenty pair of scissors, multiple flashlights (none of which worked), and when I opened one cabinet I counted 82 sets of headphones. Out of curiosity, I opened the plastic package to one of them and the felt covering the ear pieces literally disintegrated in my hands they were so old.

I called the Gwinnett Police Department and gave them his tag number and asked that they be on the lookout for him. Around 10 pm that night I got a call from an officer with the Newnan Police Department telling me they had found him and were taking him home but that I would need to come pick up his truck the next day. If you look at a map of metro Atlanta you'll see that Lilburn, where Mom and Dad lived, is northeast of Atlanta while Newnan is directly south of the airport by 20 miles. Since he was deathly afraid of getting on the interstate, I have no idea how he got there.

The phone rang the next morning and it was Dad. "Where's my truck?" he roared.

"I'm going to get it today, Dad. It's in Newnan. How did you get there?" I asked.

"You're a damn liar! My truck ain't in Newnan. Hell, I ain't never been to Newnan in my life! I want my truck!"

"Well, then, aliens must have transported it there without your knowledge cause that's where it is."

"Just go get it!" he demanded.

I tried several times to discuss with him rationally the need for him to give up his keys but there was no rationality with him, especially now in his diminished state. But finally I got the chance to take the truck away.

Another phone call, this time from the Gwinnett Police alerted me to the fact that he had had an accident. I had always dreaded this call and stayed in fear that he would hurt someone else but this time it was nothing more than him losing control of the truck and running over a curb bursting all four of his tires, which were already threadbare, in the process. He was not hurt and the officer said that they were taking him home, a practice that was becoming all too common, and would take the truck to their lot where I could send a wrecker for it.

I had the truck towed up to Winder, put four new tires on it, and never gave it back. He constantly asked for it but I held firm in my resolve.

He stubbornly refused to let me find a place for him to go so he could be looked after. I wasn't going to put him where Mom was- she deserved her peace, but I was concerned for his health and safety. He had a wonderful neighbor who would look in on him each day and make him what little he was eating but as he continued to have failing health, I knew another step had to be taken.

I hired a day nurse for him and, of course, he hated her and cursed her constantly. Thankfully, this wonderful woman had dealt with elderly people like him before so, everything he said, and believe me it was awful, rolled off her back. She took his abuse and gave it back to him threefold. I loved her.

Cindy and I went to go see him the morning of Thanksgiving, 2012. By this time, he was always in his bed but we helped him out and talked to him in his favorite recliner. Cindy attempted to fix him something to eat and I tried, once again, to get him to think about moving to a home but he was still adamant that he would die in that house. When we left, we took him back to his bed.

The next day his neighbor called me to tell me that she had found him in the den, face down under his overturned recliner with a big cut on his forehead. She had called 911 and they took him to the hospital. Apparently, he had gotten up in the middle of the night and lost his balance. He tried to grab the heavy chair for control and somehow turned it over on top of himself. I couldn't imagine how he would have had the strength to do that since he now weighed only 80 pounds.

I called Mom to let her know what had happened. She told me, "I want to go see him. Come get me."

"Mom, I don't think that's a good idea quite yet. Let's get him stabilized and then you can go see him."

"I want to see him. Come get me."

"Yes, ma'am."

The tenderness with which she held his hand while he lay in that bed will always amaze me in light of all that he had put her through during their lives together. He would drift in and out of his sleep and one time he actually recognized her. True to his old demanding ways he ordered, "Allie, get me a glass of water!"

There was really nothing the doctors at the hospital could do. He wouldn't eat and he was delirious most of the time. He woke up one time and thought I was his father. He finally went into a coma.

The phone woke me up at 3 am the morning of Thursday, December 6th. Cindy was out of town on business. I rolled over to her side of the bed where the phone is kept. There is usually nothing more frightening than a phone call in the middle of the night but I had an idea what this one was about.

The voice on the other end introduced himself as the night manager of the facility where Dad was. He said just a few succinct words, "Mr. Blalock, your father passed about an hour ago." I got all the information from him and told him I would send the funeral home to pick up his body as soon as they opened for business.

I know it may sound callous but all I felt was relief. Relief at the thought of not getting any more phone calls saying that he was lost or that he had hurt someone in an accident. Relief at not hearing him belittle and curse me or mom anymore. Relief at being free of his yoke that had been around my neck for 65 years.

Then I cried.

Harriet Beecher Stowe once said: "The bitterest tears shed over a grave are usually shed because of words unsaid and deeds undone." How right those words are.

I cried, not so much in grief, but for the lost opportunities I missed. I had always been so jealous of the guys I grew up with or met later in life that had good relationships with their dads, some even calling them their best friends. I was so jealous of Cindy because of what she had had with her dad that I never did with mine. I wanted to yell at him. I wanted to scream at him- but I couldn't. So I cried.

I think one of the reasons I enjoyed the old family sit-coms was because they all had one thing in common- a great dad. Robert Young, who played Jim Anderson in *Father Knows Best;* Ben Cartwright, played by Lorne Greene, in *Bonanza;* Howard

Cunningham in *Happy Days;* and even Bill Cosby as Cliff Huxtable were my inspirations of what a dad should be.

There are two words that we use to describe the male parent. They are father and dad. Most of the time they are used interchangeably but I think they are definitely different in scope. I talked about the difference between the two when we had the graveside service for him that Saturday.

I told the few who had gathered that the best way to describe our relationship was that we tolerated each other. I realized that he was from a generation where the man of the house didn't show emotion, either to his wife or to his children. There were certain things expected of him and as long as he did them, in his mind, he was doing his job and nothing more should matter.

A father is the one who provides for you, protects you, keeps a roof over your head and keeps food on the table. A father makes sure that you have clothes to wear and that you learn the lessons you need to be successful when you become an adult even if it comes with an extra dose of discipline.

A dad, however, is the man who teaches you how to fish and how to throw a curveball. He comforts you when your team loses the big game because he was there to see it. He takes you to the circus. He tells you jokes. He buys you an ice cream one hour before supper. And he tells you he loves you.

I came across this job description of a dad recently. Let me share with you some of the criteria for the job of dad and I think you will see even more clearly the difference between being a father and being a dad. Some of the responsibilities of being a dad are:

- must provide on-site training in basic skills such as nose blowing;
- must be able to drive motor vehicles under loud and adverse conditions while administering conflict resolution at the same time;

- must be willing to be hated temporarily until someone needs $5 to go skating;
- must be able to answer obscure questions such as "where do I come from?" and "what makes the wind blow?" on the fly; and
- must always hope for the best but be prepared for the worst.

The job description goes on to say that there is virtually no possibility for advancement; all expenses are paid for by you until the children reach 18 at which time a balloon payment called college tuition is made to them; and when you die, you give them everything that is left. However, there are some benefits. They're called hugs and words like, "Dad, you're the best."

You see, based on those descriptions and definitions, I had a father but I never had a dad. I called him dad but that was just a name- never a title of respect or one that he had earned. I cannot remember one time when he ever wrestled or roughhoused with me. We never went fishing or hunting. I only remember him taking me to one movie, other than drive-ins, in my entire life and that was only because Donny was visiting with us and he wanted to show him the Fox Theater.

Now, as I stood there in my old back yard and reflected on all this I had to ask myself what good was it doing me letting it fester and grow like an invading cancer. I heard the sweet, lilting voice of Madame Roberta in my head saying, "Let the hurt go, honey. Madame Roberta will make all the hurt go away." I agreed. It was time to let it go and it was easier to do so now that all the demons were gone because of something that happened shortly before his death.

I was visiting my Dad about a month before he had his fall that would eventually contribute to his death. Angela, his caregiver, was there and she told me he had been asking for me. I went into his room. It smelled awful in spite of Angela's efforts. Dad had lost control of his bodily functions and she spent most of her time changing him.

I sat down in the chair opposite his bed while Angela stayed in the den. Dad would babble about one subject or another making no sense of anything. He kept looking at the clock on his wall making comments about how pretty it was and how it kept perfect time. Clocks were another one of his obsessions.

Then he looked at me and his eyes got clear and his speech became coherent. There was, and is now, no doubt in my mind that he knew exactly what he was saying.

"Randy. I know I was never a good father and I was a worse husband but I do love you."

How does someone react when he hears those words from his father for the first time in his entire life? I said the words that I think he wanted to hear and the words I needed to say.

"I love you, too, Dad."

It was true what he had said. By his own admission he had not been an especially good father or husband but I will give him credit for being a good grandfather. Oh, he was never the "climb up in my lap and let me read you a story" grandfather, but he had doted on Brian and Jessica.

He only had one run-in with Brian that I recall. Brian was 16 and driving and on a visit he made to their house, Dad asked him to run an errand for him. Brian tried his best to explain that his mom had told him to be home at a certain time and if he ran the errand, it would make him late. This was long before the era of cell phones so Brian had no way of getting in touch with her to let her know the circumstances which would cause him to be late. Brian politely told his PaPaw that he was sorry but he couldn't dis- obey her orders. Dad got furious with him and did not speak to him for over a year.

I attempted to intercede on Brian's behalf many times telling him that Brian was only doing something he held so dear- total obedience. He wouldn't hear it. His stubbornness could not be swayed with logic. Finally, however, he came around and the two of them reconciled. In fact, Brian, after reaching adulthood, was the only person who could talk sense to him making him see the errors of his ways when it was needed.

Jessica, on the other hand, could do no wrong in his eyes. When she turned 16 he bought her a new car and the only criticism I ever heard him make about her was her career choice. For some reason he did not want her to become a nurse. But being a strong-willed woman, she didn't let that stand in her way.

The sun, which had shone brightly that morning in contrast to the dreary day when I had been here before, shined even brighter as I stood in the backyard of my boyhood home. You've all heard the old expression of the weight or burden that you carry on your shoulders being lifted. At that moment, the weight came off. I would never be able to erase the memories but I could erase my hatred, not of the man himself, but of the way he treated me.

And more importantly, I forgave myself for ever having those thoughts and feelings. It was only natural to feel that way because, as children, we expect so much more from our male parent than what I had received.

I don't know if my children can call me both a father and a dad. I certainly hope so but that's their decision, not mine. I know that I tried to be both to them. It was important for me not to be the type of man that he was with respect to my relationship with them. I know that the divorce took away some things from us that can't be recaptured but they have to know how happy I am with Cindy. I know one thing they can never say about me. They never had to wait 65 years to hear the words I heard that day as he lay on his bed.

Brian- I love you.

Jessica- I love you.

And, Dad- I love you.

CHAPTER 30

MY WALK TO..........

It's January 2015 as I write this. Last year was one of turbulent emotional changes for me with both highs and lows. The lows being highlighted by my illness and the death of a close friend, but with highs such as the birth of my great niece, my discoveries, the beauty of receiving a clean bill of health as well as a forgiving heart by a lady known only as Madame Roberta-all of these swirled within me last year. But now we have a new year. That's the beauty of the calendar changing over- new opportunities, new friends, new joys and, yes, maybe new heartaches to deal with but deal with them we will.

I have reached a stage in my life when there is less future than there has been past but when I get melancholy and begin thinking too much about the number of years I have left, I think about a great poem I once heard. Don't know who penned it, but it has perfect sentiment to those of us who classify ourselves as oldies but goodies.

I am fully aware
That my youth has been spent
My get up and go
Has got up and went
But I can't help
To think with a grin
Of all the great places
My get up has been

I have no idea what the future holds for me- none of us do. But whatever it brings, I plan to enjoy it to its fullest. I know that my walk is not through because I've been given more time.

More time to:

- listen to great music like Perry Como, Chicago, Streisand, great classical works, Nat King Cole, Glenn Miller, Beach Boys, Ronnie Milsap, Journey, Gatlin Brothers, Broadway musicals, good gospel quartets, and many, many others
- exercise (in small quantities)
- travel to places like Alaska, Fripp Island, Germany, Ireland/ Scotland, Indy to visit our friends, more beaches, the Holy Land, tour Italy more, the southwest part of the US, and maybe even New York
- watch Brendan and Patrick grow into young men and, God willing, make me a great grandfather
- eat wonderful meals with Cindy, whether its Hamburger Helper at home or dining experiences at places like Commander's Palace (New Orleans), Morton's (Atlanta), Last Resort (Athens, Ga.), The Stockyard (Nashville), any restaurant in The Buckhead Life Group, or the Varsity
- read great authors, classical and contemporary like Christie, King, McMurtry, Doyle, Dickens, Grisham, Stuart Woods, L'Amour, Charles Martin, Twain, Jakes, and Jeffrey Archer

- take up golf (maybe)
- rewatch classic tv shows on Netflix like M.A.S.H, Hill Street Blues, The Wonder Years, Frasier, Columbo, and the greatest tv drama of all time, The West Wing, as well as some current ones like House of Cards, American Horror Story, Mad Men, Breaking Bad, and The Walking Dead
- cheer for my Dawgs and cheer against the Dallas Cowboys each Fall
- cheer for the Braves in the Summer
- see great movies; will there ever be anything as good as Star Wars and Indiana Jones for pure movie entertainment?
- shed tears
- laugh
- sing
- dance
- go to church, because He is the reason we get to do all of the above and
- be with Cindy

I don't know where the walks of your life have taken you. I sincerely hope that most of your steps have led to happiness and wonderful memories. But your best steps are ahead of you because they are the ones you haven't taken yet. May God bless you every step of the way.

If you'll excuse me now- I have to go for a walk.

MEET THE AUTHOR

Randy Blalock has been married to Cindy for 27 wonderful years. They live in Winder, Georgia and are active members of Winder First United Methodist Church where Randy teaches an adult Sunday School Class. Randy spent his working career in the banking industry and now spends his retirement time writing, catching up on old movies, and reading. He is inching ever closer to his goal of visiting every major league baseball stadium and will satisfy that goal next year as long as they don't build any new ones. He is a self-admitted couch potato and TV junkie. And, on football Saturdays in the fall you can find him, along with 90,000+ other fans, cheering for the Georgia Bulldogs.

Randy has two children; Brian, an elementary school teacher and Jessica, an administrative nurse and the mother of his two grandsons, Brendan and Patrick. His hobbies are reading, playing trivia games, and watching sports either in person or on TV.

If you are interested in learning more about his children's books, contact him at rblalock@mindspring.com or go to the Jawbone Publishing Co. website.

ACKNOWLEDGEMENTS

Much thanks and appreciation goes to the following people who made this book possible:

Mike Lasseter and his Advanced Digital Design class at Mill Creek High School in Gwinnett County, Georgia. Mike was kind enough to make the design and production of the front cover, title page, and back cover of this book a class project and the students accepted the assignment with great enthusiasm. The following students work was selected:

Front Cover- Lily Browder
Lily is a Senior at Mill Creek High School and she plans to attend Kennesaw State University. Graphic design is one of her hobbies and as shown by the beautiful cover, one of her talents.
Back Cover- Alexis (Lexi) Baker
Lexi is a Senior at Mill Creek High School with plans of pursuing her artistic talents upon graduation. She hopes to attend the Savannah College of Art & Design and would like to have a career with illustrations or design work.
Title Page- Elaine Santoni
Elaine is a Junior at Mill Creek High School with plans to attend college and study graphic design. She enjoys reading and taking pictures. _

Joann Smith for her proofreading skills and for her critique of my first draft but, most importantly, for her constant support.

Missy Tippens for her advice and expertise in the editing of the book. Missy is an accomplished writer in the genre of Christian Romance having had several books published. She has won the 2013 RT Reviewer's Choice Award as well as other prestigious nominations. You can visit Missy at www.missytippens.com or her Amazon author page to learn more about her work.

AFTERWORD

I am solidly in the middle of taking another walk with grief as I write these words. While this book was in its interior design, formatting, and editing phases in preparation for publication, my 97 year-old mother, Allie, passed away. She had contracted pneumonia and her frail little body just couldn't handle that onslaught. I want to express my great thanks for the wonderful treatment she received at Magnolia Estates Retirement Center in Winder, Georgia where she resided for the last three years of her life; Barrow Regional Hospital; and, especially Agape Hospice House, also in Winder.

As is detailed in this book, Mom was a special lady who endured much in her 97 years. Yet, as she lay in her hospital bed in her last coherent moments, all she could talk about was what a good life she had had. She focused on her family, her work life, and her travels. She would tell all those who would listen that even though she got to go to Hawaii twice, Europe, and the Holy Land, her favorite trip was the one she and I took to New York City in 1955 where, along with all the usual sight-seeing stops, we went to a New York Giants game at the old Polo Grounds to see Willie Mays play. The brain is a remarkable contraption. She could remember every detail of this trip but 30 seconds later not be able to recall her brother's name.

I need to relate one story about her that occurred while in hospice. The chaplain of the facility came in to visit her. He would pray over her but he is an accomplished guitarist and vocalist and he would also sing hymns to her. Now, remember that by this time she was totally unresponsive to verbal communication. Nevertheless, as he sang *Amazing Grace* to her, she mouthed the words of the hymn right along with him.

I was with her as she took her last breath at 11: 02 am on Thursday, April 30, 2015. Through my sobbing at her passing, I told one of the staff at the hospice that I was so glad I was with her to see her take her last breath. She hugged me and said, "And just think, she got to see you take your first breath."

There is an old adage that says the dates of one's birth and death are not as important as what you do with the dash in the middle. What a dash she had. Mom, I will always be your baby boy.

Allie Blalock
December 19, 1917- April 30, 2015

Made in the USA
Charleston, SC
15 June 2015